AMONG the ECHOES

Aly Martinez

ECHOES

AMONG the ECHOES

Among The Echoes
Copyright © 2014 Aly Martinez

Among The Echoes is a work of fiction. All names, characters, places, and occurrences are the product of the author's imagination. Any resemblance to any persons, living or dead, events, or locations is purely coincidental.

Cover Photo by Jeremy Landis at Embracing Beauty Photography
http://jeremylandisband.wix.com/embracebeautyphotography
Cover Design by Ashley Baumann at Ashbee Designs
https://www.facebook.com/AshbeeBookCovers
Edited by Mickey Reed at I'm a Book Shark
http://www.imabookshark.com
Formatting by Stacey Blake at Champagne Formats
http://thewineyreader.com/champagneformats/

ISBN-13: 978-1500683023
ISBN-10: 1500683027

WARNING:

This content contains material that may be offensive to some readers. Including sexual abuse, graphic language, and adult situations.

Dedication

Parakeet Breath,
Without you there would be no Slate, Leo, or even Erica, my books would be boring, there would be no twists, and Sarah would be sane. Thank you for talking me off a ledge more times than I care to admit by gently telling me, "Uh, this sucks." Thank you for rewording odd sentences and saying, "This is cheesy." Thank you for actually responding to my two a.m. questions with answers like, "Cottage cheese and birds." Cottage cheese is pretty scary. Thank you for sending me random messages that say things like, "What if…" then documenting, in great detail, how you think the book should end. The plan worked! I can't imagine going through any part of this writing journey without you, and thankfully I won't ever have to. You are amazing! Now, start writing.

CHAPTER One

"KILL HER."

"No! Please! I didn't see anything!" I scream, backing into the corner.

"We all know that's a lie." His accent curls over the paralyzing words.

"I swear. Please, I won't tell anyone."

"You got this, Marcus?" he asks the large man with long, brown hair and an evil stare.

"I got it," he confirms, raking his eyes over my body with a scary calm.

My stomach rolls as I glance to the man who is no doubt going to kill me. His disgusting smirk is unmistakable, and it lights my body in a rush of fear.

"Stop. My family knows where I am. I gave my boyfriend the address before I left. They will come looking for me," I lie, wishing with all of my soul it would somehow miraculously become the truth.

"You are full of shit. We never would have chosen you if you had a boyfriend." The man in charge smiles pridefully.

"I do! He will look for me."

"No one will look for you. Sadly, my love, that's the only reason why you are here right now. No one besides elderly Rich and Margaret Lane from next door even know you exist. When they see the moving truck tomorrow morning, they will dismiss you as nothing more than just a passing memory." His grin grows even wider.

"No, wait!" I frantically try to formulate a plan or angle that will end with me alive, but his final words come all too quick.

"Kill her," he repeats roughly as his partner rushes forward.

"Please." I fold down, curling into the corner, desperate to escape his touch.

"She's attractive. Take her to the boys for a little fun first," he orders while tossing a cigarette onto the carpeted floor and walks from the room.

"They'll look for me. I swear they will!" I fight against his every touch.

"You fight and I kill you now. Your call. You come willingly, you see tomorrow. I promise you that," he says with a thick Spanish accent while holding my eyes. He curls his lips in annoyance and disgust as the tears finally escape.

I hate him, but tomorrow is more than I had a few seconds ago. I don't know what will happen if I go with him. I'm not questioning that he is absolutely going to kill me. The real question just became: how long do I want to live?

It feels like years that I've been here, but I think it's only been a day. I honestly have no clue. All I know is that I'm bound to a bed in a dark room. I know it's a house based on the silence. There are no sounds from apartments above or below us. No neighbors coming or going. No one to hear me scream. With the exception of bottles of water being brought in randomly and the man who occasionally ushers me to the restroom, I am completely alone.

I've long since been stripped naked. My hands are tied to the top of the bed, my legs spread wide and anchored to opposite posts on the footboard. I'm exposed for anyone who happens to pass by. While no one has touched me yet, I can hear the parade of footsteps passing through the room. I can feel the prickle on my skin that lets me know someone is watching. *Always watching.*

The door opens, and from the light in the cracked doorway, I make out a man's silhouette. I've never seen him before. He's older and heavy, and the stench of a cigar wafts through the room. I try to memorize his features so I can give my description to the police. Maybe. If only I live long enough to get out of here.

He pulls his lips tight, biting his bottom one and moving my way.

He walks over, assessing me. His disgusting eyes drag across my body. I know from the look on his face that this man is not here to help me. Just as I get up the nerve to speak to him, he reaches out and roughly twists my nipple. I cry out in pain, but the real tears flood my eyes as he drops his pants. If I had some silly notion of making it out of here unscathed, they vanish.

I made the wrong decision. Dying would be better than what I know is to come.

"You make her bleed, I make you bleed." I hear the voice of the man, Marcus, who brought me here. "Save some for the rest of us."

The rest of us.

A sob catches in my throat.

"I won the first fuck." The new man drags a finger down my body as I squirm, unable to escape.

"Please let me go. I'll do anything you want if you let me go." I hysterically try to reason with him. I'm not lying. In this moment, I would give this disgusting man my body willingly if it meant that I'd live through this nightmare. Survival is the only reward that could come from this.

"Shut up." He slaps me across the face, forcing my pleas to go silent, but the tears still slide from my eyes and into my ears. "Marcus, I want her on her knees!" he yells, and the door opens again.

"Not happening. You go first, but I'm the only one who gets her ass. You so much as dip a finger in what's mine and I will rip your dick off and fuck you with it myself." Marcus spits on the floor and cocks his head with a challenge. "That's the rules. Take it or get the fuck out so I can take it."

I turn my head to face Marcus, praying he will take pity and release me, but his eyes only flash to me long enough to take in my freshly busted lip. He storms across the room and, without warning, punches my abuser maliciously in his mouth, knocking him to the floor.

He leans down into his face to drive home his point. "She's fucking bleeding! I warned you, Johnny. I fucking warned you!" he shouts just before kicking him in the stomach.

"She wouldn't shut up!" Johnny yells back, holding his stomach.

"Who the fuck cares? Let her scream. The rule was don't make her bleed. Now I'm gonna get blood all over my cock while she's sucking it. Get out. You're done." The injured man stands with his nostrils flaring as he exits the room.

I breathe a sigh of relief, and Marcus swings his head to mine. His dark eyes should terrify me, but somewhere deep inside, I feel a sick safety with him—the man who is supposed to kill me.

It must show on my face because he gently shakes his head and calls out, "Lee, you're up!" before striding out of the room.

The hours that follow fade into a blur. I wish I could lose consciousness as man after man rapes me, stealing pieces of the woman I will never be able to find again. At first, I fight, screaming with every thrust, but as my voice begins to crack from hoarseness, I find a deep, dark place within myself—a place I never knew existed. I hide in the welcomed darkness.

"She's all yours," I hear the most recent man say as he leaves the room.

I steel myself for yet another round of filth, but as I open my lids, I meet the chocolate-brown eyes of Marcus. My body relaxes, but bile creeps into my throat when I remember what his turn means.

"Shut the fucking door!" he shouts over his shoulder while unbuckling his pants.

I squeeze my eyes closed, preparing for the worst.

Surprisingly, my hands are immediately untied. I should run or at the very least fight, but I'm too weak. I haven't eaten since I was brought here, not even to mention that I'm a third of his size. I'm well aware that there is no sense in trying to fight him, but I have to give it at least one shot before giving in to the culminating darkness once and for all.

I barely even move my arms before he grabs them and flips me over. My legs are still tied and my ankles cross as he spins me to my stomach, pinning me against the bed.

"Scream," he whispers in my ear with a low rumble.

I shake my head, unwilling to give him what he wants. I might be powerless in every way, but my voice is my own. I won't give him that.

"Erica, scream or you get us both killed."

I'm startled by the use of my name. I turn my head over my shoulder to meet his gaze, and finally, I'm not the one pleading.

"I'm not the bad guy. I need you to scream and make it believable."

His eyes flick to the door, and I give it everything I have left. I let out the blood-curdling sound I have been holding in since I gave up on myself. But I only do it because, for the first time since he took me, I have hope. It may be a horrible sound to others, but to my ears, it's a rejoice.

"I'm going to let you go. Don't make this difficult. I will do whatever it takes to subdue you, even if that means hurting you." He looks down at my bruised and battered body, shaking his head with disgust.

I nod, acknowledging his words. But I'm confused and not completely certain I can follow his orders.

He unties my legs and drags a blanket from the chair to cover my nudity.

"Here." He pulls a protein bar from his pocket and places it in my shaking hands. "Eat. We don't have long." He grabs a water bottle off the nightstand next to the bed and drops it in my lap.

"Are you going to kill me?" I ask, but he doesn't respond as he begins to quietly pace around the bed. "Please just let me go. I won't tell anyone."

"Eat," he gently urges while sitting down on the edge of the bed.

I'm starving. And even as my stomach threatens to revolt, I know I need this. Who knows when I will see my next meal? *If ever.* I unwrap the bar and hastily devour it.

"Here." He pulls a small tube of lube from his pocket.

At the very sight of it, I jump away as if it were a weapon. Pain rips through my tattered body when my legs painfully close together.

"No. I won't touch you. I just need you to take this and rub it all over your ass. You need to make this look legit. Go ahead." He turns his back to me as I sit frozen, holding the lube. "Erica, please! I don't have time for you to figure this out. Do it!" he growls, never turning back to look at me.

Completely unsure why I'm following his directions, I open my legs and carefully apply the lube. "There."

"More," he says, still not looking. "Rub it all over your ass, cover as much as you can reach. If you were fighting me, that shit would be all over the place. Rub it on your hands and touch places on your body, including your breasts."

"What's going on?" I ask while squeezing the lube into my hand. "Why are you doing this?"

"Because I'm going to help you. It may not seem like it now, but I'm here to help you," he whispers, facing the wall.

"I'm done." I cover myself again with the blanket.

"You tell anyone about this and I will kill you on the spot. No questions asked. No help. You understand?" He turns to face me, and suddenly, my savior disappears and the dark man who put me here returns.

Unsure what else to do, I nod.

"Lie back down. I need to retie you."

"No!" I shout as terror consumes me.

He grabs my arm, and even though I kick against him, he easily slips back on my restraints.

"There's just one more. I'm sorry," he breathes, pushing my hair out of my face.

"No, don't leave me. Please. I can't go through that again. Marcus!" I scream louder than I've been able to muster all day.

"Not one fucking word."

"I can't take it again. You said you wouldn't kill me, but that is what you just sentenced me to. I can't take one more man. I don't have any pieces left to give." I barely squeak out the words over the dry heaves.

He moves back to the bed, leaning forward on his knuckles to speak directly into my face without so much as even a hit of an accent. "I want to tell you that you'll be fine, but I can't do that. I don't think anyone will be fine after something like this. However, I will not let them kill you. I give you my word on that." He holds my eyes, begging for me believe him.

The tears stream down my face as he unzips his pants, tugs them down his hips an inch, and walks away. He tosses the lube on the floor next to the bed and opens the door.

"Marcus, please!" I scream after him. He's not much, but he's the only hope I have.

"Looks like somebody likes my cock," he laughs, walking out the door.

"About fucking time," I hear a man with an accent growl from outside. "We killing this one?"

"Yes, sir. But I'm doing it myself. Dom, gave her to me."

"Well, you don't mind if I have a little fun first? Right?" He walks into the room with Marcus hot on his heels.

"Sir, I promised Aidan he was next."

I look up to find Marcus standing behind the new man, his eyes nervously flying around the room. Tears once again make my vision swim as the realization hits me—he's powerless against this new man.

The older man prowls over to the bed, settling between my spread legs. His hands roam up and down my body. I don't look at him. I can't. Instead, my eyes stay focused on my evil lifeline silently watching in the doorway.

"Sir, allow me to get her cleaned up for you. The men have been at her all day. Hell, I just fucked her myself."

"I can see. Lube, Marcus? I didn't take you for such a gentleman."

"I'm an ass man. It's kind of a necessity." He fakes a smirk and offers a shrug, trying to play it cool, but even I can tell he's uncomfortable.

"I'm sure Dom wouldn't mind if I made this one my own. He knows I love to play with the pretty ones," he purrs.

Marcus's eyes go wide just before the pain erupts over my legs.

A scream tears from my throat as I look down to see him slicing the tip of his knife up the inside of my thighs, over my sex, and down the other thigh. I lose focus and beg for the darkness to take me. The sound of a gun deafens me, and the body of the man who just mutilated me falls lifelessly on top of me. I drift away, praying the light never returns.

CHAPTER Two

"MOVE, ERICA." MARCUS'S voice breaks through the ringing in my ears.

I open my eyes to find my hands and feet suddenly free, and the dead man has been shoved off me. I'm covered in blood, but I dive into the arms of the man who was once my captor. The same man who is now rescuing me.

There are shouts behind the door, and he shoves me into the bathroom. He closes the door, but I can't go back to the dark. I keep it cracked, watching as the bedroom door splinters into pieces. Marcus opens fire on the three men sprinting in with guns raised.

I quickly close the door and move toward the single window, but the searing pain between my legs leaves me unable to walk. I fall toward the window, pushing against it only to realize it has been sealed shut. Panic ricochets through my mind as I try to work out an escape, but I just can't focus with the sounds of gunfire banging from the other side of the door. Finally, with one last pop, the room goes silent.

"Erica, open the door. You can't get out the window."

My emotions bubble over, and I stumble helplessly back to the door. I don't know Marcus, but I have no choice but to trust him.

He walks in, throwing the blanket around me and scooping me into his arms.

He carries me from the room, stepping over the bloody mess of bodies. I bury my face into his neck so I don't have to look at the carnage.

"I want to go home," I whisper. The adrenaline fades from my system, leaving me with the shakes and tears I thought I had long since run out of pouring from my eyes.

He puts me down only long enough to snatch a phone from his pocket. "Fourteen Ulrich Ave. I need a pickup. Medical. And a whole team of cleanup. I just killed Darren Wilkes and his top three." He abruptly ends the call and cradles me back into his strong arms. "I've got you. Shhh," he whispers into my hair.

We stand for a few minutes in the doorway. He alternates between looking outside and soothing me. Finally, he yanks open the door and carries me out just as a black SUV pulls into the driveway. I prepare myself for more chaos, more pain, and more fear. My heart races even as he whispers, "Those are the good guys."

Three men and a woman jump from the barely parked truck and race towards us.

"What the fuck did you do?" the first man who arrives barks at Marcus.

"Take her. She needs medical. I have a gunshot wound to the thigh. I think it was clean through, but I'm not positive." He shifts to pass me off, but I scramble to stay in his arms. I have no idea what the hell is happening, but there is only one man I trust right now, no matter how screwed up that may be.

The man pulls me away from Marcus, but I try to hold on like a baby clinging to its mother. My legs are on fire and every inch of my body is sore, but I fight to resume my place in his arms.

"Marcus!" I scream, reaching toward him.

Despite his own injury—I can obviously see that he's bleeding through his pants—he returns to my side. "Hey, you're in good hands. This is Agent Greene from the DEA. You're safe, Erica."

I know his words should soothe me, but they only make me frantic. I'm not safe. I'll never be safe again, but Marcus made me feel that way, even if for just a minute. I need that right now more than I need the air in my lungs. I need *him* to give that to me.

He turns to walk away and I lose it, frantically swinging my arms and legs, shaking free of the blanket and the hold the supposed officer has on me. I forget about the pain in my legs and the fear I felt because of this man only hours ago. I rush ahead, slamming into his back as he makes his retreat.

"Please don't leave me. I don't understand what's going on right now. I need you. Please don't leave me like this. I..." I begin to sob, begging him to stay with me.

He spins around, wrapping me in his arms and pulling me into his chest. "Fuck. Okay. I've got you."

"Please don't leave me," I repeat as my body shakes violently.

"Hey. It's okay. I won't let you go until you're ready." He smooths down my hair as I suck in a relieved breath. "But no more Marcus, okay? My name's Leo James. Just Leo from now on."

I nod against his chest as a blanket is wrapped back around me from behind.

"Clean up is on the way. We need to get you two out of here," a woman says from somewhere nearby, but all I can see is Leo.

"Come. Let's get you to the hospital." He once again lifts me off my useless legs and climbs into the back of the SUV, cradling me securely on his lap.

CHAPTER Three

Three years later...

Slate

"KILL HIM!" I hear Jimmy yell from outside the ring while pounding on the mat. It's about the only noise I can hear. With over eighteen-thousand people crowding the arena, the cheers are almost deafening.

My opponent throws a combination of punches, catching me off guard with his sudden burst of energy. Just as his last strike hits me, he drops his hand—only for a second. But that is more than enough time for me to land an uppercut to his jaw, snapping his head back in a way that I know will end the fight. He stumbles back before landing against the ropes and falling to his ass.

The ref counts him to seven before waving his hands and calling the fight. The crowd goes wild and my corner rushes in to celebrate. This is nothing new, but I'm proud nonetheless. I haven't lost a fight in over two years. Averaging over fifty million a match and one fight every six months, I've done well for myself. More than enough for me to leave this life and never look back. But for some reason, I always return.

I'm thirty-five years old and my fighting days are nearing an end. Hell, I've made it longer than most. But one of these days, a young, rising star will be quicker than I am and put me on my ass. I better enjoy this while I still can.

"Ladies and gentlemen, your winner and *still* heavyweight champion of the world... Slate *The Silent Storm* Andrews."

My glove is lifted into the air while the belt is draped over my shoulder. I stand for a moment, nodding to the crowd with gratitude like the trained professional I am. Thankfully, Jimmy quickly pulls me from the ring. I do what has been ingrained in me over the years and tap hands and pose for pictures with fans as I make my way to the back. People slap me on the shoulder, and it takes more effort not to move away from their touch than the entire eight rounds I just went. I hate this part of my job. Always have. *Always will.*

"Good fight, man!" Chris, my trainer, says, rubbing my neck. He's allowed to touch me. Hell, I even pay him thousands of dollars to do it.

"Thanks." I push my hands toward Jimmy so he can remove my gloves. "Hey, did you get me a plane for tonight?" I ask my manager, Mitch, who is standing in the corner with an insincere smile plastered on his face.

"You sure I can't persuade you to stay? The fans would—"

"Did. You. Get. A. Plane?" I repeat very slowly in case he suddenly doesn't speak English.

"You going to finally tell me where in Ohio you disappear to after fights?" He quirks a questioning eyebrow that I swear I heard pop. "A month is a long fucking time to go off radar, Slate. You should be doing talk shows and endorsement deals after your win tonight. You could make all of us a lot of money if you acted like the superior athlete you truly are."

I bark out a laugh. "I think I make us all enough money without whoring myself out."

This is the exact same song and dance Mitch and I go through after every fight. Even before I was making millions, I still did my own thing after fights. I work my ass off for months in preparation. I don't think it's too much to ask for a little time to unwind afterwards.

I lie facedown on the table for Chris to rub down my back. "Go. Party your ass off, but I'm out of here."

"Slate, you are the heavyweight champion of the world. Act like it. Go out and mingle with the people. Maybe find a woman and break your vow of celibacy."

"I'm not celibate, you ass. Since when are you worried about my cock? Last I checked, it doesn't make you a damn penny."

"Not yet. But if you give me enough time, I'm sure I could get you a Magnum condom sponsorship," he halfway jokes.

"Oh for the love of God. I turned down Nike. You think I'd do a Trojan ad?" I groan at his ludicrous idea.

"Money isn't the devil, Slate."

"Maybe not, but you still make enough to be an evil bastard all the same." I roll my shoulders, signaling Chris to work on them.

"All right, all right," he relents. "Go on your little vacation. Can you at least take your phone this time?"

"Nope. You know the drill. You need me, send an email. Don't be a vague prick this time either. I'm not falling for that shit again. A rematch announcement does not constitute an emergency."

"It does when I need a contract signed ASAP."

"It could have waited two weeks." I push up from the table to catch his eye. "I'm serious. New rule. You don't contact me unless Jimmy deems it an emergency. Got it?" I glance over at Jimmy, who is looking down, suddenly enthralled with his shoes.

"Fuck that. This arena could burn down with us inside and he wouldn't consider it an emergency."

"Exactly," I say, pushing to my feet.

"Whatever, Slate. It's your career. You can fuck it up all you want."

"Well I've been fucking it up for over fifteen years now, all the while lining your pockets. I think my career will survive another month." I stand and head to the shower without another word spoken.

Riley

"Riley!" my boss calls, catching me off guard.

I cartoon-style throw all my papers in the air then scramble to the floor after them.

"Jeez, I'm sorry. I didn't mean to scare you." He bends down to help me collect them.

"It's okay. No big deal," I say breathlessly, more to myself than to him.

"It's just that we are taking a final head count for the Christmas party. I know you're new and I just wanted to make sure you got invited. I'm sorry. I didn't realize you were so jumpy."

"Yeah. I am pretty jumpy," I say softly. "I won't be able to make the party. I'm sorry." I stand, straightening the papers just so I don't have to meet his eyes.

"Are you sure? It's not for another week. You can bring your boyfriend if you would like." He smiles. I'm sure it's genuine, but all I can think about is what he's hiding behind that grin. He's never looked at me in a suggestive manner, but I'm sure he's thought about it.

"Yeah, I'm sorry. I can't make it." I shake my head as I quickly exit the file room.

I walk back to my corner of the cubicle I share with both of the other file clerks and snag my purse, ready to escape for the day. I pick up my phone and text out a quick message before grabbing my jacket and lunch bag and heading to clock out.

I hate this job, but it pays the bills. At least that's the way I'm supposed to think.

Dale, Derrick, Don—whatever his name is—pulls up outside in a small, older-model, silver sedan, and I all but dive into the car.

"What's your name?" I ask as soon as I shut the door.

"Fuck, Riley."

"I'm sorry. I can't remember. I'll get it, I promise. Just give it to me one more time."

"Dave," he answers shortly.

"I'm sorry," I whisper.

He shakes his head but reaches down to reassuringly squeeze my leg. "How was your first day?" he asks with a quick smile.

"*Can't Buy Me Love*," I answer, staring blankly head.

"Really?"

I nod and quickly ask, "You?"

"*Grease,*" he responds.

"Oh! Well that's not bad." I answer, finally looking over at him.

"*Two,*" he finishes, and my eyes widen in shock.

"No fucking way."

"Way. I'm a car audio installation specialist!"

"Damn. That's really bad. And here I thought a file clerk sucked."

He chuckles. "Someone out there really likes you. You've had an office job three moves in a row."

"Right. I'm so glad I spent all those years in medical school now. What would I ever do without them now that I spend forty hours a week filing auto insurance claims."

"Riley, you don't always have to be strong." He guides me into our run-down two-bedroom apartment.

"Neither do you," I snap.

I walk inside, head straight for the closet, and slip out of my heels. Suddenly, I feel him behind me. His hand starts at my collarbone and slides up my neck, forcing my head back to look up at him.

"Erica." He whispers my real name so quietly that, if I didn't know what he was saying, I wouldn't have heard it at all. But I did hear it, and it sends chills through my entire body—quickly followed by tears. I rock back into him and immediately fold toward the floor. His strong arms catch me before I fall even an inch. "I've got you," he whispers, carrying me to the tattered couch. His brown eyes pierce into mine, and I try to lock down the emotions. But no matter how hard I try, I can't seem to find the latch.

"Let it go," he urges, reading my struggling body language.

I fight it for a few more minutes before finally releasing it all. I roll over to my stomach and bury my face in the pillow, sobbing. He rubs my back for hours as I fade in and out of sleep—waking only to cry some more.

Some hours later, I wake up dehydrated, starving, and with a splitting headache. I look down and find him sleeping peacefully at the end of the couch with my feet resting in his lap. I both love and hate this moment at the exact same time. Those moments shouldn't cross for a person, but for me, they are dangerously similar.

"Dave." I push against his leg, but he remains still. "Dave." I nudge him again with absolutely zero reaction. Finally, I give up and lean in close. "Leo," I whisper.

Knowing the drill, I quickly back away as he flies to his feet—fists raised and swinging. His eyes flash around the apartment before landing on me just a few feet away.

"God damn it, Riley!" he huffs.

"You wouldn't wake up," I try to explain.

"I don't give a fuck if I'm dead. You don't call me that. Ever. Do you understand me?"

"Whatever. I'm going to bed."

I hear him growl as I march to my bedroom. "Riley, wait."

"Go to bed, Dave. We have to be at work in a few hours."

"It doesn't mean the same to me as it does you," he says from my doorway.

"Get out. I want to change clothes."

"Your name means something to you. But if someone knows mine, it just means that I've failed—and we're both dead." He runs a frustrated hand through his hair.

I suddenly feel ashamed. I know he's right, but what he doesn't understand is that sometimes I need to say his name. I need to be reminded that not everything is a lie.

"I'm sorry."

"Stop. Apologizing."

"No. I mean it. You know the first couple of days after a move are always the hardest for me. I'm sorry. I'll get my shit together. I promise."

"I know you will." He smiles so warmly that it makes me feel even worse.

We silently stare at each other for a few beats. He always lets me get away with this bullshit after a move.

"Hey, I didn't get a chance to tell you earlier. I have to go away for some training in a few days. I'll only be gone four days tops."

"What? Why?" My heart begins to race.

"On-the-job training."

"You install car stereos! You could do that in your sleep."

"Yes, but Dave can't." He walks forward and puts an arm around my shoulders. "Do you want me to call it in? Get someone to come stay with you?"

"No. Please don't. I don't want any extra attention that could draw them to us. I'll be fine for a couple of days. I have a phone if I need anything."

"God, you are a terrible liar."

"Shut up. I am not."

He laughs then tries to reassure me. "You'll be okay."

The truth is that he's a much worse liar than I am. I can tell that this is going to kill him. I'll be nervous the entire time he's gone, but he will be in a complete and utter panic until he gets back.

"Get out of here. Go to bed. Tomorrow will be better." I push him toward the door.

"Right. Night, Riley."

"Night, *Dave*!" I shout, and he throws me a wink over his shoulder.

CHAPTER Four

Slate

HOME.

I spent years trying to escape this place. All I wanted was to make a better life for me and my mother. I wanted all the crap that poor kids dream about—a grand mansion, nice cars, and fancy meals. I wanted her to retire, get off her feet, stop worrying about how she was going to make ends meet, and then I'd finally be able to pay her back for a little of what she gave me. The day I won my first title, I finally succeeded in earning enough money to get her out of here.

Twelve years later, I came back.

Who would have guessed the place I hated most in the world all those years ago would eventually become my safe haven? No one knows I bought this building three years ago. It would be a media circus if they did. Which is exactly why I bought this place to escape. Luckily for me, Jimmy was willing to put it in his name to keep mine, as owner, off public record. He even paid for it out of his own pocket to keep the paper trail from leading back to me. He did get a nice little bonus that year that more than compensated him for his efforts.

As I pull up in my economy rental car, an immediate sense of calm washes over me. Not the kind you feel after a few deep breaths or a stiff drink. I'm talking the kind of calm you feel in your bones. The eye of a tornado. The still after an earthquake. The silence after a hurricane. *Calm.*

I grab my small bag from the backseat and head inside. I never bring much with me when I come here. I never had anything before—why start now? Honestly, my whole first twenty years of life could have fit in this bag with plenty of room to spare.

I rush around the corner, ready to own that feeling for the next month of my life. It's a feeling that I will eventually lose when I have to go back to my real life, but now that I have this place, I know I can always reclaim it.

"Shit," I hear as I turn the corner. A petite woman with mousy-brown hair pulled back into a ponytail is juggling grocery bags while trying to open her front door. Her bags slip from her hands and a carton of eggs opens, spilling all over the ground. "Shit!" she screams.

I drag a baseball cap from my bag, pulling it low over my eyes, and move toward her.

"You need some help?" I ask gently.

"Shit!" she screams again and jumps away, flattening her back against the door.

"Jesus. I'm sorry. I didn't mean to scare you. It just looked like you might need some help."

"I'm okay. I'm okay." She breathes deeply, and if I'm not mistaken, talking to herself.

I reach down, pick up the mess of broken eggs, and shove it back into the plastic grocery sack. I tie it in a knot, readying it for the trash.

"You'll probably need more. Not even one egg survived." I smile, but she doesn't reciprocate. She stands silently with her back still pinned to the door. Her whole body is tight as she stares at me nervously.

Fuck. Based on that star-struck look in her eyes, I know she's recognized me. I haven't even stepped inside yet and I've already been made. I'm starting to think her choice in vocabulary seems fitting. *Shit.*

"You didn't see me. Okay. Don't tell anyone I'm here," I whisper, and she visibly relaxes. Her eyes glide over my body, and she even leans to the side to take in my small bag.

"Did Dave send you?" She finally speaks a sentence that is not a cuss word.

"Who?"

"Dave. Did he send you?"

"Not that I know of," I answer, confused.

Her eyes narrow as she accesses me. It's only fair that I do the same. I rake my eyes over her body from top to bottom and back again. She's pretty. Cute, small, nice boobs, and trim figure. She's not hard, but she is fit. Like her hair, her eyes are brown, and aside from her unusual level of alarm, there's nothing overly special about this woman.

"What's your name?"

"Adam," I lie. She might recognize me, but if she's looking for me to confirm it, it's not going to happen.

"Where are you staying?" she asks, and I narrow my eyes back at her.

"Do I need to leave? Is this going to be a problem?" I ignore her question and jump right to the issue.

"No problem for you, but I'm going to rip Dave's balls off for not giving me a heads-up." She shoves open the door and moves inside.

Clearly, this woman is unstable. Just out of curiosity, I peek around her apartment as she walks to her kitchen. The entire room is open, not even a wall to separate the entryway from the kitchen. I can tell that her place is two bedrooms based on the hallway. It's the exact same floor plan as mine, only in reverse. It's clean, but most of the furniture is older and well used. It actually looks similar to the place I lived when I was growing up. Well kept, but nothing nice. I smile and breathe in the scent of dust and mothballs.

"Are you a bloodhound as well as a bodyguard?" she asks, looking at me strangely.

"Bodyguard?" I question, and she tilts her head in confusion.

Suddenly, her eyes go wide and she takes two giant steps away from me. "How long have you known Dave?" she asks as her face pales. She slides behind the kitchen counter. I can see her head and shoulders over the bar, but her body is blocked. I can hear her digging through a drawer as fear transforms her.

I can't figure out why she is suddenly scared, but I think this would be a good time for me to leave. "I don't know any Dave. I'm sorry. I think you must have me confused for someone else."

"Cool Rider," she whispers as tears start to well in her eyes.

I shake my head as her words make even less sense. "Yeah. I'm going to go. It was nice to meet you..." I realize she never even gave me her name. "Anyway. I'm next door if you ever need anything," I throw in for some strange reason and immediately hope this odd woman never needs *anything*.

Riley

"We need to move!" I screech into the phone as soon as Dave picks up.

"What! I'll call it in now. Are you okay?"

"I'm fine, but there is a huge guy next door, and he helped me pick up eggs. I thought you sent him. I thought he was one of your guys to babysit me," I rush out incoherently.

"Wait! Do you think he's one of Wilkes's men?"

"I don't know!"

"Did you get a bad feeling?" he asks with concern filling his voice.

"I. Don't. Know!" I repeat on a frustrated shout.

"Riley, calm down."

"I can't. I thought—" I choke out a sob. "I thought he knew you, but then I said the word, and he had no idea what I was talking about," I continue, rushing out broken pieces of sentences.

"Okay. Well, did he try anything on you? Like, did he come in and look around or do anything that made you suspicious?" he asks, and I can tell he is still curious but he has already started to relax.

"No. He just stuck his head in and sniffed."

"Sniffed?"

"Yes, like a dog. He pushed his head inside and sniffed," I explain yet again, and he lets out a laugh.

"Can you blame him? That place stinks."

"So you don't think he's a threat?"

"I'll call and have someone look into it. He just sounds like our new neighbor to me. If you were obviously alone, there is not a chance in hell one of Wilkes's guys would have left you standing there."

"Maybe they were hoping you would come back." When I get an idea, I screech, "Maybe he was sniffing for you!"

He starts laughing. "Do I stink? Can you smell me?"

"Sometimes," I whine.

He lets out a chuckle before getting serious again. "Stay inside. I'll get him checked out, okay? Did he give you his name?"

"Adam."

"Hang tight. I'll get him looked into."

"Okay."

"Oh, and Riley. We need a new word now. Your choice this time."

"Parakeet Breath," I blurt out.

"Wait, are you calling me that or is that the word?"

"Both."

"Well, okay then. I guess I'll pick the word again," he replies, and I finally let out a small laugh. "I'll look into him," he promises again.

"Thank you," I breathe, and only partly because he's looking into Adam. It's mainly because, even from eight hundred miles away, he still makes me feel safe.

The knock on the front door startles me. No one knows we live here. It's not like we are expecting any visitors. I have no friends or anyone to randomly stop by. It's sad, but I have no one in this world but Dave. Although, in my old life, I didn't exactly have anyone either—but at least then I had myself. That's a lot more than I can say now.

I sit on the couch, nervously staring at the door, just waiting for the salesman to give up and leave. But this person is persistent. The knocking continues for a few minutes before I finally hear Adam's voice from the other side of the door.

"Um, I brought you some eggs," he calls out.

I cautiously walk to the door to look through the peephole.

"I wanted to apologize for scaring you earlier. I was at the store anyway, and I knew you were out," he says loudly.

"You didn't have to do that," I respond to the door without even considering opening it.

"Well, I guess I'll just leave these right here for you. Don't leave them out here long. In this cold, they are liable to freeze."

"Oh, yeah. Uh, thanks," I respond awkwardly, knowing good and damn well that I am *not* going outside to get those eggs.

Who the hell brings someone eggs? Maybe he is just luring me outside so he can kidnap me and take me back to whomever he is working for. But if that's the case, why didn't he just grab me when he had the chance earlier? Whatever, Dave told me to stay inside. That's more than enough for me.

I move to the window and very carefully peek through the blinds. He lingers at the door, seemingly uncomfortable. *Why is he nervous?*

He runs a hand through his short, black hair. "Anyway. Well. Uh…" He stumbles over his words. "Have a good night."

I watch as he walks away. He doesn't look back or try to peek in the window. He just moves into his apartment, shutting the door quietly behind him.

I pace around my living room, trying to work out every possible scenario. If he is one of Wilkes's men, why is he taking his sweet time making a move? It's possible that he's just a nice guy, but he's freaking huge. He's easily six foot four, and he must work out *all* day to keep that body. Even through a sweater, I can tell he's ripped. I just don't get it.

My phone rings from the corner, snapping me out of my quickly approaching panic attack. "Hello."

"I don't know who the hell he is," Dave says across the line, "but I don't think he's a threat."

"He just brought us eggs." I say as if that obviously proves he has malicious intent.

"What?"

"Eggs."

"Why would he bring eggs?"

24

"I don't know! Do you think they are poisonous?" I ask, and Dave lets out an infuriating laugh. "Don't laugh at me. I'm scared!" I snap across the line, and he immediately goes silent.

"I'm going to send someone. You can argue all you want, but I don't want you alone and scared. This Adam guy seems harmless. The apartment is owned by some man named Jimmy Douglas. His record is squeaky clean. He's a boxing trainer out in L.A. I'm going to assume Adam is one of his fighters, probably down on his luck and needing a place to stay."

"He's really big," I whisper across the line, "so that at least makes more sense."

"I'm sending someone tomorrow. Hang tight. It will look like a date. He'll bring your favorite flowers since we don't have a word right now. And I'm not setting up a new one over the phone."

"Okay." I bite my lip so he can't hear the tears in my voice.

"I won't let anything happen to you. I swear," he vows tenderly.

"I know you won't." I try to smile, but it only forces the tears to spill from my eyes.

"Don't cry," he says softly.

"Stop using your superpowers to read my mind."

"I just know you, Riley. No superpowers needed."

"I'm going to head to bed and read for a little while." I dry my eyes on the backs of my hands as I search the room for a distraction from reality.

"Smutty romance?" he asks as the smile returns to his voice.

"Is there any other kind?"

"Goodnight, Riley."

"Night."

CHAPTER Five

Slate

"ADAM!" I HEAR shrieked from the other side of my door.

I fly off the couch and onto my feet. I must have fallen asleep at some point. My head is groggy and my eyes struggle to adjust, but the sound of a woman's scream permeates through the darkness.

"Please. Open the door. Please!" The frantic words send ice through my veins.

I rush to the door, but before it is even completely open, my neighbor squeezes past me.

"What the hell are you doing?" I ask roughly, still unable to truly grasp this sort of shocking wake-up call.

"Someone just broke into my apartment. I..." She fades off as she slides down the wall to the floor. It's only then that I notice the gun shaking in her hand.

"Jesus Christ." I walk over and reach for the gun.

She doesn't immediately release it. Instead, she tilts her head back, looking me directly in the eyes. *Holy shit—her eyes.* Gone is the plain brown. Now they are so blue that they are almost clear. They're mesmerizing, and it takes the sounds of her crying to snap me out of my trance.

Her lips begin to quiver. "Please tell me you won't hurt me." The combination of her words with the assumption that I would startles and disgusts me.

I squat down in front of her and gently pull the gun away. "I won't hurt you. Ever. You're safe with me." It's the only thing I can offer, and they seem to be the words she needed to hear.

She drops her head into her hands as loud sobs ravage her body. I can only stand and stare. She was odd when I met her earlier, but this is more than that. This is the remnants of a broken woman. Anyone could recognize that, but especially me.

"What happened?" I ask gently, inquiring about more than just tonight.

"The...um, window by my bed was broken. I don't know if they came in. I didn't wait around. I just grabbed the gun and bolted," she tells the floor.

"Did you see anyone?"

"No."

I move to the door and glance around the breezeway. On the brick are a few sloppy graffiti tags that were definitely not there earlier. I'm sure it's probably just a bunch of kids looking for trouble, so I close it back, locking both the deadbolt and the chain just in case.

"It was just some kids," I say, reassuringly. I crouch back down in front of her, and it pains me as she recoils. Not that I would ever dream of touching her, but I understand that reaction, and it kills me to witness it firsthand.

"How can you be sure?" she whimpers.

"I can't. This neighborhood may not be the nicest, but it is relatively safe. The spray paint leads me to believe it's only some bored teenagers with slightly less than average artistic abilities." I try to make light of the situation, and for a split second, it works.

Her eyes lift to mine, and I can't stop the gasp that escapes.

"What?" she whispers as concern once again crosses her face.

"No, nothing. It's just... Your eyes. They're amazing."

"Don't look at me." She covers her face with her hands.

"I'm sorry. It just surprised me. That's all. Earlier, they were brown, but now... Why do you cover them up?"

"I forgot my phone in the apartment." She changes the subject, ignoring my curiosity.

"You can use mine if you want." I offer her a smile, but it's not from kindness. The truth is I just want her to look back up so I can see her eyes again.

"I can't. I need mine." She finally lifts her gaze back to mine, and it's actually painful. Her eyes are beautiful, but this time, I see more than just the awe-inspiring color. I see the fear and innocence in the red rims. There is a dark shadow of false strength, but what really has me reaching forward to touch her is the hopelessness. My hand doesn't even get close before she quickly slides out of my reach.

"Hey. I'll go get it for you. You're safe." I repeat the one phrase that seemed to ease her earlier.

"Why are you being so nice?" She turns her head suspiciously.

"I don't have any reason not to be nice to you. Besides, you remind me of someone I used to know," I answer, and she immediately goes stiff. Her eyes begin to frantically travel over my body—scrutinizing my every inch while desperately searching for something. "My mom. You remind me of my mother," I finish, and she holds my eyes, giving only the slightest of nods.

"Why do you live here?" she asks, and I chuckle at her random question.

"Why do *you* live here?" I throw right back at her.

"Will you walk back over there with me?" She once again changes the topic.

"Yeah, of course."

I offer her a hand to stand, but not surprisingly, she doesn't take it. She pushes to her feet on her own.

I head for the door with her tight on my heels. I suddenly turn, and she takes a quick step away. "You never told me your name," I question, and her eyes light before dimming completely.

"Riley," she says flatly.

"Nice to meet you, Riley."

She finally offers me a weak smile that never even gets close to her eyes.

"Oh, let's not forget this." I pick up the gun she came in with and pass it back to her. I immediately regret returning it. This woman is a mess right now. Arming her doesn't seem like the brightest of ideas. "Do you even know how to use that?"

"Yeah, I do. But I hate it." She reaches forward, taking it from my hands. She doesn't grasp it. Instead, she holds it flat on her palms as if it were a ticking time bomb ready to explode.

My lips twitch, and I force myself to turn away to hide the smile.

"Come on." I walk to the front door, pulling it open for her to lead the way, but she stands silently, waiting for me to exit first. I take the five steps to her door as she follows closely behind me.

She never touches me, although for some strange reason, I can't say that I would mind if she did.

Riley

"You want me to look around?" Adam asks when we reach my door.

My heart sinks, unsure of the correct answer. Do I want him to look around? I'm still not completely convinced that this guy isn't dangerous. Yet there was something in his expression when he told me that he wouldn't hurt me that made me believe him. It was something deeper than just a superficial lie. I would recognize one of those; I tell them all the time. Honestly, what choice do I have right now? He's had two opportunities to kill me if he wanted to. Both he let pass him by. He is either a normal guy or the world's worst hit man.

"Uh, yeah, that would be great," I answer.

"Just stay here." He looks down at my hands and the way I'm holding the gun. "And give me that. You look like you're serving up drinks."

I snap my head up, startled by his sudden attitude, but when my eyes meet his, he's smiling. His expression slightly falters when his eyes lock on mine.

He gently shakes his head, seemingly trying to clear his mind. "Yeah. So, I'll just have a look around."

"Can I get my phone out of my room? I really need to make a phone call."

"Let me just have a look around real quick."

I stand in the freezing cold while a stranger searches my apartment—a scenario that, only a few hours ago, would have thrown me into a tailspin. But as Adam's massive body confidently walks around, checking every room for any possible sign of trouble, an unusual feeling washes over me. A feeling only one man gives me.

I snatch my phone off the nightstand and dial Dave's number. It goes straight to his voicemail and my stomach drops. He never turns his phone off. I'm not even sure I knew that Dave had a voicemail. If I call, he answers. Plain and simple. A million different possibilities race through my mind. None of which have a positive ending.

"Hey, are you okay?" Adam walks over, and only then do I realize that I'm staring at my phone with tears running down my face.

"Yeah. This whole thing just scared me. That's all," I skillfully lie.

"Well, I think it's just your window. Everything else looks fine. I've got some tape at my place. I'll grab it and patch that window so you don't freeze tonight."

"You don't have to do that. I'll figure it—"

"I'll be right back. Put this away." He hands the gun back to me. "Preferably somewhere locked up—where you can't reach it. I saw the way you held that thing. I think the entire city would be safer tonight if you just threw it in the river," he teases, and I can't stop my lips from tipping into a small smile too.

For the next few minutes, Adam uses cardboard and tape to patch up my window. It will need to be fixed soon, but I'll have to wait for Dave to get back. Where the hell is he? I repeatedly call his phone, desperate to hear his voice. But every time, it goes straight to voicemail—skyrocketing my already climbing anxiety.

"Do you have a broom?" Adam asks, surprising me.

I suck in startled breath and jump back. My foot catches on the edge of the bed and I slip, landing less than gracefully on my butt.

30

"Shit!"

"Shit!" he echoes behind me as he rushes over. "Are you okay? I didn't mean to scare you."

"Jesus, I'm making a real ass of myself tonight."

"No you're not," he says with a smirk that tells me otherwise. "So. Broom?"

"Please, you've done more than enough. Don't worry about it. I can clean up the glass."

"Well, yeah, the glass too, but I was going to clean up your eggs."

"What?" I ask, confused.

"I'm not sure what you have against eggs, but you have single-handedly killed two dozen today. I'm guessing you trampled them on your way over to my place."

"Damn. I didn't even see them."

"It's okay. Nothing a broom and dustpan can't fix." He smiles again, and for the first time since I laid eyes on Adam, I really see him.

He's a good-looking man. I noticed that he was tall and muscular right off the bat. But as I look up at him now, I see the whole mouth-watering package. His hair is clipped short, the front just long enough to allow him to style it. His eyes are an unusual combination of brown and green, making them appear almost golden. They're undeniably beautiful. His nose is slightly crooked, but it doesn't distract from his good looks. His smile is wide, but still timid. It's as if he knows what a wreck I am and he's trying to walk on figurative—and apparently literal—eggshells around me. His white teeth are not perfectly cookie-cutter straight. It's obvious that he did not have the torture of years of orthodontics like I did. But these slight imperfections just make him look sexy and rugged. He must catch me staring because his confident smile fades as he quickly looks away.

"Really. I can get the eggs and glass. Thank you for everything. You know, letting me freak out on you. I get a little worked up about stuff sometimes. It won't happen again."

His eyes immediately lift back to mine. "If you need anything, Riley. You just let me know. Okay? Anything at all."

"That's really sweet of you, but I'll be okay. I just have a tendency to overreact. That's all." I brush off my behavior as no big deal, but it's clear that he isn't buying it.

He turns his head and gives me a knowing look that is just patronizing enough to be annoying but sexy enough for me to let it go. I don't say another word as he heads to the door.

Just before he walks out, he turns back to face me. "Anything you need, Riley. Even if you think it's silly. You know where I'm at. Don't be afraid to come to me," he says, and the honesty in his voice forces me back a step. There is a glimmer of something in his golden eyes, but before I can really figure out what it is, he steps over the mess of eggs in the entryway and closes the door behind himself. And just like that, I'm completely alone once again.

I shake off whatever weird exchange Adam and I just had and grab my phone to call Dave again. He has to pick up. He just has to. I mentally run over all the plans we have made in the past, trying to remember how long I'm supposed to wait before calling it in that he's disappeared. Twelve hours. *Twelve long hours.* I scroll through my call log to find the time of our last conversation. Four hours ago he was safe, alive, and laughing at me.

Eight more hours. I roll over to the clock on my nightstand. Seven hours, fifty-nine minutes. *Please, God, let him be okay.*

Slate

The sound of feet stomping down the hall rouses me from sleep. I fly out the door with nothing but terrified blue eyes dancing through my thoughts. Two darkly dressed teenagers jump when they see me.

"What the fuck are you doing?" I growl as they hurriedly race away laughing.

The fresh-paint smell makes it obvious that they came back to finish their underwhelming attempt at a tag on the building. *Fucking kids.* I'm less worried about the new mural than I am the woman who will be terrified by the commotion. I knock on her door, but if earlier today was any indication, she won't answer. I'm betting she is probably sitting on the other side, listening to me, maybe even peeking out the window next to her door.

"Riley. It's me. Are you okay?"

32

"Um. Yeah. I'm fine," she says quietly, but her voice shakes, giving her away.

"You sure. It was just a bunch of kids again. I'm going to call the police—" I'm interrupted by the click of her deadbolt. Suddenly, her door swings open, and those eyes—Jesus, those eyes— appear.

"No. Don't do that." Her voice quivers. Her shoulders are square and her body language is calm and collected, but I'm absolutely not convinced. It's the exact opposite of what her eyes are screaming.

"Why not? I bet they'll be back. I ran them off just now, but it looks like they are pretty damn adamant about finishing this one."

"Did you see them this time? Are you sure it's really just kids?" she asks, and no matter how hard she is trying to fake it, the way she is nervously chewing on her bottom lip gives her away once again.

"I didn't get a good look, but yeah, they were young. Ran like hell as soon as they saw me."

Her shoulders instantly fall as she releases a silent sigh.

I smile, trying to ease her. "So, I see you cleaned up the eggs."

"It was really gross," she responds humorously, but the lack of actual humor in her voice is what really gets me.

"Hey, any chance you want to watch a movie?" I ask out of the blue and against my better judgment. I'm just not okay with the idea of leaving her alone right now. She's distraught even if she's desperately trying to conceal it.

"It's late. I'm sure you would rather be sleeping than watching crappy movies with me."

"I can't sleep. And never underestimate the power of the crappy movie as a sleep aid. What do you have in mind?"

"*Vision Quest*," she answers shortly, immediately looking down at the phone in her hand.

"Who am I to say no to Louden Swain?"

A small smile lifts her perfect pink lips. "You've seen it?"

"Oh, I've lived it. I wrestled in high school. Although I never had a hot older woman fall in love with me."

She lets a quiet laugh slip, and just the sound hits me hard.

"You sure?" she asks. Her eyes lift to mine, and if I weren't already sold, her sparkling, blue gaze convinces me.

"Positive."

She nods and opens the door wide enough for me to enter. I step past her, and just before she closes the door, I notice that she takes a quick glance down the hallway.

"I promise they're gone. We really should call the cops though. I could probably get them to do a drive-by through the complex. Maybe scare the little shits into giving up for the night. I'll install a motion sensor light tomorrow," I throw in just to reassure her, but she only nods and heads to the DVD player in the corner of the room. Her small hands shake as she flips through the pages loaded with DVDs.

"You can have a seat," she says, motioning to the couch.

Only then do I realize that I have been staring at her. "Oh, right. Yeah."

I sit on the far corner of the couch, leaving plenty of room for her to sit on the other end. It's odd being here. I don't know this woman at all, but I do know that she needs someone. I'm reasonably sure she doesn't recognize me. So I can at least take comfort in my anonymity.

"You want something to drink?" she asks, but her voice is filled with distraction.

"Are you okay?" I stand to follow her to the small kitchen area.

She spins to face me and backs away a few steps as I approach. Her reaction immediately halts me.

"Yeah. I'm good. I just have a lot on my mind tonight. Drink?" she asks again, never taking her eyes off me.

"Beer?"

"Oh, sorry. No beer. I think I have a pop or something though."

"A pop would be great," I say enthusiastically, trying to alleviate her tension, but if her weak lie of a smile is any indication, it doesn't help at all.

I head back to the couch, settling in the corner again. I try to find a comfortable spot for myself in this ridiculously uncomfortable situation. What the hell am I doing here? I should be asleep right now, but instead, I'm entertaining a frightened woman who barely even looks me in the eye. On second thought, maybe I'm right where I should be after all.

"So how long have you been living here?" she asks, settling down on the opposite side of the couch and handing me a pop.

"I come and go, but I would consider this place my home," I answer honestly, careful not to expose too much. "What about you?"

"Just a few days," she says absently, looking down at her phone.

She turns around to face the TV, effectively ending the small talk.

We sit in silence as the movie begins. We both stare at the screen, but what I'm really watching is her as she anxiously dials someone every five minutes on her cell phone. My curiosity is piqued, but I don't dare ask her about it. I have a feeling she wouldn't tell me anyway.

"You don't have to stay," she says quietly. A hair slips from her ponytail as her eyes slide to mine.

"I know, but I'm going to anyway."

She nods emotionlessly and drags her eyes back to the TV. A few minutes pass before she whispers, "Thank you."

I don't respond because I have nothing to say. She doesn't need to thank me. I'm doing this just as much for myself as I am for her.

For the next hour, she continues her mission on the phone, alternating between dialing and texting. She finally gives up and curls into a ball, quietly sniffling to herself. There isn't much I can do for this damaged woman, but I can make sure she isn't alone.

Not five minutes later, her eyes close and her breathing evens out. I take a moment to really look at her. Her skin is creamy white and flawless. And her mousy hair has the slightest blonde roots peeking through. I still can't get over her eyes or figure out why anyone would want to cover them with brown contacts. But really, nothing about this woman makes sense. She's wearing fitted, black yoga pants and a plain, long-sleeved T-shirt that covers her completely. Jesus, what the hell is she hiding? She was terrified of me tonight yet so desperate for help that she was willing to momentarily trust me.

I know I shouldn't, but I can't stop myself from reaching out and brushing the hair away from her face. She releases a small gasp but only stirs for a second before falling right back to sleep.

I should really go. I could lock the door behind myself and leave her to sleep on her own. She doesn't need me anymore. But instead, I lean my head back, becoming lost in the sounds of her peaceful breaths mingling with the music of John Waite's "Change" coming from the TV.

It's not long before I follow her out of reality and into the darkness.

CHAPTER Six

Slate

I STARTLE AWAKE with a creak from the front door. I scrub my hands over my face, trying to get my bearings. It takes me a few seconds to realize where I am. I immediately glance to the woman sleeping soundly at the other end of the couch. When my eyes swing back around to figure out what woke me, I come face to face with the barrel of a gun.

"Don't fucking move," I hear a man growl, but in the darkness, I can't see his face.

I should lift my hands in submission. People always tell you not to fight, and if I were alone, I probably wouldn't. But the fact remains that I'm not alone and my fierce need to protect the woman next to me erases all rational thinking. I won't allow her to be scared again.

As fast as I can possibly move, I push the gun aside with one hand and land the other with a hard fist against his temple. He falls back with a grunt and the gun goes flying. We both jump toward it, fighting as we tangle on the ground. He rolls me to my back and lands a few punches to my face. I guard myself as much as possible, but I'm useless on the ground. I shove him to the side, knocking his head hard into the end table.

In the distance, Riley begins to scream, and the sound of her fear only fuels my fire. I land a punch to the gunman's face that dazes him, but I don't let up. This isn't a match where the ref is going to stop me; this is a fight for survival. Pound after pound, my fists land against his skull until his body eventually goes limp under me.

I need to find Riley and get us both the fuck out of here. I don't know who that was, but it's clear that she has more than enough reason to be afraid.

"Don't move," I hear her demand from the corner.

My eyes immediately find hers from where she stands across the darkened room. Her arms are raised and the gun she is holding shakes wildly in her hands.

"We need to get out of here," I say very calmly, careful not to frighten her. "Put the gun down." I push to my feet and take a step towards her.

"Don't move," she pleads with a whine as the tears stream down her cheeks.

"I won't hurt you. I promised you that. But I need to get you out of here. You have to trust me. We have to go before he wakes up."

She stares blankly at me for a second before she loses grasp of her emotions. A sob rips from her throat as she very slowly lowers the gun.

I rush forward, lifting her small body into my arms. "Shh… It's okay. Don't look."

Looping an arm around my neck, she melts into my touch. I'm almost to the door when a weak voice comes from the man lying bloody on the floor.

"Riley," he gurgles, and she explodes in my arms.

"Leo!" she screams, fighting from my grasp. I hold her tight, desperate to restrain her. "Leo! Oh God. What did you do!" she shouts at me, breaking free and rushing to his side.

What did I do?

At the last second, I catch her around the waist, dragging her away. I have no idea who he is, but I'm not letting her anywhere near that man.

"Let me go!" She kicks and hits me, all the while screaming his name.

"You need to calm the fuck down. I just woke up to him holding a gun in my face. Who the hell is he?"

"He's my..." she starts but pauses for a beat before finishing. "He's not the enemy."

"You don't know that," I growl.

"That might be the only thing I really do know," she retorts before spinning out of my arms and heading to his side. "Leo. Oh God." She kneels over his body, carefully inspecting him.

He grunts and reaches up to palm the back of her head, pulling it to his chest with a sigh. "I'm okay," he rasps.

"No, you're not. You have a deep laceration over your left eye and a possible left orbital fracture too." I listen to her ramble off medical terminology, even more confused than ever.

I watch with a sick feeling in my stomach as she begins to repair him. Is he why she is afraid? Is he the man she was searching for earlier? Or better yet, is he the man she was flinching from when I tried to touch her?

"I need ice," she demands, but I don't move an inch.

"There's some in my apartment," I say quietly, but no one could mistake my menacing tone. I need three minutes with this man. One round—that's all it would take to give him a little reminder. I would really only need half of that, but with the way Riley reacted, I have a feeling I would need the next ninety seconds to clean up.

"Well, go fucking get it!" she yells, continuing her examination of his face.

"I'm not leaving you with him. If you want ice, you are going to have to get it yourself," I say without an ounce of hesitation.

"Adam," she hisses, but he catches her attention.

"Go get it. I'll be fine," he says weakly.

She begins to reassure him, and it makes my skin crawl. "I'm not leaving you."

"Come on. I need some ice or I'm going to look like Sloth from *The Goonies* tomorrow." This fucking asshole is trying to make a joke right now. It only intensifies my rage.

Riley turns to me and asks, "Will you come with me?" I know she doesn't want to leave me alone with him. Rightly so, because I am going to fuck this asshole up the second she closes the door.

"No," I answer, never taking my eyes off the pitiful excuse of a man on the floor.

"Adam, please," she urges, but she could beg all day and it wouldn't change my mind. With or without her permission, I'm going to take care of this situation.

"Riley, just grab the ice. I promise we'll be okay," he answers, pushing up on his elbows.

"There's a bowl under the sink. Ice is in the freezer," I say emotionlessly.

"Don't touch him. Swear you won't touch him!" she orders, and my eyes flash to hers for only a second. She's pleading with me, but I don't give a damn. Her reactions over the last twenty-four hours speak louder than her words ever could.

I don't answer her demand, but *he* does. "Go. See if he has any gauze while you're at it." He pinches his nose and gently touches a large cut over his brow.

"Damn it," she swears, looking between us, but finally, marches out the door.

I don't waste any time. "Who are you?"

"Why were you sleeping on my couch?" he counters.

"Who. The. Fuck. Are. You?" I move closer to crowd him.

"Dave Roberts. I'm not her boyfriend if that's why you're trying to have a dick show," he says, spitting blood on the floor between us.

"Dave, huh? Then why the fuck does she call you Leo?"

"I don't know, *Slate*. Why does she call you Adam?"

Shit.

Riley

"Come on, come on, come on," I chant to Adam's ice trays as I quickly try to dump them into the bowl. The way Leo—I mean Dave—looked tonight tore me to shreds. I thought for too many hours that he was dead, and to see him lying lifelessly on the floor… God, I lost it. I haven't felt that level of panic in years. Not since that night when they managed to find us.

I desperately shake my head, trying to clear my thoughts. Now is not the moment to revisit the past, and it's definitely not the time to get lost in it.

I rush to his bathroom closet and search for medical supplies, but his shelves are empty. Not even so much as a Band-Aid. I give up looking and hurry toward the door, only stopping when I catch sight of his bag slung across the chair in the corner. I need to get back to Dave, but this might be my only chance to figure out who this guy is once and for all. I snatch open his bag and begin to dig through the contents. It's filled with nothing but clothes and a few toiletries, and in the very bottom is a roll of athletic tape. I twirl it in my hand for a minute before placing it on top of the ice and heading back to my apartment.

Due to the amazingly cheap doors, I can hear the guys talking and thankfully not brawling.

"I've never laid a fucking hand on her," Dave says adamantly.

"Then what the hell is she so afraid of? Who are you to her?" Adam questions, and even through the door, I can hear the accusation in his tone.

"I'm her family. Now, better question—what are you doing alone in my apartment with her?"

"I'm doing your fucking job." Adam's voice lifts menacingly without ever growing louder. "I'm looking out for her. Making sure she's safe. She's not okay. I really fucking hope you recognize that."

Dave doesn't immediately answer, and I take that as my cue to go inside.

"Hey," I say, looking between the two men.

Dave has moved to the couch, still holding his nose, but his position is relaxed. There is no alarm lingering around him. Adam is still standing only a few feet away, but I suspect his proximity is more to make whispering easier than it is to intimidate. Although, judging by the murderous glare he is flashing between me and Dave, I could be wrong.

"You okay?" I ask Dave, moving to the kitchen in search of a bag to hold the ice.

"Yep, it's not every day you get to go a round with—" he starts but is quickly interrupted.

"He's fine!" Adam spits out entirely too loudly.

I can see the silent exchange between the two men, but I don't mention it. Dave will explain it all to me later. I just pray the answer doesn't end up with us in another move. I'm not ready to start all over with a new life, even though it's only been a week in this one.

"You'll be fine. Keep ice on your eye tonight or it will be swollen shut in the morning. Hey, Riley. Can we talk for a minute?" Adam asks, motioning toward the door.

"Um, sure." I finish with the ice and head towards Dave. He flinches as I press it to his cut. "You need stitches," I snap when I get a better look at his gaping wound.

"Nah. I always wanted a scar right there. It will make me look badass. Give me some street cred, ya know?" he jokes.

His jovial tone makes me roll my eyes before dropping my chin to my chest. I fight back the tears that are vying to surface. I'm so sick of this game—the peaks of adrenaline and valleys of relief. I'd give anything for a plateau in my life.

I wipe my hands over my pants to dry them and buy myself some time while asking Dave a silent question. He tilts his head in approval toward the door, giving me the okay to move to the breezeway.

No sooner than the door clicks behind us, Adam rushes out, "I want you to stay at my place tonight."

I can't help the laugh that immediately springs from my throat. I bite my lips to cover the giggle, but it's too late.

His eyes harden when he growls out, "I'm not leaving you here with him."

"Um, excuse me for sounding ungrateful, but when exactly did my well-being become your responsibility?" I ask with a sudden flash of boldness, only because I feel safe knowing that Dave is less than ten feet away and most certainly listening to our conversation.

"How about the moment you came running to my door tonight, shaking and flinching from even the most innocent of touches? I don't know what the fuck is going on with you and him, but I do know I'm not leaving you here to take the brunt of his jealous fit just because he found a man sleeping on your couch. We both know nothing happened, but I won't leave you to pay that price."

"He's my cousin."

"Yeah, well, he was none too happy to find me in your apartment. He held a gun to my fucking head, Riley," he snaps, before leaning in close.

I immediately step away, causing my back to hit the door. "Back up," I warn, and with just those two words, the door swings open and I fall against Dave's chest.

"I have no issues making a few phone calls," Dave says bluntly, though I have no idea what the hell he is talking about.

"You can call the God damn president himself and that is not changing anything," Adam replies before directing his attention back to me. "You're not staying here tonight. Riley, I've seen this before. Just let me help you."

I shake my head, trying to find a way to make him understand, but why am I even trying to explain it to him? I have no idea who he is or why he is so determined to help me. I don't even know if he actually wants to help at all. Over the last twenty-four hours, this man has inserted himself in my life. While I appreciated having him here earlier, I'm still not sure I should trust him.

"Thank you for earlier, but I'm okay now. You have completely the wrong idea about things. Dave's very protective of me, but he has *never* hurt me. I'm sure it just surprised him to find you in the apartment."

"I bet," he scoffs. Then he reaches a gentle hand forward to grab my arm. "Listen—"

I instantly shrink away, and Dave grabs his wrist before he's able to make contact. Adam's glare is murderous as he snatches his arm from Dave's grasp. They silently stare at each other for a few seconds before Adam looks back at me.

"I don't feel right about this. I can't just leave you here."

Shit. Now I feel guilty for catching an attitude with him. He seems like a really good guy.

I take a chance and reach out to grab his arm. I give it a quick squeeze, and he immediately looks down to where I'm touching him. "I promise I'll be okay," I assure him, but he doesn't move. I hold him, willing him to understand, but a few seconds later, he pulls away. With an angry huff, he finally turns and walks toward his apartment.

It only takes a few seconds before he reaches his door, but I watch his every step. This has been a night filled with drama after drama, but I can't seem to stop my eyes from raking over his body. His sweats ride low on his hips, and the fitted T-shirt clings to his back.

"You need a napkin? You're drooling a little," Dave asks the moment Adam disappears into his apartment.

"What?" I spin around to face him.

"You know, in all our years together, I have never seen you check out a man," he says with a chuckle.

"I wasn't checking him out."

"Sorry. You're right. You were straight-up undressing him."

"I was not!" I yell, but my reaction only makes him laugh. I push past him and head back inside while he continues laughing in the doorway. "Would you shut up and sit down so I can try to get that cut closed? I think your nose is broken too." I snap, walking to the kitchen to grab my stolen tape.

"Well, there go my good looks."

"Oh, please. You would need to have them in order to lose them. Now, sit."

"Damn, you're feisty tonight," he says with a painful groan as he limps over to the couch.

I watch Leo with a soothing feeling of peace, but it's quickly replaced with anger. "Where the hell did you disappear to tonight? I was scared to death! You couldn't call and let me know you were okay?"

"Jesus, stop yelling. My head is killing me. I didn't know you would be looking for me. Last I heard, you were going to bed."

"I was until someone tried to break in."

"What?" He jumps to his feet. "Who?"

"Apparently it was just some kids. At least that's what Adam said, but it scared the shit out of me. Then I couldn't get in touch with you.

I thought…" I trail off.

"So that's why he was here." He nods as the picture becomes clearer.

"I had no idea what else to do."

"It's okay, babe. He's a good guy."

"Do you know who he is?"

"Oh yeah. And don't worry. He won't give us any trouble. I bet he'll be gone in the morning."

"What? Why?" I ask, surprised, and a knowing smile curves his lips.

"What's wrong, Riley?"

"Nothing. I just… I don't know. He helped me out tonight."

"Was this before or after he beat me unconscious?"

"You held a gun to his head! I can't exactly blame him."

"I came home to find you curled into a ball and a unknown man sleeping across from you. You will have to excuse the assumption," he snaps.

"Oh."

"Yeah, oh," he says, rubbing his head with a wince.

"Where the hell did you disappear to? I was worried sick counting down the hours," I repeat.

His shoulders fall, and I immediately feel bad for blaming him. "I was flying home. I had to turn my phone off in the air," he explains, and it makes my heartbreak.

Home.

This isn't home, but it's all we have.

I spend the next fifteen minutes replaying my night to him. I started at the very beginning and finished with *Vision Quest*. Dave didn't say much while I explained the afternoon, but at certain points, he couldn't hide the anger and regret from his face. I know it killed him to hear how Adam ended up on our sofa, but only because he feels he should have been there instead.

"So you're positive Adam isn't an issue?" I ask when I finish patching up his cuts the best I can with limited medical supplies.

"Why do you keep asking about him?" He smiles the biggest shit-eating grin I have ever seen in my life.

"I'm just worried. That's all."

"No, you're not. You are surprisingly calm as a fucking cucumber right now. You're curious about him," he says, and if possible, his smile grows even wider.

My cheeks heat to pink as I stumble over my words. "It's just… I mean… He was really nice tonight, and I don't know. He didn't have to be."

"Well why don't you go over there and say thank you." He pulls the ice from my hand and holds it to his own head.

"What? No! I can't just prance over there and bother him yet again. He probably—okay, he definitely—thinks I'm crazy as hell. But now he probably thinks we are some sort of criminal duo too."

"Just go, Riley! He'll probably be gone tomorrow. This might be your last chance to tell him." He gives me an exaggerated wink that causes me to roll my eyes.

"Why are you pushing me? I can't go to his apartment at four in the morning."

"Why not? He just left ours like ten minutes ago. I think it's safe to assume he's still awake."

"I'm not going over there, so hush. He must have hit your head really hard tonight. Usually you try to keep me away from people."

"Don't give me that crap. That is not true at all and you fucking know it. I don't try to keep you away from anyone. You're the one who is scared of letting anyone get close. You can have friends, Riley. Jesus, you *need* someone besides me."

"Maybe, but I definitely don't need the giant hot guy who lives next door," I mumble, causing Leo to choke out a laugh.

"The fact that you just called him a 'giant hot guy' leads me to believe that you do." His voice is teasing, but the hopeful look in his eye saddens me.

All Dave has ever wanted was for me to find someone—a girl-friend to chat with or even a boyfriend to move on with. He just wants me to have a life, but I've never wanted that, so he has gone through great lengths to help me keep away from everyone else.

For me, people represent one thing—danger. Who are they really? How quickly would they turn on you? And worse yet, how bad would it hurt if I had to pick up and leave them behind on a moment's notice? It's not just my life that's in danger; my heart is at risk as well.

But tonight with Adam, I felt something I've never felt with anyone but Dave—*safe*.

Damn it.

"I did steal the tape out of his bag," I say sheepishly.

"You went through his bag?" he asks, shocked, but his voice is full of pride. I peek up at him with a small smile. "Good girl," he praises.

"I just wanted to know who he was. His apartment is empty, but there was a small bag mainly filled with clothes, but it had a roll of tape at the bottom. I'm assuming he really is a boxer?"

"What gave it away? The way he lit into me tonight or the muscles that turned you into a horny co-ed?"

"Shut up! I wasn't staring at him."

"Right. Well, take the man back his tape. But put your contacts in before he falls in love. You have to at least give him a fighting chance," he teases, but I suddenly remember Adams words from earlier.

"He said my eyes were beautiful," I confess and immediately look down at the floor.

"Of course he did. Your eyes are unforgettable, Riley. Which is exactly why you need to put back in your contacts. Tell him they are prescription or something if he asks. But just go over there."

"Damn, you're bossy tonight. Can you stop telling me what to do?" I snap, but we both know the attitude isn't real.

"You went to him tonight. When you were afraid, you put down the gun and went to him," he says, holding my eyes. It's a simple statement and not at all what we were talking about, but I know exactly what he's thinking.

"It doesn't mean anything," I whisper.

"Oh it definitely means something, Riley. Nothing may come from it, but it means that, even for just a second, you opened yourself up to trusting someone else."

"I was scared." I try to defend myself.

"Right. I get why you went to his apartment, but you invited him in to watch a movie after that."

"I'm not in love with this guy or something if that's what you're aiming at here."

"I'm not insinuating that you are. I don't care if you just have a conversation with him. You need to make friends. Badly. I know for a fact that he has zero connection to Wilkes, so I'm telling you to go say thank you. You're not afraid of him, so go and enjoy speaking to another human without fear."

Damn it. He's right. Those moments with Adam, even amongst the chaos, were a breath of fresh air to starved lungs.

"Fine." I let out a huff, pretending to be frustrated when, in actuality, I'm freaking out.

"Go!" he demands then drops his head back against the couch, closing his eyes.

"You going to be okay?" I ask.

"I'll survive," he responds, but he never looks back at me.

CHAPTER Seven

Slate

"I NEED A favor," I speak into the phone the minute my door shuts behind me.

"Anything, Slate," Jimmy says, and I can envision him pacing around the room as he answers this late-night call from me.

"Hire a PI and find out absolutely everything you can about Dave or Leo Roberts. He lives in apartment 108 here. And when I say everything, I mean everything—right down to what he had for breakfast yesterday and the porn he jerked off to last night."

"Are you in trouble?" he asks in that fatherly way I've come to expect from him.

"Not me. But I think someone is."

"Maybe you should come back. Go down to the beach house or up to the apartment in Chicago."

"Nah, I'm good. I got into a scuffle tonight though and I just want to get his backstory. He's got a woman with him. Her name is Riley. He says they are related, but I'm not so sure," I respond, heading to the fridge, desperate for a drink to dull my anger. I snatch out a beer and open it with a loud pop.

"You drinking at two a.m.?" he asks, and I have to laugh.

"It's four here."

"Well thank Christ for that. I was starting to worry about you."

I laugh mid-sip, causing beer to spray from my lips. "Oh yeah? Is drinking at two worse than drinking at four?" I ask while wiping my mouth on the back of my sleeve.

"Hell yeah. Two a.m. means you haven't stopped yet. Four a.m. just means you are starting early," he says without a single hint of humor.

"I'll keep that in mind." I smile to myself.

"So, you have anything other than a name and address?"

"Nope."

"You want to explain any of this to me?"

"Nope," I repeat then take another pull from my beer.

"I'll see what I can do, Slate. If you've been jeopardized, you need to get out of there. Don't let people find you or you will never be able to go back."

"Damn it, I know," I curse, more at the entire situation than his reminder.

"Right. Well, I'll let you know as soon as I find something. I'm assuming money isn't an issue on this one since you're asking me."

"Whatever it costs, Jimmy. I just want answers."

"Give me a couple of days."

"Thanks," I say, but in true Jimmy Douglas fashion, he hangs up before I even finish the word.

I let out a relieved breath, knowing that soon I'll be getting some answers.

"Fuck." I shouldn't have left her with him, but what the hell was I supposed to do? She wouldn't listen to me, and he almost even convinced me that he isn't who she's afraid of. *Almost.* I think back to our conversation while she was getting the ice.

"My name is Adam," I said adamantly.

"No. Your name is Slate Andrews. I'm just trying to figure out what the fuck you are doing here," he said, sliding his body up onto the couch. "And better yet, why you told her your name was Adam in the first place."

"Don't say anything. Please," I pleaded.

"Are you more worried about your little secret than the fact that I held a gun to your head?"

"Yes," I answered honestly.

"And her?" His swollen eyes narrowed slightly.

His question left me puzzled. I didn't know what he was asking or what answer I could possibly give him. "What about her?"

"See, I walk into my apartment tonight to find Riley curled into a ball. You were sound-ass asleep, and so was she, but her hand—" He paused to shake his head. "She had one hand reaching out, holding the arm you were propped up on. Damn it. I should have killed you when I had the chance."

"Oh yeah? How'd that last attempt work out for you?" I asked just to be a dick while wiping the nonexistent blood from my bottom lip.

"You could have killed me if it meant that she was okay," he announced oddly, and it quite honestly floored me. *Who the fuck is this guy?*

"Why the hell is she so terrified of everything? She was a fucking mess tonight. I've never seen a woman so afraid in my life. I swear to God, if I find out you had anything to do with that fear…" I stopped only to step in close. I know the walls are thin, and she was right next door. "I won't stop next time," I solemnly swore. "There is not an army in the fucking world that could save you if I find out that you're responsible."

He cocked his battered and bruised head to the side with a sick sense of approval. But what really pissed me off most was the slight tip in his lips when he said, "I've never laid a fucking hand on her."

"Then what the hell is she so afraid of? Who are you to her?" I screamed as loud as my whisper would allow.

"I'm her family. Now, better question—what are you doing alone in my apartment with her?"

"I'm doing your fucking job. I'm looking out for her. Making sure she's safe. She's not okay. I really fucking hope you recognize that." I glared at him and his eyes immediately dropped to his lap.

"Hey." Riley suddenly appeared in the door, halting any further conversation.

I did everything I could short of dragging her away from him. And I would have done that if I'd thought it wouldn't make me just as bad as he is. A barrage of images from the night flashes through my mind. I'll never be able to forget how scared she was tonight, but the one picture in the forefront of my mind is that single moment when she smiled. Now that was amazing.

Riley

I have no idea how I let Dave guilt me into this. But somehow, I find myself nervously knocking on Adam's front door. It's still dark outside but the sun is starting to peek over the horizon. It's been a really long night.

"What the hell am I doing?" I ask myself. This is ridiculous. He's probably asleep and I'm going to be the crazy neighbor who wakes him up yet again.

Just as I turn to walk away, I hear the click of his deadbolt.

He opens the door and his eyes quickly check over my body from head to toe. His angry demeanor sends me back a step, but he immediately softens.

"Shit, Riley. Are you okay?" He reaches out to pull me inside, and normally I would be afraid of such a sudden movement, but the tenderness in his voice keeps my fear at bay.

"I'm fine," I say as he closes the door behind me.

"Did he hit you?" he growls, and my head immediately snaps up to his.

"Dave? No way! I promise, Adam. He would never hurt me. You have the wrong idea about him. I swear."

"Well I'm not sure exactly what idea I should have. You're terrified of everything and he came home wielding a gun. Sorry, that doesn't exactly scream your normal, average life to me."

"He's my family."

"So I've heard," he replies sarcastically, and I suddenly feel like coming over here was even worse of an idea than I'd originally thought.

"Well, okay then. Here, I took your tape. I wanted to return it and say thanks for putting up with me tonight, including right now. I won't bother you again," I rush out and turn to bolt.

Before I make it even a step, he asks, "Why'd you put back in your contacts?"

"They're prescription," I answer with my practiced lie.

"You didn't wear glasses when we were watching the movie earlier," he quickly responds with apparent disbelief and a surprising amount of attitude.

"What is this, an inquisition?" I snap back at him. "My glasses are broken. You don't have to be a dick."

He sucks in a breath before running a hand through his hair. "I'm worried about you," he admits, catching me off guard.

"You don't even know me."

"Which is what makes being worried about you difficult and ridiculous."

"Why do you care?" I inquire when curiosity gets the best of me.

"I told you. You remind me of someone I used to know." He lifts a single muscular arm and grabs the back of his neck. I can't help but watch the way his bicep flexes.

"Really. I'm okay. I get a little out of sorts when he goes out of town. I'm sorry he almost shot you," I say in all seriousness, but even I can hear how silly and inadequate that apology sounds.

He begins to laugh, and I smile up at him through my lashes.

"Well if that's how we are doing this…I'm sorry I almost killed him."

"Apology accepted." I finally look up and his smile fades.

"You should really get clear contacts." His eyes flash back and forth over mine as if he is searching for a glimpse of the true color. An unexpected flutter tingles in my stomach, forcing my eyes to the ground.

"Yeah. Anyway…" I try to change the subject. "Here's your tape." I reach out to hand it to him, but he doesn't immediately take it. He stands staring at my outstretched arm.

"So not only are you my weird neighbor who forces me to watch '80s movies and gets me into life-threatening situations, but you're also a thief? I know that tape was in the bottom of my bag." He lifts a questioning eyebrow and crosses his thick arms over his chest. He looks pissed, but the twitch in the corner of his mouth gives him away.

"Something like that. I was trying to find some gauze."

"In my bag?"

"Okay fine. I was being a nosy woman and trying to figure out what your deal is," I rush out, embarrassed.

"And did you?" His friendly tone disappears completely.

"No."

"Our good friend Dave didn't fill you in?"

"Huh?" How does he know that Dave looked into him? We stare at each other, both of us just as confused as the other. "Well, Adam, this was fun," I say awkwardly. "I should go. I just wanted to say thanks for tonight, and I'm sorry about everything—including stealing your tape."

I turn and head for the door when I hear him ask from behind me, "What's your last name?"

I freeze for a moment, knowing how I want to answer, but instead, I say, "Peterson. Yours?" I question.

"Andrews."

I turn back to face him with a true smile. "Adam Andrews is quite the mouthful. I like the alliteration though."

"Yep," he answers without emotion, and it appears he's lost in thought.

"Okay, well…I'll see you around."

"Yep," he repeats while staring blankly over my shoulder.

Without another glance, I open the door and head back to my apartment.

No sooner than I walk in does Dave start in with the questions.

"How'd it go?"

"Weird," I answer, perplexed.

"Weird good? Or weird bad?"

"Weird weird," I respond, heading to my room.

I need some sleep and a whole new day. Unfortunately for me, I'll

only be getting one of those tonight. Even if my alarm weren't scheduled to go off in approximately one hour, there is no way my mind would allow me to fall asleep tonight. Not when there is obsessing to be done. And I have a full twenty-four hours' worth of things to obsess about—all of which start and end with muscles and golden-brown eyes.

Slate

"Wake up, sunshine!" I hear from the other side of my front door, quickly followed by a loud knock.

I pry my eyes open and notice that it's well past noon. Jesus, I can't remember the last time I slept this late, though there were a lot of firsts for me last night.

"Oh, Mr. Andrews?" he calls and it sends me rushing toward the door before the asshole on the other side has a chance to repeat it.

I crack the door to find that prick from last night holding a drink carrier containing two large coffees. Before I have a chance to slam the door in his face, he slides a foot inside, braces a hand against the top, and says, "We need to talk, *Slate*." He says my name as if it were a threat, and it only serves to enrage me. The smile on his swollen face has me wanting to reopen every single wound Riley no doubt closed last night.

"I have nothing to say to you," I respond, looking down at his foot, silently ordering him to remove it or lose it.

He smiles wider while stepping even closer to the door. "Maybe not. But there are a few things you should know about Riley and her past."

I watch him for a minute, trying to figure out what the hell to do. I know I should close the fucking door, pack up, and head to my apartment in Chicago. I should chalk this place up as a loss and never look back. But instead, I open the door and usher him inside. Hopefully, I can get some answers about the small woman I can't seem to stop worrying about.

"Good choice. My next move was calling the tabloids to let them know where you were hiding."

"I'm not paying you off to keep quiet if that's where you are trying to go with this," I say firmly. I love it here, but not enough to give him a single cent.

He begins to chuckle and shake his head. "I'm not trying to blackmail you. So can you tone it down a notch? Let's talk."

"Right. Talk." I motion away the coffee he pushes toward me.

With a shrug, he puts the drink on the table then flops down on the couch. "Well okay then," he says, propping his hands behind his head and crossing his legs at the ankles, making himself completely at home. *Fucking dick.* "Riley is my cousin. Our moms were sisters and we were both only children. I think of her like my sister."

"Get to the point," I growl to speed him up so I can kick his ass out and hopefully catch the next flight to Chicago. I can't imagine that this is going to have a positive ending. A retreat to my apartment in the Windy City is inevitably in my future.

"She's had a shit past. Her last boyfriend beat the shit out of her. I, in turn, beat the shit out of him, which didn't make him too happy. So we moved here to get away. So yes, Riley is always afraid, but it's not of me."

"You know, you two are spending an exorbitant amount of time trying to convince me of this. I honestly don't give a shit anymore. Your life is just that—yours. I'm glad I was there for her last night, but consider that the end of my part in that fucked-up situation." I don't flat out lie. I would love some answers about what is really going on with them, but I'm not trying to insert myself into their shit. I just want to make sure she's safe.

I can't close my eyes without being consumed by the images of her shaking and crying. I need to get out of here, but I sure as hell can't just walk away without being sure nothing else will harm her. It's not that I'm on some fucked-up savior mission now. I just want to do for her what I wish someone had done for my mother all those years ago.

"See, that is what I was hoping for too. But I got a phone call this morning from a buddy of mine informing me that someone was looking into my background." He quirks a knowing eyebrow at me. "You wouldn't happen to know anything about that, would you, Slate?"

"I have no clue what you are talking about, *Leo*." I sling his name back at him, and he reacts as if someone lit him on fire.

He flies to his feet and closes the distance between us. "Shut the fuck up!" He steps up into my face with a challenge.

"Oh, so it's okay for you to toss my name around like a God damn cussword, but I can't say yours at all?" I grin, leaning in even closer.

"It's not my fucking name. It's a nickname she used to call me when we were kids. And it means painful things to both of us now," he explains, and there's an odd tinge of pleading underneath his angry tone.

I think back on the night before and remember the way she called him Leo when she freaked out initially, but the second she calmed down, she immediately went back to calling him Dave. I'm starting to believe that there might be some truth to his words.

I exhale a frustrated sigh. "What the fuck do you want from me? Why are you here and telling me all of this? I don't know you. We're not friends. We just happen to share a wall between our apartments. Can we go back to that?" I step away, just wanting this bullshit to end.

I'm supposed to be here relaxing and winding down after months of rigorous training. I'm supposed to be experiencing my calm, but instead, I'm shoving my nose into places it doesn't belong all in an effort to be some sort of knight in shining armor to a woman who may or may not need to be rescued. Maybe I'm just making this whole thing harder for her by asking questions. No one wants to relive their abuse, and definitely not in front of a stranger.

"I won't expose who you are, Slate. Not even to her. But I'm going to need you to back off your little search into our past. I know about your mother." His words have me stepping right back into his face. "So I completely understand where you are coming from with this. But I promise, your digging up the past won't help her. I'm trying to help her move forward, not backwards."

We stare at each other for a few minutes, neither one of us willing to back down. Finally, he turns on a heel and heads to the door, pausing just before he leaves.

"Oh, and one more thing. This part really is kind of blackmail. Riley feels bad about involving you in all that mess last night, so she wants to cook you dinner at our place tonight."

"She doesn't have to do that. She already said thank you."

"Yeah, but you know women. They think nothing says thanks like good food, and if you've ever tasted her fajitas, you would be inclined to agree."

"I can't make it. Sorry," I say dismissively. If I'm going to forget about this whole damn rescue mission, I'm going to do it completely.

"Well, figure out how to make it. Riley is really excited. You do this one thing and we go back to being neighbors, *Adam*." He grins.

I take a deep breath and scrub a hand through my hair. I absolutely don't want to go over there tonight, and I think he's just fucking with me about the blackmail part, but the idea of disappointing Riley is really what has me reconsidering. I can go, eat her food, pretend to be social, and then head home early. Maybe then I can really put all of this behind me.

"Sure, yeah. Whatever. What time?" I respond with an exaggerated sigh.

"Six. See ya then! Oh, and don't let that coffee go to waste. I got it just the way you like—two cream, no sugar." I don't even have a chance to ask before he answers my unspoken question. "I Googled you." He tosses me a wink and walks out the door.

Of course he did.

CHAPTER CHAPTER CHAPTER CHAPTER CHAPTER Eight

Riley

"WHERE ARE YOU?" Dave barks over the phone as I pull up in front of our apartment.

"I just got here. I had to stop at the grocery store to get the stuff to quell your sudden craving for fajitas," I smart back at him.

"Well I would have gone myself but you took the car to work, and I wouldn't have had any clue what the hell you put in that delicious yellow rice."

"It comes in a box. You've watched me make it a million times." I laugh, dragging out the bags and heading up the sidewalk.

"Yeah, but don't you put those little green and red peppers in the rice?"

"Nope, all in the box." I laugh again. "Hey, I'm outside. Can you get the door?" I ask before ending the phone call. He pulls open the door and I suck in a startled breath. "Jesus, you look horrible."

"Pretty burly, huh?" he replies, taking the groceries from my hands.

Using his chin for leverage, I inspect the various cuts and bruises Adam left on his face last night. "Come here. Let me clean that one over your eye again before I start cooking. I got butterfly bandages to hopefully keep it closed a little tighter than just the tape."

"I told you I was okay with a scar."

"Sorry to disappoint, but I don't leave scars if I can help it."

"I'll be fine. Besides, you need to get cooking." He looks down at his watch impatiently. "Did you get the stuff for guac too? You want me to get started on that?" he hurries out, causing me to give him a questioning look.

Dave hasn't offered to help me in the kitchen since the early days. He sometimes cooks, but if I'm in the kitchen, he steers clear.

"You must be starving if you're offering to help."

"I really am. So hurry up and get to cooking. It's almost six."

"I know you are getting old, but is this a nursing home? Do we need to start eating dinner at, like, four these days?"

"No, six is more than acceptable." He flops down on the couch, propping up his feet on the coffee table and engrossing himself with whatever is on TV.

Fifteen minutes later, a knock at the door causes me to jump and my pulse to race. I spin around, and Dave must read my fear because he immediately shakes his head.

"I was expecting this one, Riley."

I let out a relieved sigh and watch as he confidently strolls to the door.

Just before he pulls it open, he looks back at me. "Promise you won't poison my food. You know fajitas are my favorite."

I don't even have a chance to ask what the hell he is talking about because he opens the door, revealing Adam Andrews standing in the hall.

"Hey," Adam says awkwardly.

"What's up, man?" Dave replies, extending a hand.

Adam stares for a minute before taking it in a firm shake. "Hey,

Riley." He offers me a quick nod.

"Uh. Hi," I stumble out.

"I wasn't sure what to bring, so I brought some beer and wine and also some bandages and antiseptic for your face."

"Well aren't you a gentleman," Dave says humorously, taking the bags from his hands and bringing them to the kitchen.

Shoving his hands in his pockets, Adam rocks back and forth on his heels uncomfortably. I've never seen him actually dressed before. Every time I've had the pleasure of embarrassing myself in front of him, he's been dressed in some combination of sweats. But tonight, he is wearing perfectly tattered, dark jeans with washed-out thighs and a navy-blue sweater over a white button-down. It stylishly clings to his every curved muscle. If Dave thought I needed a napkin last night to wipe away my drool, I probably need a super-absorbency mop tonight. *Jesus, Adam is gorgeous.*

"Dave, can you help me for a second? Adam, please make yourself at home. Can I get you something to drink?" I ask, faking the Suzy Homemaker bit, all the while dabbing at the corner of my mouth just to be sure nothing is actually leaking.

"Just a beer," he answers, looking around the apartment.

"Dave," I warn with an overcompensating smile.

"Excuse me for a minute," he tells Adam before following me down the hall.

"What the motherfucking hell is he doing here?" I snap the moment we get out of hearing range, which is honestly a joke. This apartment is so cheap that you could be standing three doors down and still hear me whisper-yelling.

"Slow your roll, babe," he responds with a wicked grin.

"Slow my roll? Really? What is he doing here, and why didn't you tell me he was coming over? I loathe surprises. Damn it." I begin to pace back and forth down the hall.

"I invited him over because I wanted to get to know him a little better." He tries to explain, but his words catch me off guard.

"What? I thought you said he wasn't an issue."

He lets out a frustrated groan. "He isn't, Riley. I just meant that it wouldn't hurt for us to know more about our neighbor. I'm talking on a personal level."

"So this is a social call?"

"If it were 1920, yes, it would be a 'social call.'" He smirks at me. "But since this is 2014, I'm just going to say I invited the neighbor over for dinner."

"Ha, ha. Freaking hysterical. You should have told me, jerk," I whisper and look back over my shoulder to make sure Adam isn't watching us.

"Understood," he responds with an unapologetic smile.

I let out a huff, knowing that there is no use in arguing with him about this. I walk back toward the kitchen to find Adam standing over the cutting board, slicing up bell peppers.

"Oh jeez. You don't have to do that," I rush out.

He looks up and offers me a half smile and shrug. "It's okay. I actually really like to cook. I'm not great, but I can slice a mean vegetable," he jokes with a crooked grin that's so kind it makes my annoyance disappear. "You want me to open the wine?" he asks, putting the knife down on the cutting board.

"Oh, um… Thanks, but I'm not a big drinker. I bet Dave would take one of the beers though."

"I absolutely would," Dave confirms, appearing behind me. "Hey, Adam, what are your thoughts on the Lopez vs. O'Neil fight tonight?"

"Shit. Is that tonight?" Adam pulls two beers out of the fridge, where he apparently placed them earlier.

Dave quirks an eyebrow and tilts his head in confusion. "You forgot?" he asks in disbelief.

"I've been busy," Adam responds shortly.

"Whatever. This is probably the biggest fight of the year!" Dave laughs, and Adam gives him an unimpressed eye roll.

"It's hardly the biggest fight of the year. But I think O'Neil really has a shot this time."

"No shit?" Dave asks, surprised.

"Yeah. He's been working out with Mike Greene. It's always been his speed that kept him back, but Mike…" Adam continues to talk, but I turn back to the food while they bond.

The guys sit in the living room, watching the pre-fight interviews. They fall into a casual comfort with each other, but neither ever truly drops his guard. I steal glances at Adam every opportunity I get, and on rare occasions, I catch him watching me too. Even though I have no idea what he's talking about, I find myself jumping in and out of their conversation.

"Can I help with anything?" Adam asks when he comes to the kitchen to grab another beer.

"Nah. I'm good. Thanks though."

I move so he can squeeze back past me in this postage stamp of a kitchen. But instead, he leans his hip against the counter and tips the beer to his lips. I watch from the corner of my eye, not sure what to say or how to react to his sudden attention.

"You're weird," Adam says, catching me completely off guard.

"Excuse me?"

"You're weird," he repeats with a serious look, but his eyes are dancing with humor.

"Um, where I come from, that is not exactly a compliment."

"It's not a compliment where I come from either. But that doesn't make you any less weird."

I blink at him for a minute, trying to figure out how the hell I'm supposed to respond to something like that. "Well, I officially think you're weird now too. Who says that to someone they barely know?" I snip, causing him to laugh.

"I've met you maybe five times now and you are either terrified or awkward every single time."

"Yeah, sorry about that. I'm not always—"

He interrupts me. "But just now, when I showed up, you were bossy and filled with attitude while talking to him." He lifts his chin in Dave's direction.

"Were you eavesdropping?"

"Oh please. These walls are so thin I can hear you chewing your food every night at dinner. But in this case, yes, I was eavesdropping." He pulls another sip from his beer.

However, Adam doesn't just take a sip like your average person. No, that would be too easy on me. He lifts the beer to his luscious lips and tilts it up—his smoldering eyes never leave mine. His glare is intense and, if I'm not wrong, a little bit teasing. I look back and forth between his eyes and lips before turning away.

"You hear anything interesting?"

"Just that Dave lied when he told me you wanted me to come over for dinner."

"Son of a bitch," I mumble under my breath.

"It's okay. Watching you stand up to him back there was worth it. Makes me feel a little better about leaving you last night."

"Adam, he loves me. He wouldn't hurt me."

"Well, sometimes those lines can get blurry. I'm just glad to see this fiery and pissed-off side of you. It looks better on you than the woman I met last night." He grins and his eyes slide over my body in an obviously flirtatious way.

"Well, it's good to see that you actually own clothes and don't just live in sweats." I smile, raking my eyes over him in the exact way he just did.

He laughs, and his easygoing smile steals my breath. "What can I do to help?"

"Go entertain Dave. Any minute now, he's going to start whining for dinner."

"Ugh. I'm still not sure how I feel about him," he says honestly while glancing over to where Dave is watching TV.

"He's a good guy, but if you want to hang out in here, I'm sure I can find some way to put you to use. You botched my peppers, so chopping anything is out. But if you want to stir the meat, I won't stop you."

"I did not botch the peppers. That is how they were supposed to look," he says defensively.

"I've minced garlic with bigger pieces than the peppers you crushed."

"Hey! How about you stop complaining and perhaps give me some credit for multitasking. I was eavesdropping while I cut those." He smirks, and it makes my cheeks heat.

"Well, regardless. I'm benching you from knife duties. Grab the spatula, tough guy, and make sure the meat doesn't burn."

He puts his beer down and moves to the other side of the kitchen, and just as he squeezes past me, his hand drags across the small of my back, sending an unfamiliar shiver over my entire body.

I look away and silently mouth, "Oh my God!" as he begins flipping the meat.

What the hell just happened? Where did this funny and charming man come from? This Adam is a far cry from the one I met yesterday. Sure, he was kind and gentle, but this is different. This is a man who seems to be interested in me as a woman, and the best difference of all is that fact doesn't scare the hell out of me. I bite my lip and turn my head away from him to hide my giddy smile.

Dinner comes and goes, and I'm not sure I've ever smiled so much. Adam never reverted to the quiet guy I originally thought he was. He's smart and witty, two traits that made him even more attractive to me. Our conversation flowed easily, and my naturally shy disposition vanished. We chatted like old friends. God, it felt amazing. I can't even swear to you that Dave was even at the table while we ate. It seems Adam and I dominated every conversation.

"Riley, that was delicious," Adam says, standing to clear the table.

I quickly try to stop him. "You don't have to do that!"

"No, sit. You cooked. I can manage the dishes."

"We should hire him," Dave leans over and loudly whispers in my ear.

I giggle for a minute before heading toward the sink to stop him.

"I have a trick," I say, stepping beside him. I catch a whiff of his cologne, and it takes my every conscious thought not to sway toward him. "Watch." I fill the sink with warm, soapy water and pull the dirty dishes from his hands, dropping them unceremoniously into the water. "There. They're soaking," I announce.

A slow smile creeps across his face. "Who's going to wash them after they *soak*?"

"I'll guilt Dave into doing them in the morning." I return his smile.

"She really will," Dave confirms from the couch, but Adam's eyes never leave mine. It's unnerving but exhilarating all at once.

"Make sure you do that." Very gently, he reaches a hand forward to brush a hair out of my face.

I freeze, but not because I'm frightened. I can't move as I watch his hand tenderly moving toward my face. It's so slow that I know I could easily stop him if I wanted. It's a purposeful speed that makes my heart skip a beat. He knows I'm skittish and he decided to take a risk, but he made sure to make me feel comfortable while he did it. The flutter in my stomach returns at full force.

"So yeah, I bet the fight is starting soon." I look down and step away, wishing I could have stayed. *Story of my life.*

"Right," he responds without moving an inch.

I look up to find him staring down at me with a sudden and unexpected heat in his eyes.

"You really need to get new contacts," he mumbles before walking away.

I collect myself for a few minutes before following him over to the couch. I look between the two men sitting on either end before settling for the tattered recliner nearest to Dave.

"No way!" Dave shouts, and Adam's lip lifts a miniscule amount. "Did you see Lopez tonight? He's huge!"

"He made weigh-in though," Adam challenges.

"Maybe with one leg off the scale." Dave begins to laugh, and Adam joins him in the most amazing and unexpected show of humor between the two men, who before this moment have been cordial at best. I can't help but laugh right along with them.

The announcer begins his exaggerated introductions that vibrate over the speakers of our cheap TV, causing us all to automatically hush. Both of the competitors enter the ring and I sigh to myself when I think about how delicious Adam would look crossing through those ropes.

"I'll be right back." Dave stands up and heads down the hall, rubbing his stomach, but Adam never drags his eyes from the TV.

A few moments later, the fight begins and he immediately slides forward to the edge of his seat. I don't particularly care for boxing, but watching Adam get excited about it makes me curious. He doesn't speak or even cheer, but as the rounds progress, I watch him more than the TV. I begin to think he's forgotten I'm even in the room. With every punch thrown on the screen, he twitches to the left or right, and at one point, he dips completely. I use a hand to stifle my laugh, but he immediately swings his gaze to mine. I try to wave him off and excuse my laughter with a hand gesture, but he cracks a knowing smile that makes me blush.

"Something funny, Riley?"

"No. No." I continue laughing. "It's just I wasn't sure which match to watch—the one on TV or the imaginary one you were fighting."

He gives me a quiet chuckle and leans back against the couch, scrubbing his hands over his jeans. "Sorry. Habit."

"So you really are a boxer, huh?" I ask, and his bright smile fades.

"I am," he answers shortly.

"You ever been to one of these big matches? I bet it would be exciting to watch one of these in person."

A glimmer flickers back into his flat eyes and he nods. "Yeah, I've been to a couple. It's always…fun."

"Cool." I say awkwardly, looking down and plucking imaginary fuzz from my pants. "Hmm. I wonder where Dave went?" I peek down the hall to see the bathroom door shut but the light glowing from the crack under the door. I fully expected Adam to go back to watching the fight, but instead, he crosses his legs, knee to ankle, and tosses an arm over the back of the couch.

"So where are you from, Riley?"

"Florida," I answer without thinking. My eyes go wide when I realize what I just admitted, and no matter how hard I try, I can't catch the truth as it flies across the room.

"Florida? Really?" He appears shocked.

"Well, at least that's what I like to tell people. I'm actually from here in Ohio, but doesn't Florida sound like more fun?" I nervously laugh as he narrows his eyes.

"Yeah, that does sound more exciting than Ohio. You ever been down there—to Florida, I mean?" He asks suspiciously.

"Yeah. I went to Disney World once when I was in college. I loved it. What about you?" I attempt to change the focus of the conversation to him.

"I've been to Disney a couple times."

"No, I mean, where are you from?"

"Oh, I grew up right near here actually, but these days, I'm kind of a nomad. I stay in Chicago a lot," he responds, glancing back at the fight. I could be wrong, but I think it's more to avoid the conversation than to actually catch up on the action.

Normally, I would enjoy the silence. I can't screw up anything else like I did with my little Florida slip up if I don't talk. But I'm too curious about him to keep myself from starting another conversation.

"So, how'd you get into boxing?"

He turns back to face me, and a staggering warmth slides over his face. "My mom put me in boxing when I was a kid. Apparently, I was quite the handful when I was young, and she wanted to give me an outlet to get out the pent-up frustrations." He pauses to laugh to himself.

"You stuck with it all these years?"

"I did. By the time I hit middle school, I was a good bit larger than most of the other kids my age, and while football seemed like the likely sport, I just wasn't interested. I grew up with just my mom, and I took the role of man of the house very seriously. I wanted to be able to protect her. I took up wrestling and enrolled in every self-defense class the community center offered, and when I wasn't there, I was at the boxing gym." He stops to look over at me knowingly. His words from that first night flash into my head.

You remind me of my mother.

"Oh." I look down at my hands, twisting in my lap.

"Have you ever taken any self-defense classes, Riley?"

"Um. Yeah. Dave's taught me a good bit. I swear I'm not always frightened like I was last night," I say unconvincingly.

"Was he the same one to teach you how to handle a gun?" he asks sarcastically.

"Hey! I know how to shoot. I just hate guns," I laugh, trying to defend myself.

"Let me teach you some self-defense stuff."

"What? Why?"

"Because I think it would make you feel a little more secure to know how to properly defend yourself. I mean, combine that with your stellar skills behind the barrel of a gun and you wouldn't have to fear anyone," he teases.

If he only knew how much I really have to fear. No self-defense class will make me feel secure, but I still laugh at his silly comment. It feels good to make light of it even if I'm the only one in on the joke.

"It's okay. You don't have to do that," I answer, but he leans in close to catch my eye.

"Dave seems like he means well, but I promise I can teach you better, Riley. Let me help you feel safe," he implores and the gentleness in this huge man's tone has me immediately agreeing. "Good. I'll get a mat and move aside my furniture. We can do it in my apartment."

"Oh, God. That sounds like a lot of trouble. You don't have to do that."

"No trouble. Tomorrow after work, okay?"

"Um, I guess."

He nods and turns right back around just in time to watch the last thirty seconds of the fight. "What happened to Dave? He missed watching Lopez get destroyed."

"You know, I'm not sure." I get up and head down the hall. I knock on the bathroom door, but I hear his voice from behind me.

"Over here, babe," he says from inside his room.

I walk to his doorway to see him lying on his bed, reading a book. His legs are crossed at the ankle and he's wearing those nerdy glasses I tease him about all the time.

"What are you doing?"

"Reading," he states obviously.

"Okay, why are you reading? You missed the entire fight."

"I needed some fresh air," he says with a smile.

"In your bedroom?"

"The sexual tension was strangling me."

My head snaps back in surprise. "What the hell are you talking about?"

"All those little side glances and flirty smiles you two were tossing around the room were suffocating me." He makes a gagging gesture before giving me a wide smile.

"You have lost your damn mind! I was not flirting with him." *I was totally flirting with him.*

"No, you were mentally undressing him while *he* flirted with you."

"Shut up!" I whisper while reaching back to pull the door to his room closed.

"Don't get all uppity. I was just giving you two some alone time to talk. That's all."

"Well can you come back out? It's awkward that you just disappeared."

"It can't be that awkward considering I've been in here for over a half hour and you are just now coming to look for me." He winks and stands up off the bed. "I'll be right there."

I head back to the den and find Adam sitting on the couch, fighting back a laugh while toying with the label on his beer.

I let out a loud sigh and ask, "Eavesdropping again?"

"Nope." He shakes his head but never looks at me. I let out a breath thankful that he didn't hear— "But I did hear the conversation."

"Seriously! Why the hell does this crap only happen to me?" I shout in frustration.

He finally looks up, and the glowing smile he's wearing is infectious. We both burst out laughing, because really, what the hell else can you do? My face is bright red with embarrassment, but neither one of us can stop long enough to acknowledge it.

I calm only to plead with him, "Please pretend you didn't hear that."

"Okay. But it's more fun to assume you are mentally undressing me every time you look at me." He begins to laugh again.

I throw my hands up to cover my face. Fire trucks have nothing on the color red my cheeks are sure to be right now.

"Oh my God. You really did hear. He's an idiot. You can't believe anything Dave says," I say from behind my hands.

"Okay, okay. I should really go. I need to get a move on ordering those mats. " He stands, and I immediately move my hands, not ready for him to leave yet. His eyes are warm, and the smirk on his gorgeous face warms a few of my own places too. "So tomorrow night. My place, okay?"

I nod, and he turns to walk away. Just before he gets to the door, he pauses.

"For the record, you can believe some things he says, because I was absolutely flirting."

My eyes go wide, but before I have a chance to squeak out a witty retort, he leaves.

"Told you," Dave says from the hallway, leaning up against the wall.

"I'm going to kill you!" I shout at him only to hear Adam laugh from outside the door. *Fantastic!*

69

Slate

I don't know what the hell happened last night. When I accepted Dave's invite to dinner, I expected to go over there, have dinner with a shy, frightened woman and her asshole cousin. Instead, I met the amazing Riley Peterson. Smartass extraordinaire. Sarcastic aficionado, and hands down the sexiest woman I've ever laid eyes on. She's not like the plastic women who usually throw themselves at me, but that only made her more appealing.

Who was that woman? Even from the first moment when I arrived, I could tell something was different with her. She stood taller, smiled more, and she wasn't apologizing for everything. She didn't look defeated. No. This version of Riley was full of life. She was, well…*beautiful.*

I can't begin to tell you what a turn-on it was to see her stand up to Dave. It kills me to know there is a layer of pain hiding under this woman. I wanted to help her the minute I met her, but it appears I was all wrong about what kind of help she needed. Tonight, hopefully, I can give her that—just a little confidence in her own abilities to protect herself.

Self-defense isn't a one-stop shop that will make her invincible, but I'm hoping I can light a fire inside her to maybe explore this further. It doesn't hurt that I'll have to touch her while we do it. While I think that may make me an asshole, I can live with that fact. I would never hurt her, but I wouldn't mind making her come a time or twelve. Yeah, that absolutely makes me an asshole, but I'm still okay with it.

I'm an introvert—and that is being generous—but I can't wait for her to get here tonight. It's an unusual feeling at best. The absurdity in this level of excitement at seeing a woman I barely know isn't lost on me. I may not be weak or insecure, but the struggle I see in Riley's eyes is oddly familiar. It draws me to her, but it took seeing her as a woman and not a victim in need of rescue for me to realize it.

So today, I have pulled out all the stops. First, I called an out-of-town athletics supply store and ordered the mats. I ended up paying more for immediate delivery than the actual mats, but whatever. Then

I ordered conservative takeout from my favorite restaurant. Or at least that is what I paid the delivery boy to say when he shows up. I actually hired him to put ridiculously expensive Italian food from the best restaurant in a fifty-mile radius into cheap takeout boxes and bring it over at eight.

Okay, so maybe that isn't *all* the stops, but it's more than *Adam* would ever be able to realistically do. I'm not going to push my luck. I still have no plans to tell her who I am. I don't think she would rush out and tell the tabloids or anything. Hell, if Dave hasn't done it by now, I'm sure Riley wouldn't either. But I'm really fucking enjoying being broke-ass Adam Andrews—boxer wannabe who is down on his luck, just trying to get his head straight.

At 6:01, there is a knock at my door. Not that I was watching the clock or peeking through the window or anything. *What the hell is wrong with me?*

"Hey," she greets as soon as I pull open the door.

Her eyes are unfortunately brown as she looks up at me with a nervous smile playing on her lips. And like a jackass, I watch her mouth for a beat too long. I have a feeling that being forward isn't going to help me at all with this woman.

I wait for her to shyly look down. But not this Riley. She bites her lip to restrain a smile and says, "You're wearing sweats again."

"Ah, yeah. Sorry. My three-piece suit was at the cleaners," I tease, and this time, she really does look away, but it might be for the best because her bright smile is blinding even from this angle. "And I have to note you're wearing sweats too."

"Mine are pink though. So it's okay," she says matter-of-factly.

"I'll keep that in mind next time I head to the mall." I push the door wide for her to enter, and she does a quick glance over her shoulder before walking inside.

"Um, not any trouble, huh?" She looks around my apartment at all my furniture precariously shoved into every spare inch of the room while thick, blue wresting mats cover the floor.

"None at all." I smile, but she doesn't seem convinced.

"These are new."

"They're on loan," I answer, and it's not a lie. I fully intend to donate them to the local high school as soon as we're done.

"So what now? Do I try to tackle you and then you fall unconvincingly to the ground under my slightest touch?"

"No. Now we talk. I know you are a little...*timid*. But I'm not going to go easy on you tonight. I wouldn't be a good teacher if I did. So I will be mindful of your emotions, but I want you to remember that I'm only trying to help. I don't want to scare you, but if someone truly attacks you, they aren't going to coddle you."

She nods her head and immediately looks back toward the door. I don't think she is really considering leaving, but judging by the look on her face, she definitely wants to escape.

"Do you think you can you trust me?"

"I don't know. I want to say yes, but the moment you pin me to that mat, I'll probably lose it," she says with a sad smile that causes her eyes to water.

Her answer doesn't break my heart; it pisses me the fuck off. Who the hell pinned her somewhere, and where can I find them to destroy their life? Maybe I don't want to know this stuff about this woman. I'd rather focus on her smile and how amazing her ass looks in those yoga pants.

"Then I won't pin you," I respond casually as if an inferno of rage isn't burning inside me.

"I think I'll be okay then." She nods, but her eyes are screaming otherwise.

"What about my touch? Any areas I should know about that will set you off?" Her eyes go wide and she takes an immediate step back. "I don't mean anything sexual," I quickly clarify. "I just mean your arms, shoulders, legs, or even ankles. Riley, I don't want to accidentally hit a trigger of yours, so please just tell me where not to go. This isn't going to be a free-for-all by any stretch of the imagination, but I will have to touch you. I need to know if there is any place that is off-limits for you. Like, if I grab your ankle to move your foot into a better position, would that be an issue?"

Is this the normal round of questioning during a class? Hell no! However, what I'm about to show her isn't your run-of-the-mill self-defense class either. And above and beyond all of that, I really want to know her personal boundaries.

"Um. My ankles are fine, but maybe not above my knees—like

my thighs," she says so quietly that it's barely audible.

God damn it! I have to remind myself that I wanted to know this, but a million different scenarios about what someone could have done to this woman's thighs sends fire through my veins.

"Hang on. I'll be right back," I say roughly while heading to the bathroom in order to collect myself.

I shouldn't have asked. I'm a freaking masochist for torturing myself like this. I'm also curious and, for some reason, utterly drawn to her. I could have done this little lesson by the book, but I want her to feel safe. I'm reasonably sure Dave has taught her the basics, but I want to give her more than that. Riley is stronger than she thinks she is, and I want to show her that. I want to renew the strength that her ex took from her.

I have absolutely zero tolerance for any man laying a hand on a woman. I know a lot of that is because of the difficult situation in which I grew up, but I hope that, even if I had grown up under different circumstances, I would still feel the same way. I fight for a living. I get paid millions of dollars to punch a man to the point where he is no longer able to continue standing. But my opponents step into the ring willingly and with full knowledge of what is about to happen. He will have a similar paycheck in his back pocket and the exact same goal I have. I don't hit him out of anger or dominance, and at the end of the fight, no matter who the victor may be, there are no hard feelings.

Men who physically, mentally, or emotionally abuse women, are the ones who really deserve to look into my eyes from across the ring. Solving violence with violence may not be the best course of action to end the cycle, but it would definitely make me sleep a little sounder at night. If I ever find this so-called ex-boyfriend of Riley's, I cannot be held responsible for what I might do to him. I don't even know what really happened to her, but I hate him all the same.

I splash some water over my face and get myself back into the right mindset. "This is for her, you dumbass. Get it together," I whisper to myself in the mirror before going back out to face her. I find her sitting Indian style in the middle of the mat, inspecting her fingernails. "Hey," I say softly so as not to scare her. "You ready?"

"Am I allowed to say no?" she asks, surprising me.

"Absolutely. I won't force you to do anything. I'm only trying to help."

She looks at me for a few seconds before pushing to her feet and dusting imaginary dirt from her pants. "I'm ready. Teach me, oh great one!" she says with a teasing smile.

For the next ninety minutes, I teach Riley numerous defensive techniques. Some she picks up fast and some she bumbles completely, but no matter what, she keeps trying. What starts as a simple clinical session quickly turns into something totally different. Riley sheds her protective shell, exposing an unexpected fierce and raw side to her. Her every move is planned and calculated, and behind the contacts, I can see her determination.

It's by far the sexiest thing I have seen in my entire life.

For those moments while we are moving against each other on the mat or when she is blocking my false attacks, she truly comes alive. Gone is the victim, and in her place is the shadow of a warrior. If I wasn't interested in Riley before, I'm awestruck by her now.

"Shit," I cuss when her leg sweeps mine, catching me off guard. I've given her a few dramatic falls before now, but this is one hundred percent real—and completely worth it as she lets out a loud laugh and falls to the mat beside me.

I watch as she loses herself in hysterical laughter, rolling from side to side in a show so spectacular that nothing could ever drag my attention away. God, this woman is incredible. She must catch me staring because she suddenly sobers and settles on her side to face me. She's a good two feet away, and I've never hated personal space more. I want nothing more than to reach out and touch her. Slide my hands over her white, exposed flesh or glide them over the small curve of her waist and up to her breasts, where her peaked nipples are showing through her thin sports bra. Most of all, I want to trace my tongue over her plump, pink lips and into her—

Luckily, the knock at the door stops me before I can make an actual move.

"Are you expecting someone?" She immediately jumps to her feet. I watch as, before my own eyes, she transforms back into the frightened woman I met a few nights ago.

"Hey." I reach out to grab her arm, but before I even have a chance, her hand nervously grips my forearm. I look down, and she's squeezing me so tight that her knuckles are beginning to turn white. It doesn't burn like when most people touch me—but it sizzles all the same. "It's okay, beautiful. I ordered takeout."

I move my arm from her grasp, but only so I can loop it around her waist and pull her to against me. I expected her to be stiff from such an overt gesture, but she immediately relaxes into my side. Riley is small but not tiny. I'm six foot four, and she fits perfectly tucked into my side. My hand rests on her lower back, and it takes all the restraint I can possibly gather not to naturally slide it over to her ass.

"You like Italian right?" I ask, looking down into her camouflaged eyes.

"Yeah," she confirms in a shaky voice.

"Good, because I ordered a ton." I smile reassuringly.

And instead of the smile I was hoping for in return, she quickly steps away.

"Sweet mother of Italian food. That was amazing," Riley says, rubbing her flat stomach. "You have to give me the name of this place."

Dinner was a hit. Listening to Riley moaning to herself with every bite was pretty much excruciating. Thank God there was a table between us, because I'm not sure how else I would have been able to hide my hard-on. It wasn't just her moans that sent blood sprinting toward my cock. The way she leaned forward to eat the pasta gave me a generous view of her cleavage. I tried not to stare, but Jesus fucking Christ. Thankfully she never caught my glances. Or at least I don't think she did.

The conversation flowed easily between us, and the woman who panicked when she heard the knock at the door quickly faded away. After our brief moment of closeness, Riley has unfortunately kept her distance. It sucks, but I'll change things soon enough. One touch was enough to hook me.

"It's my favorite, " I reply, placing my napkin on the table.

"I can't remember the last time I had food that good."

"You didn't even taste the gnocchi either. It's unbelievable."

"Well I was going to taste the gnocchi, but by the time I unfolded my napkin you were already licking the bowl."

"Oh shut up. I offered you a bite at least twice."

"Yes, but something in your eye made me believe you would have literally snapped at my hand if I'd tried to snag a piece."

I bust out laughing, but she remains humorously silent. Only the hint of a smile gives away her attempt at being serious.

"So how do you feel now?"

"Stuffed."

"No, I mean after what I taught you tonight. Do you feel a little better?"

Her smile immediately falls and her shoulders tense. "Oh, um… Yeah. I think I do."

"Why don't you come back tomorrow? We can go over some more stuff." I reach across the table and casually touch her hand. It's meant to be encouraging, but she still pulls away.

"Yeah, I don't know about tomorrow. But…um, maybe later this week. When do you have to give the mats back?" she asks, standing to clear the table.

"I have them on indefinite loan." I take the plates from her hands.

"Oh. Well. Sure. I'll look at my calendar. Let me take care of those before I leave."

"No. I've got it. A beautiful woman recently taught me a trick about letting them soak." I wink, and her eyes go wide at my compliment.

She tries to change the subject, but as always, her smile is obvious. "I should go. It's getting late."

"You sure you don't want to stay and watch *Vision Quest*? We never finished it the other night."

"Nah. Tonight isn't a *Vision Quest* night. *Sixteen Candles*, maybe. But definitely not *Vision Quest*." She giggles to herself. Just as I begin to ask what she is laughing about, she looks up at me with the most amazing twinkle of truth in her eyes. "Thanks for tonight, Adam. I had a lot of fun."

I don't know how to respond without pulling her against me and kissing her roughly. However, I need to touch her. I reach out and gently stroke her forearm. She doesn't back away and her eyes hold my gaze.

"Riley," I whisper, taking a step closer.

Her eyes heat, but she doesn't respond. I take her silence as my signal to continue. I carefully grab her hip, pulling her toward me. She sways, but her feet don't budge. I take it upon myself to close the distance between us. She sucks in a shaky breath as she rests her hands on my chest. We continue staring until, finally, her eyes flash to my mouth.

I can't take this anymore.

I slowly lean in, giving her every opportunity to back away, but she remains still and unmoving. Her tongue darts out to dampen her lips, and that's my cue. I brush my lips over hers, but at the last second, she turns her head and buries her face in my chest.

"I'm sorry," she whispers. "Shit. Shit. Shit."

"Don't be sorry. It's okay." I run my hands reassuringly over her back.

"I need to go. Like now." She pulls away and darts out the door.

"Riley, wait!" I follow. "It's not a big deal!" I tell her back as she sprints inside her apartment, closing the door behind her. "Come on, Riley." I knock, but she doesn't respond. "Damn it," I mutter to myself.

What the fuck just happened?

CHAPTER Nine

Riley

"FUCK. FUCK. FUCK." I stand with my head in my hands, thinking to myself that Adam Andrews might be the best reason we have ever had to pick up and move.

"What the hell are you doing?" Dave asks from the couch.

"He tried to kiss me," I answer, still in a daze.

"And?"

"And he tried to kiss me!" I shriek, suddenly snapping out of it.

"You didn't want to kiss him? Because I have to be honest, you've been throwing off all the signals. Hell, I even caught them, Riley. And let me just tell you, that was awkward," he says sarcastically.

"No. I mean, yes. Shit, I don't know," I answer, and he gives me the who-the-hell-do-you-think-you-are-kidding look. "Fine, I do. I just didn't expect *him* to want to kiss *me*. Shit, I panicked. I wasn't prepared for that. Oh, God, he is going to think I'm even weirder now. Do you think I should apologize to him?" I rush out at a mile a minute.

"Where's the wine Adam brought over last night?" he asks out of the blue.

"In the kitchen. Why?"

"Come on. We're drinking." He grabs my hand and pulls me over to the bar stool at the counter.

"No, we are *not!*"

"Oh, yes, we are! When was the last time you had a drink?" he asks, grabbing the wine from beside the fridge. We don't even have a corkscrew to open it with, so I'm intrigued as to how he is going to pull this off.

"A while," I answer while he scrambles around the kitchen, snatching open drawers and plundering through them.

"Do we have one of those little corkscrew thingies?"

"No. Which is precisely why we aren't drinking."

He shrugs. "Desperate times." He heads to his toolbox in the corner of the pantry and comes back carrying a screwdriver. "No spare cork. I guess we'll have to drink it all." He winks.

"What?" I ask, confused, just seconds before he uses the screwdriver to push the entire cork into the bottle.

He pours wine into one of our regular plastic cups and places it in front me. "Drink."

"Nope. Not happening." I push the cup away.

"Why not?" he asks then takes a sip. I can't even begin to explain how much I wish for a camera when he makes the most wretched face as he swallows. "Sweet hell. That shit is terrible." He gags as I burst into laughter.

"I'm not drinking," I manage to get out between laughs.

"Yes, you are."

"Jesus, I'm going to bed." I turn to walk away, but he gently stops me before I can make my retreat.

"I want you to drink because I think you need to do something ridiculous and irrational. Something stupid that will probably make you hate yourself tomorrow but will bring you the highest of highs in the meantime. Because that is what normal people do. They make stupid choices without thinking them through for months at a time. Riley, I want you to fucking live. I'm sick of watching you make the right decisions and smart choices that only keep you down and feed your fears. Screw up, babe. Make a God damn mistake and feel it." He takes a breath and shakes his head at me. "Drink the fucking wine and go kiss that man. Hell, have sex with him. He likes you. And, Riley, you are not always the most likeable person." He tries to close with a joke, but it makes my eyes water. Okay, fine—it makes me cry big, fat, ugly tears.

"What if something happens while I'm making these mistakes? Something I can't control. What if they find us and I'm drunk and making out with Adam?" I mumble, trying to compose myself.

"Then it happens!" His voice rises slightly before lowering again. "You can't spend your whole life preparing for the worst. You are just next door—with a man who has proved he would protect you at all costs. If there was ever a fucking moment to make a rash drunken decision, this is it. I'm begging you. Drink and act like a fool. Please stop hiding and actually live your life." He pauses long enough to squeeze my shoulder. "It's killing me to watch you fade into the background. Last night, while we were all hanging out, you were amazing. It's no wonder he tried to kiss you." His eyes are desperate and kind…and loving. *Oh yeah… Ugly. Tears.*

"Dave, I love you. And I know you hate it when I tell you that, but I do. So you're going to have to hear it again. I love you." He nods but doesn't say a single word back. I push my cup even farther toward him, and he readies for an argument. "Fill it up," I order, and the fight freezes on his tongue. His shoulders relax as his head falls forward in relief.

"I remember you saying you used to love wine." He pours my glass to the rim.

"I did. Wine was my reward at the end of a shift."

He pulls one of the beers Adam brought over out of the fridge. "Cheers, babe. It's been a really fucking long shift."

"Cheers, babe," I repeat back to him, unwilling to call him Dave in this moment. I take a sip of wine, acting carefree for the first time in three long years.

Slate

Son of a bitch. I should have known better than to try to kiss her, but for fuck's sake, she was giving me all the signs—even if I weren't desperately trying to read into them. She was so strong and confident that, even if I wasn't sure what she wanted, I probably would have tried to kiss her anyway. My only complaint is that she had her eyes covered up by those atrocious brown contacts all damn night. I would have paid millions to see her true color.

I pull my iPod out of my bag and scroll through the playlists, searching for something calming. I need a distraction, perhaps something that won't leave me thinking about Riley all night. Two nights ago, I sat on this couch worrying about the frail woman next door, but tonight, visions of her naked and moving under me threaten to force me into a cold shower. She may have rejected me tonight, but she has no idea who she is dealing with. I have no plans to give up, even if it means taking a step back from our already nonexistent relationship. I'll give her the space to figure things out, because based on how she acted tonight, I know she's interested in me too.

I find an old playlist labeled 'Chill' and decide to take a chance. Counting Crow's *Colorblind* slides through the sound system I had installed last time I was here. *Yeah, this will definitely do.*

I settle on the couch and stare at the ceiling, replaying the entire night like an adolescent girl after her first kiss. Shit. That was not what I had been expecting from this evening. I must sit on the couch for half an hour listening to music and enjoying the calm around me. Just as I begin to drift off, I hear a quiet knock at my door. I jump to my feet, knowing that only one person comes to see me these days.

I yank open the door to see her standing outside with a sweater pulled tight around her shoulders and a nervous look on her face.

"Riley? Are you okay?" I ask as she tips her head up to look at me. The moment her blue eyes hit mine, a huge smile spreads across my face and travels down my torso and into my pants. Jesus Christ—those eyes.

"You tried to kiss me tonight," she announces as if I hadn't been there when she pushed me away.

"I did, and I'm sorry if that made you uncomfortable. I won't apologize for actually trying though. I've never wanted to taste a woman more than I did you, Riley."

Her cheeks pink, but she looks up at me playfully. "Is the offer still good?"

I know what she is asking, but I can't stop myself from taking it a step further. "The offer to kiss me?" I ask, trying to both clarify and restrain the smile that is threatening to swallow my face.

"Yeah, that one."

"For you. Always." Before the words even finish coming out of my mouth, she dives into my arms.

Her mouth crashes into mine, and the taste of wine lingers on her tongue. Somehow, in the half hour since she left, she managed to get drunk? I'm not too proud to admit that I don't give one flying fuck how much she has had to drink. I'm taking this opportunity.

I pull her against my body and she stills for a second before my tongue coaxes her back into a rhythm. Her soft lips glide over mine and her hands roam up my chest and over my shoulders. I can't stop my own wandering hands from pushing down the back of her pants and squeezing her firm ass. I hold her tight as her tongue meets mine thrust for thrust. I need to slow things down before my dick forces its way out of my pants, but this woman…

I thread a hand into her hair and suck her bottom lip into my mouth, all while holding her tight against me. "Should I start leaving the door open for you?"

"It wouldn't hurt," she responds, moving her attention to my neck and sucking her way up to my ear.

Chills spread over my body, forcing a groan in their wake.

"I should go," she whispers into my ear.

"You really should." I lift her with both hands on her ass. We both know she isn't going anywhere.

She immediately wraps her legs around my waist, rendering me completely silent. A groan wouldn't even come close to doing justice to the moment when her fully clothed heat rolls over my cock.

Only one word will suffice.

"Fuck," I breathe, pushing her against the wall. She may have heard my curse, but she shows me absolutely no mercy with her mouth.

Her pace is wild and her intensity is confusing from the woman who blew me off less than an hour ago. Her hands slide under my shirt. God, her touch feels so good. I need more of it. I use my leg and hips to support her against the wall while I tear my shirt over my head. Her breath catches in her throat as her eyes grow wide. Even if I didn't get paid to keep in shape, her reaction alone would have me adding hours a day in the gym.

"God, Adam," she gasps, sliding her hands up my chest and back down again.

I focus on her lips as her fingers explore over my body. She moans into my mouth when they reach my abs. We both need more room to play. I palm her round ass and pull her away from the wall.

"I thought you didn't drink?" I ask as I turn and gently lay her down on the mats still covering my floor. I'm careful to never break our full-body connection.

"Liquid courage," she answers before resuming her wandering hands.

I flinch when she traces them down my sides. I can't take it anymore. Her touch is overloading my senses. I can't focus on anything but how fucking good the tips of her fingers feel as she drags them over every inch of my chest and stomach.

"You're killing me, Riley."

I reach down and grab her hands, pushing them over her head. Before I even have a chance to fully restrain them, she jerks them out of my grasp. I look down, expecting a playful smile, but her eyes are wide and flashing around the room. I lean back and give her a questioning eyebrow, but she doesn't respond. She takes a deep breath and offers me a weak smile before tugging my head back down into another kiss. Her tongue rolls against mine as she seemingly shakes off whatever I just did wrong.

"The moment you pin me to that mat, I'll probably lose it."
Fuck.

I try to apologize as I immediately roll to the side. "I forgot. I'm sorry."

"It's okay. Don't," she whispers, kissing me again.

It doesn't take but a second before she begins to lick her way down my neck and over to my shoulders. She wraps her arms around my back, but she never resumes her wandering hands. I'm careful not make any more attempts to restrain her, even inadvertently, with my body. We make out for a few minutes while trying to regain the heat we just momentarily lost. Finally, she lifts her hips, and they grind against me, sending my straining cock into the 'painfully hard' category.

I shove my hands down, but just before they slide into her pants, she quickly pulls them back up to cup her breasts. *How the fuck did I miss her tits?* I'm out of practice, but that's no excuse. I lift her shirt and she lets out an encouraging gasp when my fingers brush across her bra-covered nipple.

"Can I take your shirt off?" I ask, pretending to be a gentleman. She's lucky I'm not stripping her bare right now, but after she has stopped me twice now, I have a sneaking suspicion that ravaging Riley wouldn't go over too well. This is going to have to be slow and tortuous, but I'm willing to do whatever it takes to keep her under me.

"Roll over," she whispers, moving to the side so we can change positions.

I lie down and she straddles my hips. Before this moment, I had control over how often she could press against my cock. Now, I'm helpless, and as she settles on top of me, there has never been a better or worse feeling in the world. Well, that is until she peels her shirt over her head, revealing two pale-white breasts that are unfortunately still covered by a bra. I quickly sit up, causing more friction between us. We both groan from the connection. I drop my head to her chest as I reach around her back to unclasp her bra.

As her bra falls away, I waste not a single second before pulling her pink nipple into my mouth. My tongue circles over her sensitive flesh. Kneading with one hand, I use the other to hold her against my mouth. She takes a deep breath, forcing her breast even farther into my mouth, and I greedily take every inch she is willing to give me. Her nails rake over my back and into my hair as she purposefully grinds against my cock. I hold her waist to still her movements. I can't take even one more touch without being inside her.

"Just to be clear, how out of the question is sex tonight?" I ask before resuming my assault on her breasts.

She freezes above me and I mentally chastise myself for saying the words out loud. I'm a dumbass. I know she has issues, yet I still asked the question all the same.

"Completely," she answers firmly, looking down into my eyes with discomfort and embarrassment covering her beautiful face.

"Okay," I say, smiling up at her. "I just wanted to make sure we were on the same page." I shrug, but her look of failure bothers me. "So here is how this is going to work. I'm about to pick you up and carry you to my room. You are going to squeal and pretend like it's a fun surprise when I toss you over my shoulder. Then I'm going to lie on my back so you don't feel trapped or pinned down, and you can do whatever you would like while we are in there. Pants stay on, but shirts are strongly discouraged." I wink and glance down at our naked chests pressed together.

Her clear, blue eyes sparkle with relief. "Can we shut the door?" she asks, making me smirk in confusion.

"Um, there's no one here but us, beautiful. But yeah, if you want the door shut, I'm okay with that."

"Yeah. I don't do well with open doors. I need to know I would hear it if someone tried to come in."

Son of a motherfucking bitch. I'm going to kill this asshole when I find him!

"When you're in that room, no one is coming near you but me," I vow, meaning it with every fiber of my being. We may be nothing more than just tonight, but I'll be damned if I ever let her be hurt again.

"Then let's go," she says. I immediately stand, swinging her tiny body over my shoulder. She laughs and gives me the surprised squeal I was hoping for.

"Oh, wait. Slapping your ass?" I ask as I turn to head down the hall.

"Have at it." She continues to giggle the most beautiful and unrestrained sound.

I give her a gentle tap and head to my room.

I want to tell you that things got crazy hot from there. Maybe that I worshipped her body with my mouth all night long until she couldn't stand it anymore and was forced to strip me naked and beg for my cock. But the truth is that we were both laughing so hard when we got to my room that, as soon as I deposited her on my bed, she curled into my side and we actually talked. I know. It's a novelty. But I loved every fucking second of it.

Riley is unlike any woman, or even person, I have ever met. She's funny and smart, but I can't quite put my finger on her. No matter how hard I try, I can't figure her out. Sure, on the surface, she's incredible, but for some reason, I always feel like I'm missing some integral part. I've only known her for a few days, but in that brief amount of time, we've been through some shit together. I feel like I should have a better grasp on her by now. But I can feel that she's hiding something, and I'm not just talking about her fears.

For two hours, Riley and I lie in my bed, shooting the shit. For two hours, I stare at Riley's amazing eyes while tracing my hands over her naked chest. For two excruciating hours, I lie still while her hands move over my own chest. It's not excruciating because she's touching me; it's torturous because I want more.

"I should go," she whispers into my neck as she's curled into my side.

I give her a tight squeeze. "I vote you stay."

"I can't."

I let out a groan but release her from my side. If I try to force it like I want to, it will only spook her more. "Okay."

"Okay?" she questions, sitting up suddenly.

"Um…what else am I supposed to say?"

She smiles a glowing, white smile that causes my cock to stir back to life. "Thank you for not giving me shit. And for making out with me like we were in high school," she says nervously.

"I won't push you, beautiful. Anything that happens from here on out is completely up to you."

Her eyes begin to twinkle with humor. "You didn't let me finish. And thank you for working out twenty-*five* hours a day. I've thoroughly enjoyed the benefits tonight," she finishes with a kiss to my chest.

I drop my head to her hair just to breathe in a whiff of all that is Riley before she leaves. "Come over tomorrow night?" I ask as though I haven't already asked this question tonight.

"Yeah, okay. But promise you'll wear sweats even if your three-piece suit comes back from the cleaners," she teases barely containing her laughter.

Ten minutes later, after a gentle kiss and all-too-brief hug, Riley leaves.

Forget my rescue mission to save her… Who's going to save me?

Riley

"All right. Spill it," Dave says, scaring the ever-loving shit out of me when I walk back inside.

I scream and jump back against the wall. "God, you scared me! What are you still doing awake?"

"I've been waiting up for hours for you to kiss and tell. You know…girl talk," he says with a shrug, and I burst out laughing. "Don't keep me waiting, Riley. I read an entire Cosmo in preparation for this moment. My manhood is in serious jeopardy right now. I think I can pull off the BFF role if you hurry up and start talking before I remember I have a dick." His face is so completely serious that I can't help but double over in a fit of laughter. "Less laughing, more sharing!" he shouts, but he joins me.

When I'm able to stand back up, I walk over and throw my arms around his neck. "Thank you."

He returns the hug. "I'm assuming it went well."

"Yeah. It went really well."

"I'll buy more wine." He squeezes me painfully tight.

"Nah, I think I'm good from now on." I let him go and take a step away. "Is it okay if I go back over there tomorrow night?"

"You don't have to ask me, babe. I'm not your daddy. You can do whatever you want. Just let me know when and where so I won't worry."

"Okay. We're just going to be at his place. Why don't you…ya know…go out tomorrow night too?"

"Nah, not quite yet. Only one of us can get laid at a time. Besides, I don't do that kind of stuff." He feigns innocence that forces me to give him a knowing look.

"Oh please. For a man who never gets laid, you sure do run through quite a few condoms. You forget I was with you when you bought not one but two ginormous boxes last month."

"I told you those were for a friend!" he yells, but his eyes are laughing.

"Of course. You really are a thoughtful friend."

"I know. I scored a ninety-three on Cosmo's BFF quiz."

"You did not take a quiz!"

"I totally did, and it just further proved how awesome I am."

"You are ridiculous is what you are." I head for my bedroom. "Wait. Where the hell did you get a Cosmo?"

He looks down, pretending to be shy and somehow managing to keep a straight face. "I hid it under the condoms at checkout."

"Oh my God! You are such a loser!" I call over my shoulder as he continues to laugh behind me.

"Night, Riley."

"Night, Dave."

CHAPTER Ten

One week later…

Slate

TIME HAS BEEN flying by with Riley in my life. We can't seem to get enough of each other. Our relationship isn't rushing ahead at light speed; it's more crawling at a junior high pace. That's okay though, because there isn't a day that passes where she isn't knocking on my door. That makes it all right with me.

Since that first night, we've been inseparable, but I still don't feel like I'm getting the whole picture of who Riley really is. We talk for hours, but some of her stories just don't add up. There's always a blur on the lens when I look at her. I feel like I am missing just the slightest detail that would bring her completely into focus. However, I don't push it because I still haven't even told her my real fucking name.

It's an asshole move, but I just wanted to get to know her a little better before screwing it all to Hell and back. She seems like a quiet, low-key girl who isn't going to want to be thrown into the spotlight that unfortunately is my life. But the fact of the matter is that I can only stay here in Ohio as Adam Andrews for so long.

I've been trying to work out as much as possible to buy myself a few more weeks before I have to go home and get back on my training schedule. I could hang around here for a bit longer if I found a way to keep on track. Maybe see if there is a boxing gym nearby that would allow me to come in at night. It's not ideal, but it might buy me just a little more time with her. I could sleep during the days while Riley is at work, spend my nights with her, and train while she's sleeping.

I bought all new bedding the very next day after we were together in hopes that she would spend the night. But around midnight every single night, she kisses me at the door and goes back to her apartment. I hate it, but I can probably make it work for a while longer.

At six p.m. sharp, Riley and her brown contacts are knocking at my door.

"It's open!" I shout from the kitchen.

"What if I were an ax murderer?" she asks the minute she walks inside.

I drop the knife on the counter and head over to wrap her in my arms. "Well then, I guess I'd have to fight the ax from your hands before kissing you." I lean forward to press a gentle kiss to her mouth. "Hey."

"Hey," she responds as her cheeks heat to pink.

"How was work?" I ask, still holding her.

Her hands trace up my forearms and under the sleeves of my T-shirt to my biceps. "I hate my job."

"Well okay then." I laugh.

"I would rather be unemployed than spend another day in that file room. But a girl's gotta eat, right?" She shrugs and moves out of my arms. "Whatcha cooking?"

"Lasagna."

She breathes in deeply, sniffing the aromas. "Homemade?" she questions with shock.

"Yep."

"Wow. All because I showed you my boobs last night?"

"No. Well, kind of no. It's one of the few things I know how to cook. But the boobs definitely didn't hurt."

She leans up on her toes to kiss me again. It's a sweet kiss, but nonetheless heated. And when I move to deepen it, she immediately opens and strokes her tongue against mine. It's a dance we have mastered, and while we still haven't had sex or really done anything below the waist, these moments are more than enough.

I can tell that Riley wants more, but she's pretty freaked out any time I try to take it further. The mixture of fear and longing in her eyes doesn't sit well with me. It worries the hell out of me when I try to figure out what she could possibly be afraid of when she so obviously wants to be with me. However, besides those few moments in bed before I decided to stop trying to push her, I haven't seen Riley scared at all. She doesn't flinch from me anymore, even when I make sudden movements. It might have only been a week now, but I would say, given how we started, Riley and I have made great strides toward achieving something normal.

"Holy shit, Adam. That lasagna was amazing," she says, curling up on the couch after dinner.

"Better than my shrimp?" I ask, sitting down next to her and pulling her into my side.

"You burnt the shrimp. So I'm going to have to say yes."

"I did not burn them! They were blackened. It's a real, honest-to-God flavor."

"Right. Whatever you need to tell yourself." She begins to giggle as I drag her across my lap, tickling her. "Stop! That's not fair! You're bigger than I am" she squeals, trying to break out of my arms.

"What's wrong, Riley? Not so fond of my body anymore?"

"I didn't say all that." She continues to laugh but finally relaxes, lying down with her head on my lap.

I look down at her, wishing her blue eyes were staring back up at me. "Let me buy you clear contacts."

"What? No way. Adam, I told you. The kind I need are expensive. I'll be fine with the brown ones until I run out." She awkwardly looks away, once again making me feel like she's hiding something.

"I can afford them. Just give me your prescription and I'll order them tomorrow."

"No. I can't let you do that. Trust me, they are fine. Besides, I actually like the brown."

"No, you don't. There is no way in the world someone who has eyes like yours would want to turn them brown. Same thing with your hair. I know you're a blonde, Riley."

She bolts straight up out of my lap. "Shut up, Adam. You don't know what you're talking about. Besides, you're an unemployed boxer. I'm sitting in your apartment, remember? Buy new pots and pans before worrying about my contacts," she says with a bitchy tone I've never heard her use before.

"If I had the money, would you let me buy them for you?" I snap back at her.

"Nope." She crosses her arms and leans away from me.

I let out a sigh and rub my eyes. "Why do I always feel like you're using those fucking contacts to hide from me?" Her eyes go wide with surprise before she turns away completely. "See? Just like that."

"What is your obsession with my eyes?" she mumbles.

"They're beautiful! And more than that, they are you. I already feel there is a lot I don't know about you. At least *show* me something real."

"There's a lot I don't know about you either, you know," she snaps. Then she sucks in a deep breath and her frustration begins to fade. "We're just getting to know each other. We'll figure it all out over time." She offers me a weak smile before crawling back across the couch and into my lap. She peppers kisses over my face and down my neck. "We'll get to know each other eventually."

"Jesus." I give her a half smile, knowing that there has never been a more perfect moment to tell her the truth. Shit. This is going to suck. "What's your middle name, Riley?" I ask then lean in for a deep kiss.

"Um, Jean," she stutters out when I pull away.

"Was that a hard question?" I tease, but she stills.

"No. I just… I mean, I wasn't expecting it. That's all."

"Well, Riley Jean, my middle name is Adam."

"Really? What's your first name?" she asks.

I lean in for one last kiss, giving it everything I've got and praying it's not the last. "Slate."

"Oh, well, I can definitely see why you go by Adam," she says with a shrug that makes me laugh and my chest ache.

"Actually, no one calls me Adam but you. My name is Slate Andrews, and I'm not an amateur boxer down on his luck. I'm actually a very successful professional boxer."

"What?" She leans away in disbelief. "What do you mean very successful?" she asks as her face pales.

"I mean, I'm currently the heavyweight champion of the world. For two straight years now."

"Yeah, right. Are you messing with me?" The color slightly returns to her face as her lips tilt in a small smile. But it all disappears when I shake my head. "Why the hell are you living here then if you're some big-time fighter?"

"I grew up in this apartment. A few years ago, I bought it so I could escape the celebrity lifestyle in LA. I'm not built for that kind of life. I just needed somewhere to hide after fights."

"You're a celebrity?" she breathes as tears spring to her eyes.

"I'm not Tom Cruise, but I have a certain following."

"Oh my God. I'm going to be sick." She jumps from my lap and runs to the bathroom.

"Wait a second." I stand and race after her, but she slams the door in my face. "Talk to me. It's not as bad as it sounds. I swear."

"You lied to me," she chokes out, crying.

"I didn't lie. We were just getting to know each other. That lifestyle makes things complicated. When I first told you my name, I had no idea we would end up here. I thought you recognized me, and I didn't want my cover blown."

"Yeah, we wouldn't want your cover blown. Where the worst thing that happens is your adoring fans shower you with love. We definitely wouldn't want that cover blown," she bites out sarcastically, but her voice cracks at the end.

"It's not like that. The paparazzi follow me, and I never have a minute to just breathe and be myself. I'm always looking over my shoulder," I try to explain.

She snatches open the door and stares at me with tear-stained cheeks. "Now that, I understand." She bumps into me, forcing me to step out of her way. "I have to go."

"Riley, wait. This is not something to freak out about."

"Adam—fuck…I mean, Slate. What the hell do I even call you? You have no idea how big of a deal this really is."

"Why? Tell me why this is such a huge deal. This is my job. I can't change it. Trust me, I hate the lifestyle."

"Well, you know what? Right this fucking second, I think I hate it more. I can't live like that, Adam. Like, literally. I can't *live*." She laughs without humor while shaking her head. "It's funny the way the world works. The one person I'm magically not scared of is probably the most terrifying of them all."

"What the hell does that mean? Stop talking in fucking code and let me in on your hang-up. Yeah, it's a hard life, but you haven't given me one fucking reason why you are freaking out right now. Stop hiding and tell me what the hell is going on with you!" I yell in a way I swore to myself I would never speak to her. But I have a terrible feeling about where she is going with this.

"This…whatever this is…is done. Stay away from me," she says, walking out the door. Luckily for me, I know exactly where she lives.

"Tell me what you are afraid of. Tell me why my occupation has you on the run. I can keep you out of it."

"We can't take that risk," she calls over her shoulder.

"Why do I feel like I'm missing a puzzle piece here? Because nothing about this makes sense. I can protect you from your ex-boyfriend if that's who you are worried about!"

She comes to a complete halt and turns around to face me. "My ex-boyfriend?" she questions with an expression I can't quite figure out. But she stops moving away.

"You don't have to hide from him, Riley." I take a step forward and push a hand into her hair to tilt her head back. "Look, you're right. This is all new. We are just getting to know each other, and who the hell knows if it will work out. But I will swear on my life that I will make you safe. Whether this works out or not, I will never let anyone hurt you again."

She closes her eyes and her chin begins to quiver. "You have no idea how much I wish I could believe you," she says with a sob and drops her forehead to my chest.

"I swear to you. I'll get you a good attorney, a restraining order, and a security detail—whatever you need. I want to be with you, but more than that, I want to see you live without fear."

She sucks in a long breath and shakes her head against my chest. "You're a good man, Slate Andrews."

Sliding her arms up my chest, she wraps them around my neck. The tears steadily fall from her eyes as she stands on her tiptoes and pulls me down for an agonizing kiss. It begins slow and gentle, but it doesn't take long before it becomes wild. I push her up against the brick just beside her front door. Her hands trace over my body and back up and over my shoulders. I hold her tight against me and she clings to my back, digging in her fingernails in the most positively arousing way possible.

"I'll fix that part for you. Then we can figure the us part out together," I say, trying to reassure her again.

Suddenly, she steps out of my arms and rubs the heels of her palms over her eyes. "I can't even begin to tell you how much I wish we could make that happen. It's just not possible. Goodbye, Adam." Before I even have a chance to react to her words, she opens her door and slides inside, locking it behind her.

"Don't do this. Don't let this go because of who I am!" I shout at the closed door.

"I'm not. I'm letting it go because of who *I* am," she says in a voice so broken that it physically hurts to hear it.

"Damn it! Just talk to me, Riley," I plead, but she never responds.

I wait for at least fifteen minutes, but I never hear another word from her. I try to figure what the hell just happened. I knew she was going to be upset that I hadn't told her about my life sooner, but her cryptic little messages about why we can't be together worry me the most. Finally, the cold forces me back to my apartment. But I leave knowing that I'll be back. This is not a fight I'm willing to lose.

Riley

"DID YOU KNOW?" I ask, storming into Dave's room. He's asleep, but after the night I've had, he's going to have to wake the fuck up. "Did you fucking know?" I scream at the top of my lungs as he flies out of bed.

"Know what? Jesus, are you all right?" he asks, trying to scrub the sleep from his eyes.

"That I was dating a God damn celebrity!" I yell again, but it catches in my throat.

"Fuck." He sighs.

"Oh, God! You knew." The threatening tears spill over my eyes.

"Yeah, I knew," he admits.

"Wonderful. You encouraged me to put our lives at risk. Both of us could be exposed at any minute and you encouraged me to do it. What the fuck were you thinking?"

"I was thinking he made you smile and you weren't afraid of it. You acted like a woman instead of a piece of glass so shattered it would never be able to be pieced back together. So yeah, I took a chance and pushed you towards him. I have watched you smile more over the last week than I have seen in the three years we have been forced together. You acted like a normal person for seven full days, and it was the best moments of my entire fucking life to watch you do it."

"That's bullshit. This is not fucking fair! You shouldn't have kept something that big from me. All it would take is one fucking picture and we would both be dead." I stomp my foot in frustration. "When the hell do I get to make some decisions about my own life? You don't always get to decide what's best for me, damn it!"

"Well, you need someone to do it!" he growls, sitting back down on the corner of his bed. "You're doing a shit job at managing all of this. I've been stressing since we got word of this move about what to do with you. You've regressed back to those first few months after the trial. Then, all of a sudden, Slate fucking Andrews walked into your life and something changed. It's like you came alive in a way I have never seen before. So yeah, I pushed you towards him. I also stayed close and had the big boys send in a detail to keep an eye on things while you were with him. You know I would have pulled you out if I thought you were in any danger whatsoever."

"You asshole! That isn't your call! You threw me into an impossible situation. You know better than anyone that he is not a chance we can afford to take. Say what you want. Your heart may have been in the right place, but you put us both in danger. We can't trust a man like that!"

"Slate Andrews is the only man I would have ever trusted you with. He's the God damn patron saint of abused women." He lets out a string of curse words and runs a hand through his hair. "I'm sorry, Riley, but you needed someone."

"What?" I ask, completely confused.

"You can't do this all alone."

"No! I mean the abused part."

"Look him up, babe. He spends millions of dollars every year advocating for women. He privately funds three rehabilitation programs and a safe house for women who have been victimized by physical or sexual abuse. Riley, Slate himself is the product of a rape."

"No," I gasp, throwing my hands to my mouth.

I think back on when he told me I reminded him of his mother, and it makes my stomach turn at how right he really was. I can't even imagine how it would have felt to relive my past every day in the eyes of an innocent child. And for him to know that about how he was created makes my heart break for him too. I can only imagine how he grew up feeling.

For the briefest of moments, I find a feeling of hope swelling in my chest. Maybe he really could understand bits and pieces of my life if I were allowed to open up to him. But then again, that can never happen.

"Shut up. I don't want to hear this."

But Dave continues. "So yeah, I threw you at him. And he took to you—hook, line, and sinker. And before your mind goes there, that had nothing to do with your past, because he has no fucking idea about what happened to you."

"Shut up!" I scream. "Shut up. I don't want to hear any of it. I don't care who he is. The only thing that matters is I can't be with him...ever." I sway as anger wages war with the longing I have for Adam.

"I love you," Dave says for the first time—ever. It startles me, and I jerk my eyes up to his. "Riley, I need you to be happy more that I need blood in my veins. I need redemption. I saw the way you looked at him and…" He drops his head into his hands.

My anger is quickly replaced by sadness. Dave may not have the physical scars I do, but I'm not the only one of us who was shredded by that night. He's given his life up too. Sometimes, it's hard for me to remember that.

"I love you too. Thank you for looking out for me, but from here on out, I relieve you of your duty. You can't live my life and you sure as hell can't force me into the arms of a man just because you deem him worthy. I should get a say in this. As much as I like Adam-slash-Slate, I wish I could go back to before I met him."

He smirks over at me before announcing, "I will continue to set you up with as many *good* guys as I can find. The good news for you is they are few and far between. Slate was kind of the jackpot. It's all downhill from here."

He's right. Slate really was the jackpot.

"I felt safe with him," I admit not only to Dave, but to myself as well.

"I know, babe. And for what it's worth, I think we could make things work. It's completely a risk, but you say the word and we'll figure a way for you two to be together."

"That's a terrible idea," I say, sitting on the bed beside him.

"I know. It really is." He gives me a sad grin.

"Promise me you'll let me handle this from here on out. You want to see me get better? Then let me control at least this part of my life. It's not like I can control anything else."

"I had to try."

My moment with Dave is gone and reality comes crashing back down on my shoulders. What Adam and I had may not have been some great whirlwind romance, but it was more than I've had in years. I've had plenty of boyfriends in the past, but I've not wanted to get close to anyone until Adam. *Damn it.* Now, just like everything else in my life, he's gone too.

For two weeks, I avoided Adam at all costs. But that doesn't mean he avoided me. He stopped by my apartment almost nightly. Dave always turned him away, and on more than one occasion, they had not-so-kind words about it. But I didn't have any other choice. Spending time with Adam, even on a limited basis, just wasn't an option.

I started leaving super early in the mornings and going to the gym after work just so I wouldn't accidentally run into him in the hallway. I missed Adam more than I'd ever expected, but more than that, I missed the person I got to be when we were together. I got to laugh, smile, and feel sexy without fear. For a full seven days, I got to be Erica again.

I'm relaxing in bed when a sudden tap on my window scares the shit out of me. I scream and rush toward the door until I hear his voice.

"Riley. It's just me. I didn't mean to scare you," Adam says to my window.

The blinds are closed, but that doesn't mean I don't try to squint to get a glance at him. I don't respond, but tears pool in my eyes. I stare at the window, willing it to open. I wish he would climb through, pull me into his strong arms, and tell me that it's all going to be okay. Even while I'm wishing, I begin to pray he will just leave. I don't know how much longer I can stay away from him.

"I'm leaving," he tells the window while apparently reading my mind. "I have to go back to LA. I just wanted to..." He pauses. "Look, when I first met you, all I wanted was to help you. Then I really met you and all I wanted was to get to know you. You're hiding, Riley. Whether you know it or not, that is exactly what you are doing. Okay, fine. We can't be together. And while I don't completely understand your reasons, I accept them. But what I won't accept is you locking yourself away from living a real life. If you won't let me help you, promise me you'll let someone else. You're an amazing person, Riley Peterson, and you are doing the entire world a disservice by keeping all of it to yourself."

The tears steadily fall from my eyes. It takes every ounce of my willpower not to climb through the window myself at this point. But there is one emotion more powerful than any other—*fear.* And it's the only reason my feet remain rooted in place.

"If you need anything, Riley, you have my number. Day or night, all you have to do is call. Take care of yourself. Bye, beautiful." With his final words, I hear his footsteps walking away.

I rush to the other window so I can catch a last glimpse of him as he leaves. His muscular body moves slowly towards the car. With a small bag thrown over his shoulder, he looks nearly identical to the day when I first met him. Just over three weeks ago, Slate Adam Andrews walked into my life. I thought I was scared that day, but as I watch him drive away, I'm suddenly more frightened than ever.

CHAPTER Twelve

Six months later...

Riley

"SPECIAL DELIVERY!" DAVE shouts from the den.

"Flowers or eggs?" I reply.

"Italian food."

"Shit!" I groan to myself.

"I'll take care of it, Riley."

"Don't you dare touch that gnocchi!" I yell as I head to the kitchen.

For six months, Slate Andrews has been sending me gifts. Every week. Every. Single. Fucking. Week. A box arrives at my door. It never comes on the same day, so I can predict it and avoid it. Nope, he keeps me guessing. It's always something different too. But one thing always remains constant. Each week, there is a box of clear contacts of a different prescription.

It all started at Christmas, exactly a week after Adam moved back to LA.

"Oh, Dave. It's perfect," I say, pulling the new jacket from the box.

"It's got a secret little pocket I was thinking you could hide your phone in." He takes the jacket from my hands and begins to show me all the bells and whistles. I can't help but giggle at his enthusiasm.

Suddenly, there's a knock at the door and Dave's head snaps to mine. The surprise in his eyes lets me know that he was definitely not expecting this one.

"Go to your room, babe." He orders.

"No," I defy, but I rise to my feet anyway, knowing that this is not something to be argued.

"Go," he whispers.

I move to my bedroom, preparing for the worst. I cover my ears in fear of what I might hear, but the disturbing sounds never come. I finally lift my head from my shaky hands as Dave walks into my room.

"It's okay," he says, but he approaches me with apprehensive eyes.

"Dave, you're scaring me."

"Slate sent you a present." He holds out a silver box with a bright-blue bow.

"Why?" I jump to my feet. I want to immediately rip the contents from the package and, at the same time, hide it for all of eternity.

"You know why, Riley."

"What is it?" I ask, knowing that Dave opened it, especially since I'm assuming it was addressed to me.

"Flowers."

"Okay." I breathe a sigh of relief. I can handle meaningless flowers.

"And new sweats. They're pink," he says, and it makes my eyes water. Sweats may not be the most romantic gift, but the memory makes the tears appear. Though his final words are what make them fall freely. *"And clear contacts."*

"What?"

"I think you need to read this." He pushes a handwritten note toward me.

Riley, you can hide from me, but don't hide from the world. We all lose when you do.
Merry Christmas, beautiful.

—Slate

"What is wrong with him?" I put the note down on the bed beside me.

"Um, I think he's a man who likes you."

"Asshole," I mumble under my breath.

For six long months, my weekly contacts arrive, unwelcome. They either wind up in the trash or sitting on top of my bed—depending on whether Dave or I get the mail that day. It never fails. They always come with some random accompaniment. At first, it was cliché flowers, but then I think he got serious. One day, I came home to a special delivery of three-dozen fresh, organic eggs. Don't ask me why three dozen, but regardless, there they sat in a cooler on my doorstep. I had an overwhelming urge to throw them at his front door, but I knew I would be the one who had to clean them. Instead, we had omelets for dinner. After that, his gifts ranged from flowers and candy, a case of wine, and sometimes even mace. But today… Today, I got Italian food.

"Fuck," I hear Dave moan as I walk in the room. "Riley, this food is amazing!"

"Yeah, I know," I say, pulling two plates from the cabinet. "Why does he keep sending stuff? We barely knew each other. It's been six freaking months."

"I don't know, babe. Probably the same reason why, every time I open the computer, you've left open some article about him or why you secretly ordered the pay-per-view of his fight last night."

"What? How'd you know about that?"

"Because when I went to buy it, the cable company told me it had already been purchased." He gives me a big smile while popping a piece of garlic bread into his mouth.

"Yeah, well. At least I'm not being creepy and sending him gifts all the time."

"Ah, yes. Stalking him from afar is so much less creepy."

I roll my eyes and walk away, knowing that he's right. I can't seem to help myself when it comes to Slate.

For the first few weeks after he left, I was a mess. I missed him more than I ever would have thought. Slate was my escape. When I was with him, I wasn't constantly reminded of my past or my current life on the run. I felt alive and happy. And most of all, I felt like a woman again. He desired me, and with him, that didn't scare me. Slate was a completely separate facet for me. And then…he was gone.

"Riley, what are you going to do if he comes back?" Dave asks unexpectedly.

"Why would he come back?"

"You know this is where he runs to after fights."

I jump to my feet. "What?"

"Okay, so apparently this is new information for you." He sighs.

"Don't fuck around. Is he coming here?" I yell, desperate to know if I need to prepare to face Slate—or better yet, start packing my bags.

"I have no idea. The way you two left things… I just don't know."

"You know, if he comes back, we have to move, right?"

"So you don't have to face him, or because it would be dangerous to stay?" It's a real question, but I know he's prodding me.

"All of the above!"

"Right." He shakes his head with a look of disappointment.

"Don't bullshit me. Do you think he will come back?" I ask, nowhere near ready for his answer.

"Probably."

I put my untouched food in the sink and head directly to my room. I can't handle seeing Slate. Even if it means moving again, I would pack up right this very second just to avoid him. At the same time, I would give up everything I have just to feel his touch again. Maybe feel the warmth and safety he gives me when he says my name—even if it is the wrong one.

"Riley," Dave calls as I walk away, but he doesn't follow me.

I fall into bed with golden eyes blocking my every distraction. I miss Adam, but I'm terrified of Slate.

"Damn, I'm sorry!" Slate exclaims when I slam into his chest as I round the corner to my apartment.

"Shit!" I jump back, overreacting as usual.

Running into Slate Andrews is the realization of my every nightmare as well as the answer to my every prayer.

"It's okay, Riley. It's just me." He immediately tries to soothe me. Even after all these months, I know exactly who *me* is without even having to look into his face.

"Jesus," I gasp, trying to catch my breath.

"Hey, beautiful." I look up to catch a sweet smile on his gorgeous face. Damn if I don't want to kiss it.

"What are you doing here?" I snap.

"Um, I live here?"

"Um, no, you don't," I say with more attitude than I originally planned.

He laughs and gives me a knowing smirk. "I believe I own this place. That kind of makes me a resident." He shoves his muscular arms into the pockets of his jeans.

"Well, you need to leave, I live here and we can't stay if you're here."

"Riley. I'm not going to bother you. I'm not here to rekindle something with you if that's what you're worried about. I just want to lay low and enjoy some downtime." I'm sure he didn't mean those words as an insult, but they punch me in the gut all the same.

"I'm sure you're not here to bother me, *Slate*," I hiss, and he phys-ically dodges the blow of his real name. "But that doesn't mean I want to be your neighbor."

"Are you pissed?" he asks, clearly confused. Well, he is absolute-ly not the only one.

His huge, sexy body is muddling my head and screwing with my resolve. However, based on his last statement, whatever hope of being with him again is obviously one-sided. I let out a loud exhale and look up at him. His eye is slightly swollen and there is a small cut under his other from his fight, but beyond that, he is just as sexy as I remember. But I wish attraction were all I felt for him.

"No, I'm not pissed," I say while becoming, well...extremely pissed.

"Right. How about this? I'll stay out of your way. You won't even know I'm here."

"Your just being here is the problem. You're the freaking heavy-weight champion who just successfully defended his title for the fifth time. Every cable TV station would trip over their own dick just to cover the story of whether you like Coke or Pepsi."

"Neither. I'm not really a pop person." He smiles, which only serves to piss me off even more.

"You're an ass."

"Because I don't like pop?" He tosses his hands out to the side in frustration.

"No. Because I'm being serious and you're joking around. I can't live next to you. So either you go or I do."

"It's a month, Riley. Twenty-nine days from now, you will be free of me. I'm pretty sure the world won't come crashing at your feet in that time."

"You are assuming I'll live to see the world crash at my feet!" I scream irrationally, way overstepping what I'm allowed to tell anyone.

"What is that supposed to mean? Has he threatened you again?" Slate takes a step forward, crowding me.

"Oh, sweet Jesus. No, *he* hasn't done anything. Everything is fine. No one tried to *threaten* me. My life is all unicorns and puppy dogs."

"Stop fucking lying. You are always lying to me about something, Riley." He barely raises his voice, but his tone is angry nonetheless.

"Oh that's rich, *Slate*. Last time we spoke was when you were telling me your name wasn't Adam and that you were actually a millionaire recluse boxer with the whole world at your fingertips.

"Actually, I didn't tell you any of that, beautiful. Have you been doing some research?" he says with a playful wink that makes me want to physically harm him—with my mouth.

"You're impossible." I spin away and head back to my apartment.

"It was a real pleasure seeing you again," he calls behind me as I slam the door only seconds before the tears spring to my eyes.

"Riley!" Dave calls as I storm through the den and into my bedroom.

"Leave me alone," I say over my shoulder, desperate to escape his curiosity.

"Are you okay?" He finally catches up to me as I flop face-first on my bed.

"No. I'm a bitch and I hate him."

"So I see you ran into Slate?"

I dry my eyes only long enough to give him the death glare. "You knew he was back?"

"Yeah. I got a call from the big boys last night after you went to bed."

"You can't keep this shit from me! Stop trying to run my fucking life!" I curse at him, but he doesn't seem to acknowledge my attitude when he walks into my room and crawls into the bed next to me. He doesn't touch me—he never does. Instead, he throws his arms behind his head and crosses his legs at the ankle.

"We're leaving," he announces.

"What?"

"You're right. We can't stay here if he is going to be coming and going. We need to hit the road. I've already let everyone know it's time." He turns to look at me. "I mean, that's what you want, right?" I swallow past the lump in my throat and give him a silent nod. No, it is absolutely not what I want, but it's the smart decision. "I'll get the ball rolling. Seven days max and we'll be heading somewhere new. You'll need a new name, so start thinking." He pushes to his feet and strides to my door. "That is, unless you decide you want to take a chance with Andrews. You say the word and I'll make it happen."

"I can't even begin to tell you how bad you are at this. He's going to get us both killed," I respond.

"Maybe," he says entirely too nonchalantly. "But maybe *we* are already gone. Maybe he'll just save *you*." His voice is alarmingly sad.

I quickly flip over, trying to figure out what the hell he is talking about, but I can hear his bedroom door close before I even have a chance to ask.

Thirteen

Two days later…

Slate

IT'S OFFICIAL. I have crossed the line. I've somehow turned into a stalker.

I haven't spoken to Riley again since I literally ran into her in the breezeway, but that doesn't mean I haven't seen her. I've seen her plenty as she comes and goes to and from work. Okay, this is definitely not my finest hour.

Sure, I came back to Ohio looking for a getaway. But mainly I came back looking for Riley. I can't figure out what she is hiding or, better yet, why is she hiding so desperately from me. That fact just doesn't sit well with me. None of this does. My lifestyle sucks, but it's nothing that can't change. I've wanted to escape the spotlight for a long time now. It's not like I'd be giving anything up by slipping into oblivion.

I have nothing left to prove. I haven't needed the money in a long time. If it weren't for the fact that I love the sport, I probably would have retired from boxing as soon as I won the title for the first time. I can honestly say that I don't know that I will ever return to the ring, and that has nothing to do with a beautiful woman who wants absolutely nothing to do with me and everything to do with the fact that I think I'm finally done. It's a liberating decision in and of itself.

Now, I just have to figure out what the hell I want to do with the rest of my life. The good news is I have a whole month to not think about it. I flip on my iPod and head over to my couch for a night of solitude.

"You son of a bitch!" I hear shouted from outside my apartment. I recognize Riley's voice and immediately rush to the door, readying myself for whoever she is screaming at.

Just as I pull it open, a box sails past my head. It's quickly followed by a bouquet of flowers that hits me directly in my chest.

"Jesus, what the hell is wrong with you?" I brush the stray petals off my shirt.

"Stop sending me crap!"

"You're welcome?"

"I'm not thanking you," she says in the bitchiest tone I've ever heard outside of LA.

I can't help but laugh at her. "So I've gathered." I smirk, and she narrows her eyes. "I can also see that your eyes are still brown, so apparently I haven't gotten the right prescription yet. I'll try again next week." I shrug and pick up the box off the ground.

"Call your little assistant or whoever you have sending me this shit and make them stop. I don't want it. Damn it, Slate. I don't want anything from you."

I toss the box back at her feet. "I don't have an assistant. Well, I do, but I don't even know her name. I sure as hell don't have her out shopping for you. That's my handwriting on that box. Now, if you just gave me your damn prescription, I'd stop sending you random contacts."

"Whatever. We're moving, so send away. Maybe the next tenant has poor vision and your stupid contacts will finally get put to use."

"Where the hell are you going?" I step forward, fully expecting her to retreat. But she stands her ground and even squares her shoulders.

Her attitude and fearlessness makes my cock stir to life. Even with her bitch face, Riley is still beautiful. I've missed her so fucking much. It's absolutely absurd, but looking at her now makes it all so rational.

"Pssh. Yeah right. Like I'm telling you that."

"Riley, are you scared of me?" I ask, taking another step forward.

"What? No." She rolls her eyes, and I swear it makes my cock go ridged.

"Good." I suddenly loop an arm around her waist and pull her hard against me. She goes stiff, but she doesn't resist. "You're not moving. I'll leave if I have to, but you are not going anywhere." I quickly turn and her shoulders fall back against the brick beside her door.

Her arms remain at her sides as she stands silently against me. She may not be afraid of me, but she definitely isn't lighting up under my touch like she did in the past. *Shit.* I prop myself on a hand next to her head.

"Beautiful, you're not moving. I have other places I can go—other places I can live—but nowhere I want to be as much as *here.*"

She slowly lifts her head to look at me, and no matter how much I want this moment with Riley, I am not ready for the level of pain on her face.

"Slate," she says softly. It's only a single word, but it wrecks me. I'm done with the bullshit. I've played her games for six months; it's my turn now.

"I lied. I absolutely came back for you. It's stupid, but, Riley, I can't think of anything but you."

"Slate," she whispers again.

"Shut up." I gently grab her ass, forcing her against me. "Riley. I don't even know you, but I spent a week with you, and if that was any sort of preview of who you really are, I want it all."

"You need to forget about me," she says, but every muscle of her body tells otherwise.

"Not happening. Try again."

"Forget. Me."

"I'd love to. But you see, we have a little problem, Riley. Not a single night has gone by where I didn't lie in bed and envision your blue eyes. You have haunted my dreams. For six fucking months, I've worried about you. Every time I heard even a car door shut outside my apartment, I would fly out of bed, frantic because I knew the noise would have scared you." I drag my nose up her neck and smile to myself when her breath catches. "Do you know how fucked up that is, beautiful? You never even spent the night with me, yet I wake up in a cold sweat, worried about you. It's fucking ridiculous! But as the days passed, it was the memory of your smile that gutted me. So don't tell me to forget about you, because trust me, I've fucking tried."

"I can't be with you. You don't understand." She tries to walk away, but I refuse to release her.

"Then explain it to me!" I yell beyond all frustration. I'm only inches away from her face, and she immediately shuts down. "I'm sorry," I begin to apologize when she explodes.

"Don't you dare yell at me! I want to be with you, but I can't. It's just not possible, and it's not fucking fair for you to try to make something happen. Walk away. Leave me alone, and stop sending me gifts so I can go one damn week without having you consume my every thought." She throws her arms up, batting my hands away.

"Damn it. Stop," I say just as she cracks open the door. "I'll make it possible, Riley. Just give it a chance. I will make you safe."

"I'm not some damsel in distress you can just swoop off her feet and save, Prince Charming. I'm lost in a world so dark you wouldn't be able to find the light of day again. But make no mistake, you're the poisonous apple in this fairytale, Slate."

"Fuck your fairytale. I just want you. I'll make my own God damn happily ever after. But you're the one who is mistaken. You'll be at the end of that story, beautiful. You either come willingly or you force me into the dark after you. It doesn't matter to me, because either way, I'll find you." I turn to walk away, and as I near my door, I decide to take a risk. It's a gamble that could leave me looking like an arrogant prick, but I've been called worse. "Get your head together, because this is happening. My door's open. I'll be waiting for you."

She doesn't try to stop me, but I don't need her to. One thing has been constant since I met Riley. She's always knocking at my door.

Even unconsciously, since the very first time I laid eyes on her, she hasn't been able to stay away from me either.

I cross my arms over my chest and stand inside my apartment, watching the door and willing her to bust through it. But as the minutes pass, that wish goes unanswered. Finally, I drag a chair over to face the door. She'll come. I know she will. But when the clock hits the one-hour mark, I begin to lose my confidence. I lean forward, placing my elbows to my knees, and cup my hands over my mouth.

"Fuck. Come on, Riley. You want this. I know you do," I say to myself.

Finally, over an hour and a half later, I hear the slam of her door and the thumps of feet running toward my apartment. I jump up and ready myself for something so big that I don't even know where to start preparations. Once she walks back into this apartment, she's mine. I let her go once. I won't make that mistake again. I'm ready for her—ready for us.

Suddenly, my door swings open and her eyes are red rimmed but blue as the Caribbean ocean. Her chest is heaving with anxiety, and the mix of longing and insecurity mingles in her face.

"You ready?" I ask calmly.

"I'm really fucking scared. I don't know how this will ever work."

"That's not your job to figure out. I'll take care of you, Riley. Just tell me you trust me."

She might have shown up, but I can tell that she isn't *here*. She's nervous and jittery. However, just the fact that she came at all proves that she's trying to get there. Fuck it. I'll make her ready.

I stand my ground, careful not to move any closer, completely unsure which version of Riley is standing in front of me. The timid and broken girl I first met or the bold and beautiful woman from the hallway.

With a gentle yet stern voice, I tell her, "I want to touch you, but I'm not going to want to stop. So tell me you trust me, beautiful."

"I don't even really know you," she breathes, clearly doubting her decisions.

"You know enough, or you wouldn't be here at all."

"I think this is going to be really fucking bad."

"Probably. Now tell me you trust me."

"I trust you."

"Then come here." I curl my finger at her, but she just blinks at me for entirely too long. "Riley…" I growl.

"Don't call me that. Just call me beautiful. Please."

"Anything, beautiful," I purr.

Before I have a chance to say anything else, she rushes forward. I'm only a few feet away, but she runs at a full sprint, diving into my arms. Her unrestrained mouth crushes against mine.

Riley

I can't fight this with Slate anymore. It's messed up and I have no idea how anything good could ever come of us being together, but I absolutely can't stay away from him any longer. It was one thing when he was hundreds of miles away, but knowing that he is right next door and feeling the spark that still burns between us has me throwing every single one of my fears into the wind and praying he can make good on his promise to keep me safe.

I push a hand into his hair, desperate to be closer. It's been too long without him. Way too many months without the blaze that only *he* can cause within me.

"I want you naked. Can you handle that?" he asks, pulling his shirt over his head and discarding it on the floor. I can't even bring myself to stress that this is about to happen. I just want to feel him.

"Door shut. Lights off," I demand between kisses.

I move my hand to trace the muscles of his stomach. *Fuck.* Slate Andrews is an amazing specimen of a man. I've never had self-esteem issues before, and I'm not about to start now, but what the hell this man wants with me is mind-boggling. Yet his hand slides over my breasts with the same intensity that I touch him with.

"Door shut. Overhead off. Lamp on," he counters while carrying me toward the bedroom.

"This is not a negotiation." I drag off my own shirt.

He doesn't say another word, but the grumble in his chest makes it quite apparent that he's not pleased. He'll have to get over it though because in all the stories Dave and I have memorized, we have never once discussed what I would tell someone about my scars. I'm bad at telling the lies we have practiced a million times. I can't even image how I would explain away the raised scars up each thigh and over my sex. And I have no plans of letting Slate see them tonight. Having sex with a man for the first time in three and a half years is big enough for tonight. I'll figure out the rest later.

As he places me onto the bed, he follows me down, devouring my mouth in a scorching kiss. I lift my hips off the bed, desperate for contact or, at the very least, friction. Slate props himself up on one arm and the other dives between my legs, still safely covered by my jeans.

"I'm going to lick this pussy tonight, beautiful," he growls, and my eyes immediately fly open. It's a shame I can't let him because I instantly go wet at just the idea.

"No, you're not, but tell me what you would do," I ask, and he looks up, surprised but barely managing to tear his eyes away from my core grinding into his hand. I can't experience it, but that doesn't mean I can't enjoy his ideas.

He blinks for a few seconds, seemingly unsure of what to make of my rejection and even more confused by my request. I reach forward and drag my nails up his rippled abs, moaning when he increases the pressure of his hand.

"Tell me."

He clears his throat and stands all the way up. I'm lying on my back across the bed and he's standing against the corner. One of his hands is playing between my legs, pressing the seam of my jeans against my clit like his own personal sex toy. But what really drenches me is when he uses his other hand to stroke his very promising cock through his own jeans.

"I'd start by taking off these fucking pants, but not your panties. Beautiful, I bet you've soaked completely through them right now, huh?" he asks, and he definitely isn't wrong. I nod my head, urging him to continue. "I want to feel that on my hand. The wet cotton sliding against your pussy as you ride my hand. I could feel your lips, and it would drive me out of my mind. I wouldn't be able to stop my fingers from sliding your panties aside and pushing inside you." He lets out a moan and leans down, tugging my nipple out of the top of my bra and sucking it into his mouth. My back arches off the bed as he continues talking against my breast. "I bet your pussy's so tight. I'd start with just one finger, pushing deep to get you primed. What do you think? Should I add another finger?" He pauses both his hand and mouth.

Holy shit! Slate gives good dirty talk.

I groan and begin to grind against him. I'm desperate for him to continue. This phone-sex-meets-dry-humping thing we have going on right now might just be the hottest sex I've ever experienced.

"No more fingers. Get to the part with your mouth," I say wantonly, surprising even my own ears.

"Is someone eager?" he asks with a slight chuckle and a huge, knowing smile. "I've got a better idea. Let me show you." He reaches down, unbuttoning my pants.

I cover his hands to still them. "Please just tell me," I whisper.

"Beautiful, if this is some sort of foreplay for you, then I am all too willing to give it. I'll tell you absolutely everything I've dreamed about doing to that sexy little body of yours, and trust me, I've thought about it a lot. But if you think for one second this is all that's happening tonight, you've lost your damn mind. I won't let you talk yourself out of this. You want me. I know you do."

I absolutely do.

I immediately sit up and strip open his jeans. I might be afraid of a lot of things, but being with a man on my terms is not one of them. It's just that, up until now, I've never trusted someone to let me have my own terms. I'm not scared of Slate. I never was, even when he was just Adam. I boldly reach into his pants, only stopping when my hand meets hard flesh. It seems everything about Slate is huge, his cock being no different.

"Fuck, Riley."

"Don't call me that," I say, sliding his hard cock through my hand.

"I think you need to get naked." He reaches down again, but I stop him by moving across the bed.

I immediately miss his touch. "Tell me. You didn't finish telling me." I drop my legs open, inviting him to join me on the bed. He doesn't waste a single second before his hand is back between my legs.

"Damn it, beautiful. The first time I make you come, it's not going to be through denim." He begrudgingly flips off the lamp next to the bed. "There. The lights are off."

I smile to myself and shimmy out of my jeans. He was right—my panties are soaked. Slate quickly follows suit and pushes his own pants to the floor. His cock slides against me as he crawls up the bed. He leans over and gently kisses my mouth. I can tell that he's restraining himself, but it doesn't take long before he loses it.

"You have to take control of this, beautiful. What I want to do to you right now is not something you could handle."

"You don't know what I can handle."

"Okay, how about this? I want to strip you naked and drill into your tight pussy until we are both sated and numb. I want to cover you completely, to touch every part of your body. I want your chest pressed against mine while you writhe under me. And it's going to be rough because I won't be able to control myself when I get inside you. I want to fuck you until—"

"Okay, stop!" I shout, cutting him off. My eyes are wide, and while absolutely everything he just said sounds amazing, I know myself. Without question, I would shut down on him.

"I thought you liked to talk?" he says with a smirk that I can barely make out in the darkness.

"I'm nervous," I admit, and his smile instantly fades.

"Tell me what to do to make you comfortable."

"Don't touch me below the waist. I'm sorry. I'm just not there yet," I say, embarrassed. I ready myself for his reaction. I mean, what man wants a woman they can't touch? But Slate doesn't say a word. He just stares through the darkness, seemingly lost in thought.

"I'll give you tonight. But I won't do this again. You either trust me or you don't. I want all of you, beautiful. I'll earn your trust tonight, but tomorrow, there will be no more rules. No more nerves and especially no fears—not in this bed with us. And before you start getting any ideas about retreating again, there *will* be a tomorrow." He grabs the back of my neck and pulls me in for a gentle yet unapologetic kiss. "Now, do your worst."

His hard body relaxes on his back. His hand roams over my chest but never even begins to travel south. Jesus, he is sexy. I'd give anything to forget it all and just enjoy this moment with Slate, but that's not the way my life works.

"Can I—" I begin to ask, but he quickly cuts me off.

"See, the difference between us is that I unquestionably trust *you*. You can do anything you want, beautiful."

Conversation is officially done. I crawl down his body and suck his hard cock into my mouth.

"Fucking hell," he curses while his hands clench the sheets.

I lick and suck Slate over and over until he is on the brink of orgasm. I take it further because I love the way he feels and looks under me. His every muscle ripples with my every upstroke and quakes on the down. Just as I begin to really enjoy myself, he drags me up his body. Shoving a rough hand into my hair, he pulls me down for an uncontrolled kiss.

"Are you wet?" he asks between kisses. I nod against his mouth. "Thank Christ for that." He reaches to the nightstand and pulls out a condom, making quick work of sliding it over his length.

Finally, his hands resume their places on my breasts. He very gently rolls my nipple between his fingers, igniting me unlike ever before. I rock back and find his stiff cock at my entrance. Fuck it. *I need this.* I push back firmly as he slides inside me with a cuss. The familiar bite of pain threatens to transport me back in time, but Slate grounds me.

"Look at me," he demands, and my eyes immediately flash to his. "I don't know much about you, but I know something is playing in your head. Let me fix it."

The tears threaten to spill from my eyes. It's not fair to bring all of my baggage into his bed. I want to forget that it even exists.

"Take me away from it all," I whisper.

A small smile grows across his mouth as he lifts off the mattress, pushing deep inside me. The burn fades, but I'm consumed from the heat left in its path. We both groan as he fills me. Slowly, he begins to thrust in and out of me from the bottom. I fold over him, kissing every inch of his neck and mouth. And for those minutes with him moving inside me, I forget.

He tries to move his hand between us, presumably to rub my clit—a feeling I would pay thousands for—but he stops just inches away.

"God damn it. I want to taste you," he growls.

I push up, using his hard pecs to brace myself. I reach between us and rub my clit, forcing myself perilously close to the edge that Slate is driving me toward.

"I'm sorry," I say as I slide a finger into his mouth. His tongue swirls around, savoring my arousal.

"For fuck's sake, don't tease me with that." He grabs hold of my hips, forcing me down as he thrusts inside me. His movements become frantic. "Come on, beautiful. I want to feel that tight pussy pulse around me."

Oh yeah, Slate gives really good dirty talk.

With one final push, I do just that. I stop fighting and embrace the high that no one, including myself, has been able to give me in three and a half agonizing years. I lean over on his chest, riding the wave of my orgasm down while he finds his own release inside me.

The inevitable tears spring to my eyes.

"That was really good." I half-laugh, half-cry into his chest.

"Shit. Are you okay?" he asks, and I silently nod, not trusting my voice. "Riley," he growls and sits up taking me with him.

"I didn't freak out," I barely squeak out.

"What?" He relaxes again, pulling me down tight against his side.

"I always thought I would freak out when I was with a man again. But I didn't with you."

Slate's eyes flash dark and he swallows hard, yet somehow he manages to be gentle as he says, "Why would you freak out, beautiful?"

"It doesn't matter why. It only matters that you made me comfortable enough to forget it."

"Son of a bitch," he mumbles, pressing a soft kiss to my mouth.

I go willingly into his arms, squeezing as close as possible while trying to stop the tears of relief and happiness that are openly flowing from my eyes.

"Riley, I'll never ask, but one day, you are going to have to tell me."

I don't respond because I have nothing to say. I can't tell Slate—ever. I just curl in even closer, lying with my body instead of my voice.

He holds me for hours as I drift in and out of sleep, but from what I can tell, he never even closes his eyes. His fingers constantly glide over my back and up my sides.

"I need to go. Dave will worry."

Slate lets out a laugh. "You're not going anywhere. We aren't doing this you-running-home shit anymore. You sleep in my bed, or I sleep in yours after we make love. And even when we don't. I've never even slept *with* you, but I refuse to sleep without you again."

"You're bossy." I stretch up and kiss the underside of his chin.

"No, I'm just not going to sit back and watch you distance yourself from me again. I missed you—something else I'm not willing to do again."

"Slate, I—"

"Sleep, beautiful," he says with a sexy grin.

"I need my pants," I shyly whisper.

"No pants."

I immediately clam up. I'm no choirgirl. I know middle-of-the-night sex happens, and I'm not positive how I would react if he woke me up like that. He must notice my anxiety because he immediately rolls me over and folds his hard body behind me.

He whispers in my ear, "I won't touch you, but I want to feel you." A tender sentiment that makes me melt against him.

"I trust you," I whisper back.

"No you don't, and we'll talk about that tomorrow. But at least you believe me tonight. Now go to sleep, Riley." He kisses my head and buries his face in my hair.

If he only realized how much I'm trusting him by being here at all.

Slate

MY BLOOD IS fucking boiling. Holding Riley is the only thing keeping me from destroying the entire apartment complex right now.

"I always thought I would freak out when I was with a man again."

I knew she had been abused in some way or shape, but this? I was not prepared for this little revelation tonight. I need to talk to Dave. Then I need to find her ex-boyfriend and ruin him.

She's been sound asleep for two hours, and I've finally been able to inch my way out from under her. I grab some sweats and my phone off the nightstand. I take one last glance over my shoulder before leaving, but she doesn't budge as I silently sneak from the room.

"What's up?" I hear Jimmy's sleepy voice answer the phone.

"Riley Peterson. I know I called you off her last time, but I need *everything* this time. I'm looking for her ex-boyfriend. Spare no expense. Fucking find him."

"Should I also start stashing away bail money now?" he asks humorously.

"It wouldn't be a bad idea."

"Slate," he warns.

"I'll text you as much information as I can tomorrow and a picture of her so they can ask around. I don't care what you have to do. Just get me his location," I snap.

"Shit." He sighs. "Yeah, I'll get on it in the morning."

"Thanks," I reply, scrubbing a hand through my hair, but he has already disconnected the line.

I toss my phone onto the table and head out the door. One man holds the answers. I'll be damned if I'm going to let him keep them from me.

I leave the front door open just in case Riley wakes up.

I quietly knock on Dave's door, but he doesn't answer. It's the middle of the night, but tough shit. He's waking up. I knock a little louder, and finally, his eyes peek through the window. He swings open the door and shoves a gun down the back of his pants.

"Where is she?" he asks with concern etched across his face.

"Do you always answer the door with a gun?" I ask, crossing my arms over my chest.

"Where the fuck is she? Or you might never get to knock on another door again," he snaps taking a step closer.

"Sleeping."

He instantly relaxes and small smile tips the corner of his mouth. "Good night, huh?"

"Fuck you. What's her ex-boyfriends name?"

His eyebrows pop up in surprise before falling flat again. "I took care of him."

"If he is still breathing, you did not take fucking care of him. Now tell me his God damn name!" I roar.

"Jesus Christ, Slate. Calm the fuck down. First of all, you are going to do more harm than good if you try to become some celebrity vigilante. Just focus on her. She doesn't need you out there trying to make this guy pay. She needs you to help her rebuild."

"Don't fuck around with me, Dave. I'll never be able to sleep again knowing he is out there. Not after what he did to her."

"Then don't sleep, but you can rest easy knowing she can."

"I swear to God, you people talk in code. What the fuck does that mean?"

"That woman never sleeps. Yet it appears, with you, it's not an issue."

"She have nightmares?" I ask, trying to seek out the logical explanation for her sleep issues.

"No. But I'm not ever going to tell you her business. You want answers? You ask Riley."

"Or you could just tell me so I don't have to make her relive that bullshit."

He stares at me, obviously weighing a decision. But the sudden scream that comes from inside my apartment halts the conversation.

"Slate!" Riley cries, forcing us both into action.

Side by side, Dave and I sprint the few steps down the hall towards her. Just before we get to the door, he pushes me to the side, narrowly making it inside before I do.

My eyes fly around the apartment, searching for any possible trouble, but only Riley is standing in the middle of the room, sobbing with a sheet pulled tight around her naked body. Dave is the first to reach her, but she breezes past him, slamming into my arms.

"Oh, God. You left the doors open. I just…" She stops talking but continues to cry into my chest.

"Talk to me, beautiful. Are you okay?" I ask, rubbing her back. Her arms are locked around my waist and her body trembles against me. "Riley, you have to tell me what's going on."

She doesn't respond, and I turn to Dave, who is standing with his mouth hanging open. I give him a confused glance, and his eyes just go wide in return. He shakes his head and looks down, only to look back up with a huge smile.

"She doesn't like open doors," he tells me before turning his attention to Riley. "It's okay, babe. We were just out in the hall talking. Slate just wanted to let me know you were staying at his place tonight. You know, so I wouldn't worry." He winks at me.

She turns her head to face him. "I'm sorry. I just got scared."

"No biggy. Nothing to worry about." He shrugs, and her whole body relaxes in my arms. "So are you staying here or coming home?" he asks as he turns toward the door.

"She's staying," I quickly respond, and she tilts her head back to look at me.

"I am?" She tries to ask with attitude, but her voice is still on edge.

"I already told you not a single night again, and especially not after that. So yeah, you're staying."

"You're bossy," she complains, dropping her forehead to my chest.

"Yeah, we covered that too."

She turns her attention back to Dave, who is still smiling. "I'm going to stay with Slate."

"All right, babe. I'll see you in the morning." He waves over his shoulder as he closes the door behind him.

I pull her in for an all-too-brief kiss. "Go get in bed. I'll meet you there."

"I'll wait," she answers while chewing on her bottom lip.

I walk to the kitchen and retrieve a notepad and pen. As I head back toward her, I rake my eyes over the sheet she has pulled tight around her body. The tips of her nipples are barely showing through the thin, cotton material. Riley's body is amazing, and I have a sudden and desperate need to touch her.

"I want to be inside you again." I brush the back of my thumb over her breast as I stop in front of her. Her eyes instantly heat, telling me that I'm not alone in that desire. "I rushed it the first time. I think we need to give it another shot." I wink, and she finally gives me a smile that I recognize as the strong woman I see in flashes between the fears. And it's simply amazing. "But first, we need to talk." And just like that, her smile completely disappears. "Oh stop. It's nothing bad. It will help, I swear."

"I don't want to talk."

"Okay, then write." I hand her the pad and pen and guide her toward the bedroom.

Once inside I shut and lock the door behind us, I look in her direction to make sure she saw it. She responds with an embarrassed grin.

"I never would have left that door open if I knew it scared you. I remember now that, a few months ago, you mentioned something about keeping it shut, but I honestly didn't remember until Dave told me. I actually purposely left the front door open in case you woke up. I was just outside and I thought it would be better if I could hear you. I'm sorry." She shakes her head and dismisses my apology, but that doesn't change the fact that it happened. "Tell me what you're scared of, Riley."

Her eyes widen with anxiety as she backs away. "Please don't do this."

"No, just listen. I told you I wouldn't ask, and I won't. I don't need to know why you're scared of it. I just need to know *what* you're afraid of so something like tonight doesn't happen again."

"I've never made a list. A lot of stuff is just situational," she answers nervously.

"Okay, well just give me the definites." I shrug and lean back against the pillows.

She lets out a groan but curls under my arm and spends the next five minutes writing.

"Uh, I think that's it. But you promised you wouldn't ask why."

"I already told you that. You have to start trusting me." I snatch the list from her hands and intently study it. I am actually surprised at how short it is and how much I already know off it.

Open doors
Unexpected knocks on doors
Being snuck up on
Being touched below the waist
Being physically restrained
Birds
Cottage Cheese

"Riley, this is bad. Really fucking bad," I say seriously while dragging her onto my lap. She immediately shies away from me and swallows hard. "There are some things you should know about me. Things that could change everything." I kiss her mouth reassuringly as my cock grows between us. I graze her lip with my teeth, sucking it into my mouth before leaning back and holding her gaze "I have a pet bird and an obsession with cottage cheese."

She slaps my chest and rolls her eyes. "No, you don't, jerk."

"No, but you were the smartass who put them on the list."

"Those are legit fears of mine. Cottage cheese is all clumpy. I mean, why is it so freaking chunky? And don't even get me started on birds. They are all flappy and they could fly at you at any moment." I bust out laughing, but she remains silent. "Can I ask you a serious question?"

"Yes, I like cottage cheese," I answer matter-of-factly but then smile and signal for her to ask away.

"Why don't you like to be touched?"

"Wow. You really did do your research on me." I roll her to the side and prop myself up on an elbow, facing her.

"I read it in a few articles. Then I watched some of your old fights online and noticed you always flinch when fans touch you." She leans forward, giving me a reassuring kiss of her own.

I take full advantage of her mouth for a moment. I'm willing to take whatever comfort she is offering—even if I don't need it.

"I wish I had some grand story to tell you, but the truth is, I just don't like it. I'm a really quiet guy. I like my privacy *and* personal space. When I was growing up, my mom was very loving but not very affectionate. I guess I just got used to it. What is it with everyone needing to touch people? All that hugging and touching. A wave and a friendly smile work just as well."

"You let me touch you." She wraps her arms around me, dragging her nails up my back in the way she knows I love.

"That's because I wanted to touch *you*. I'm not some hermit who can't stand the human touch. It just makes my skin crawl when people I don't know feel the need to grab me or hug me. I'm a person, not an animal who needs to be petted."

"I like to pet you." She throws a sheet-covered leg over my hip.

"Show me." I reach around and grab her ass, grinding my cock into her core. "And get rid of that damn sheet," I growl as she rolls over on top of me. I quickly flip off the light.

I glide my hand over her breast. I would rather slide it between her legs and into her pussy, but I saw the list. I fully intend to shred that paper soon, but for now, I won't push her.

"One of these days, beautiful, you're going to trust me."

"I do trust you." She leans forward, pressing her breasts against me.

"No, I mean *really* trust me. And when you do, I am going to fuck you with the lights on and door open while touching every inch of you." Her whole body stiffens on top of me. "But despite my initial reaction, I'll wait for you to be ready." She gives me a weak smile that I can barely make out in the darkness. "Now, tell me. Are you wet?"

"I would be if you got naked again."

I quickly peel off my clothes and roll on another condom from the nightstand. Riley watches my every move, licking her lips.

"Show me you're wet. Give me another taste."

She takes my mouth in a rough kiss. Her tongue slides over mine, and I can feel her hand brush over my cock as it moves between her legs. A second later, her fingers are snaking between our tongues. I groan, sucking her fingers all the way into my mouth just as she slides down onto my cock.

Riley slowly rides me until she finds her own rhythm. Her pace quickens, and I grab her ass to slow her, but she throws her head back, lost in the feeling. It's fucking beautiful to watch this woman, who is normally so closed off, unravel around me. I pull her forward to take her mouth. Gripping her hips, I thrust hard, taking complete control of the situation even though she's on top. It doesn't take long before she begins to tremble through her orgasm.

"Slate," she moans, dropping to my chest.

"Fuck, beautiful." I thrust into her one last time before finding my own release.

We lie down, sated, trying to catch our breaths for a moment, but Riley suddenly sits up with a bashful smile.

"I love that you called me beautiful when you came."

"Well, it's fitting, and you told me not to call you Riley." I reach up to tuck a hair behind her ear.

"I also really like when you take control from the bottom like that." She pauses to look away.

"That's good to hear too, because one of these days, I want to kneel between your legs and watch you take control of my cock while you fuck me from the bottom."

"Jesus, Slate," she sighs. "You know, for a quiet guy, you have a deliciously filthy mouth." She begins to giggle, and I can't help but laugh along with her.

Just to watch her subtle transformation from only hours ago is amazing. No tears this time, and that hits me deep. I'm fucked—literally and figuratively.

CHAPTER Fifteen

Three weeks later...

Riley

"HEY, BEAUTIFUL," SLATE says, walking in the door.

He never knocks, but he always shouts my name from outside the door. At first, I thought he was crazy, but then he produced that silly list clearly documenting my fears.

"Hi," I respond, looking up at him through my brown contacts.

He gives me a deep, lingering kiss and scoops me up off my feet, causing me to immediately wrap my legs around his waist.

"How was your day?" he asks, kissing my neck.

"Terrible."

"*Pretty in Pink,*" Dave answers from behind us. He's wearing the same smirk he does every time he sees Slate and me together.

The day after Slate made things clear that we were building a relationship, Dave called off the move. I told him that I didn't want to leave, and he spent the next thirty-six hours shouting at people over the phone. I didn't ask and he didn't elaborate, but if possible, I fell in love with him even more because he fought to give me more time with Slate.

I still haven't showed Slate my scars, but he doesn't push me. We have this amazing balance of him letting me squeak by with no questions answered and me asking him everything about his life. I've never broached the topic of his mom though. I'm not that brave yet. I also don't want him to pour his heart out about his past and have to look directly into his eyes and lie about my own.

Since the first night, one thing remains consistent—Slate sleeps with me every night. Whether we are at his place or mine, he's always there when I close my eyes. And I always sleep, a magical feat of its own. Before I met Slate, sleep was a bit of an issue for me. I was an insomniac to say the least. Stress has a funny way of screwing with you. I've never been a huge sleeper, but the five to six hours I get a night in his arms is more than I ever would have thought possible. Noises in the night still terrify me, but now it's because I'm worried someone will take him from me. I lost myself, but I don't think I could survive losing Slate. However, every day that we are together, I put his life at risk.

"Riley, you going to explain the movies?" Dave says, snatching a piece of bacon off the plate.

"Stop eating the bacon or you're going to end up with just an LT sandwich for dinner!" I shout, and Slate slides me down his body, placing my feet back on the ground. I look up at his golden eyes and smile, squeezing him one last time before heading back to the frying pan. "So Dave and I rate our days based on '80s movies. The worse the day, the worse the movie."

"Wait. Shouldn't it be the worse the day, the better the movie?" Slate asks, stealing his own piece of bacon.

I give him an evil glare that does nothing to intimidate him as he pops it in his mouth. "Um, no. I don't want to watch a good movie and let my attitude ruin it. I want to watch a piece of shit that I can scream and cuss at for being...well, a pile of shit. I want to complain about

130

the actors and make fun of the director and basically just flip them all off," I finish and look up at Slate, who is standing beside me with a disgusted look on his face.

"Riley, are you telling me you think *Vision Quest* is a terrible movie? The night I met you, that was your movie of choice, and I have to say, even from my point of view, that was a really fucking shitty night for you."

"Um, I mean..." I stutter teasingly.

"I want you to consider this very carefully, because I'm not sure we can continue this relationship any longer if that is really the way you think." He looks at me in all seriousness, but I know he's joking.

"It's growing on me?" I question with a shrug.

"Oh hell no." He leans down and tosses me over his shoulder. He pushes the pan of bacon off the burner and strides to my room.

"Slate, stop!" I laugh.

"Say goodnight to Dave," he says, slapping my ass.

"No! We haven't eaten yet! Fine. *Vision Quest* is pure cinematic genius. Matthew Modine is a God."

"Oh, thank the Lord. I'm fucking starving." He puts me down just outside my bedroom door.

"You are such an ass," I say with the same perma-grin I've been wearing for weeks.

"I can deal with that." He wraps a thick arm around my waist and tips me back for a heated kiss that leaves me wishing I hadn't caved. I'd be more than happy with abandoning dinner and heading to bed at this point. "Actually, can we talk for a second anyway?" He tilts his head to my room.

"Yeah, sure." I move to my bed and plop down on my side, but Slate stands at the foot.

"I have to go back to LA in the morning," he announces.

My hands immediately knot. "Oh, um... Yeah. Of course."

"Don't get all shy on me, Riley. I'm retiring."

"What? No, you are fucking not!" I jump to my feet and shout entirely too loud.

"Riley?" I hear Dave yell from the den.

"I'm fine!" I snap then level my eyes back at Slate. "You are not retiring!"

"Oh really? I'm not?" he asks with a smirk. Yep, a fucking cocky-ass, sexy-as-hell, panty-drenching *smirk*.

"You are not giving up your career for me! No fucking way. I know what it feels like to give up your life, and trust me, you will resent me. It's not happening. We can figure it out long distance, but you are absolutely never, not one question about it, giving up your career for me."

"You ready?" he questions oddly.

"What?" I ask, but it's too late.

Slate rushes me, lifting me off my feet once again and pushing me down to the bed. His huge body is careful to land beside me instead of on top of me, but with a hand in my hair, he gently tips my head back to look into his eyes.

"Who said I was giving it up for you?" He pops a questioning eyebrow before roughly taking my mouth.

"Well, this is embarrassing," I say against his lips while dragging my nails up his back.

"I'm done, Riley. And the only part of that that has anything to do with you is how you have made me feel over the last few weeks. I was still on the fence when I came back this time, but after spending numerous quiet nights with you…I have zero desire to go back to that life. I love the sport, but I hate pretty much everything else that comes along with it. That life? It's not me, beautiful"—he tucks my hair behind my ears—"any more than this life is you," he finishes, surprising me.

I instantly freeze at his words, completely unsure of how to respond. His eyes search mine for an answer, but I have nothing to offer. He sees right through my lies—he has since the day I met him.

"Yeah. That's what I thought." He pushes off me and to his feet.

"Slate, wait!" I call after his sudden departure. He didn't leave the room, but he left me all the same.

I grab his waist and plant my head against his chest. His arms immediately wrap around me, and he lets out a resigned sigh.

"I'm not going anywhere, beautiful. But tell me something real. I think I know you, but I always feel like I'm missing something. It's like you are some seven-billion-piece puzzle, and every time I find a corner tile, you change the entire picture."

I laugh, knowing exactly what he's saying. I feel the exact same way too. I've lost so much of myself over the years that I don't even know what the picture is anymore.

"What did you mean you know what it feels like to give up your life?"

"I just meant, I don't want you to give up something for me," I lie. "We can make this work without you having to do that." I give him a fake smile, but once again, Slate calls my bluff.

He takes two giant steps forward, forcing me to fall back against the wall. Not because I'm scared but because I have nowhere else to go. "Bullshit. Bullshit. Bullshit." He leans closer with every word until his mouth is only a breath away from mine. "I won't ask. But just so you know, I think you are full of bullshit."

"I gathered that by the excessive use of bullshit." I smart off while looking at his mouth.

He quickly closes the gap, mumbling against my lips, "Well, as long as we're clear." His tongue snakes into my mouth, claiming me as his own. He slides a hand under my shirt and over my breasts. I eagerly reach down to unbutton his pants, but his hands still me. "I'm starving. So unless you plan on feeding me something else"—he pointedly looks down at the button on my own jeans—"I need to eat."

"Tease," I mumble and head for the door.

It's probably for the best that he stopped things from progressing. It's light outside, and even with my curtains drawn, there is no way I could have hidden my scars from him. Dave and I developed a less than convincing story about how I got them in an accident, but Slate is already suspicious about my past. There is no way he would have believed some weak-ass story. That is just not a bridge I'm ready to cross yet.

"I don't want you to go," I say, lying naked, wrapped in Slate's arms.

"It's only for a few days, beautiful."

"You know you are going to have to lay really low for a while. No more going to that gym at night anymore when you get back." I drag my fingers over his hard abs. "And you know I'm only using you for your body. How will we ever manage that if you can't work out?"

He laughs, squeezing me hard against his chest. "I'll have some equipment delivered while I'm gone. Make a little gym in the spare room. You want to start working out with me? Clothing is completely optional."

"Well as sexy as naked lunges sound, I'm going to say yes to working out but no to the naked part."

He suddenly rolls me over, hovering on his elbows above me. "When I get back, I will just be Slate Andrews. Not professional boxer or celebrity. Just Slate. Can you just be Riley? No more hiding or secrets. I need some truths, beautiful. I don't want you to relive any details for me, but even the general idea of who you really are would be amazing."

"Slate," I whisper, swallowing around the newly formed lump in my throat.

"I want you. All of you. Not these little bits I hear echoing around the room. I just want you, Riley."

Tears well in my eyes because that's exactly what I want to give him too. But I'm not totally sure that woman even exists anymore.

"I can try," I respond hesitantly, just to appease him.

"Mmm, good answer," he sighs.

CHAPTER Sixteen

Three days later…

Riley

"PACK YOUR BAGS," Dave says, storming into my room.

"What?" I jump to my feet.

"First, I'm going to kill your fucking boyfriend. Then we have to move," he barks.

"Wait. What did Slate do?"

"He's hired an entire fucking network of PIs to investigate you!" he roars.

"No," I barely breathe. I fall back onto the bed and my legs start shaking as my worst nightmare comes true. "How? I mean, did he find anything?"

"Well, one of his guys found Jessica Lynn and Chris Webb."

"Oh, God. No, no, no!" I begin to pace as my breath stills in my chest. "How is that even possible?"

"I have no fucking idea, but I guess, when you have unlimited resources, anything is possible. Point is, if Slate can do it, so can Wilkes. We have to go."

"I'm not leaving him."

"I'm sorry, babe. We don't have any other options. We need to go."

"I'm not leaving him!" I scream.

"Riley, we don't have any options. I'll see what I can do in a few months about getting back in touch with him. But right now, the safest thing for everyone is to put some distance between you two. Let's set up a new life, get settled, then maybe see if we can figure out how to bring him back into the picture."

Tears spring to my eyes at the very idea of going months without him. I just got him. "He can come with us. Please. I can't. I just. I…" I begin to stumble out irrationally.

"I'm so sorry," Dave whispers, folding me into a hug.

I suck in a deep breath and try to collect my thoughts, but my mind is spinning. "Wait. Please just stop for a minute. I can't think. How do you know this isn't Wilkes? Maybe Slate has nothing to do with it?" I plead, looking for any possible way to keep him in my life.

"One of the big boys moved into our old apartment in Utah, hoping Wilkes would come looking for us there again. Well, lo and behold, a PI showed up at his fucking door yesterday with a picture of you and asking a million questions about Jessica Lynn, a.k.a. Riley Peterson. Feds brought him in, traced it all back to Jimmy Douglas, Slate's trainer and owner of the apartment. Jimmy doesn't have access to that kind of money, Riley, but I'll give you one guess who does."

"No." I reject his theory. "Slate's not dangerous. He's just curious. Maybe I can tell him to back off. He'll listen to me. Please, just let me talk to him."

"We have to leave before he gets back."

"No!" I yell again. "I am *not* leaving him!"

"He's going to get you killed!" he shouts back in a way Dave has never spoken to me. It startles me at first, but suddenly, it dawns on me that he's actually scared this time too.

"Yeah, well. I told you that months ago. And you said we could make it work. Make. It. Work."

"Fine. I'll take the blame. But pack your shit!" he snaps, stomping out of my room. I know he's not mad at me. He's pissed at the whole situation, but his tone still stings.

I sit on my bed, staring into space for over an hour. Shifting from tears to fear, but I finally just get really angry. I have zero control over my life, and I'm sick and tired of it. They want me to recover and live again. That's a joke. How can anyone be expected to truly live with the knowledge that they can lose everything with only a moments notice? *Fuck that.* I'm not losing Slate. I rush out of my room to find Dave sitting on the couch, whispering into the phone.

"Give me the phone." I snap my fingers at him and his eyebrows lift in surprise.

In all the years that we have been on the run, I have never once spoken to anyone at the US Marshal's office. Dave handles everything when it comes to the Witness Protection Program, or "big boys" as he calls them. I'm so fucking done with hiding though.

I don't wait for his response. I just snatch the phone from his hands.

"Who is this?" I bark into the phone.

"Miss Peterson, it's so nice to finally talk to you." I can hear the smile in the woman's voice on the other end of the line.

"Screw you. I'm not leaving."

"I'm sorry. You don't have much of a choice in the matter. You have been compromised by Mr. Andrews."

"Nothing has happened. All we know is you didn't do your job at covering our trail. So what if Slate found out we have a past. He's not working for Wilkes. He's not a fucking threat, so I'm not fucking leaving!"

"My, my. How you have changed since we last met." She almost laughs.

"You listen to me now. Do your fucking job. Erase the past and ensure our safety. If a couple of high-price PIs can find me, it seems to me you are failing. We can move across town, fine. But I am absolutely not leaving Slate, so figure it out."

Just as I begin to hand back the phone, she shouts across the line.

"Miss Peterson, you are allowed to leave the program any time you would like. Your identity can be reinstated. But just know that comes with zero protection. You will be completely on your own."

I laugh at her. If there is one thing I have learned, it's that they need me. They won't let me go. "But then who would you use as bait?" I throw the phone at Dave and storm back to my room, slamming the door behind me.

I'm lying on my bed, staring at the ceiling when Dave casually opens the door to my room. "That was some serious attitude."

"I'm sick of it. I hate this fucking life. I finally found someone who makes me feel like me again and they want to take him away from me too." I don't even bother looking up.

"Damn it, Riley. I shouldn't have let this happen. I should have taken you far away from here before you ever had the chance to get to know him, but the night that I walked in and saw you holding his arm, a part of me was freed."

"What?" I roll over, and the expression on his face shocks me. I always knew the events from that night had affected him too, but this? I never expected this level of devastation.

"When I walked in that first night, you were sound asleep but gripping his arm as if your life depended on it. Then, when he first got back, you ran right past me and into his arms. God, it was liberating watching you come alive again."

"Leo, I..." I fade off, and he painfully closes his eyes at the sound of his name.

He puts a finger to his mouth, signaling me to be quiet. "Erica, I have relived your screams while I stood outside your door all those years ago for too long. And when I saw just the tiniest flash of hope that you really could be a person again, I wanted you to take it. I told you once that I never thought you would be okay again, but that doesn't mean I've ever stopped hoping you would." His voice catches in his throat and his brown eyes fill with tears as he tries to fight back the emotions.

He clears his throat and continues. "Then I found out who he was and realized that he not only had the time, money, and resources to protect you, but that he could give you something I never could. He could repair you from the inside out. I've always made sure you were safe, be he can truly fix things for you—give you back all the things I stole."

The tears are streaming down my face as I whimper, "You didn't steal anything from me. You saved me."

"I love you, but I hope, one day, he fixes that mentality too."

"Leo, you did the best you could."

"I don't want to talk about this anymore. I just wanted to tell you I'll figure it out. You talk to Slate. Make him stop searching or we will have no choice but to leave. We may have to move. I'm not really sure what to do at this point, but I won't make you give him up. Just make him stop asking questions." He gives me a weak smile.

"Okay."

He turns to walk away and pauses at the door. "When's Slate getting back?"

"Couple of hours."

"Is it cool if I take off for a bit? I need a drink and I think you need some privacy."

"Yeah. Privacy sounds good." I try to dry my eyes, but the tears won't stop flowing. Leo James is an amazing man. What I wouldn't give to have met him under different circumstances. I can only imagine how incredible it would be to have a friendship with him that wasn't based on guilt and pain.

"See ya later, babe."

"Night, Leo." I purposely use his name once again. He needs to hear it as much as I need to say it.

Slate

Fucking weather. My flight was delayed for two hours, and worse than that, Riley isn't answering her phone. It's killing me not being able to get back to her and away from the craziness of Slate *The Silent Storm* Andrews yet.

I announced my official retirement a few days ago, and you would have thought the world had imploded. I know it was unexpected. I was at the top of my game, and a rematch was already in the works, but I'm done. The media went nuts, and it took a lot longer than I'd thought it would to escape the attention. My plan is to see if I can convince Riley to go on an extended vacation with me. Get away for a while, somewhere we can escape until the attention dies down. Maybe even see if I can get her to open up and stop hiding.

I learned quite a bit about Riley while I was gone. The biggest part being that her real name is Jessica Lynn. I had a sneaking suspicion for a while that Riley wasn't really her name, mainly because she insists that I call her beautiful in bed. But also because, if she is reading late at night or watching TV, she never answers you immediately when you call her. And then there is the whole Dave/Leo thing from when I first met them. It doesn't take a rocket scientist to figure out that something is going on with them.

My guys have never found this ex of hers, and by all accounts, Jessica was a hermit, never leaving the house. If she did, she was always accompanied by her *cousin*. The good news is neither she nor Dave seems to have a criminal history. My agent, Mitch, spent hours trying to convince me she was some sort of con-woman. Obviously, they have never met Riley. She is a terrible liar.

"Riley, it's me!" I shout when I get to her door. I don't bother knocking. It will only scare her.

But as I swing open her door, it appears I'm too late for that. She's standing with her hands knotted in front of her and her eyes are red and puffy as if she has been crying all day.

"Jesus, are you okay?" I quickly glance around the room, but nothing seems out of place.

"We can be together but only if you stop asking questions."

"What the hell are you talking about? What's going on, Riley?" I drop my bags and slowly walk towards her, but for the first time in months, she backs away.

"I know you hired investigators to look into my past. You swore you wouldn't ask, Slate. You promised me." Her face crumbles.

"I wasn't trying to find out what happened to you. I was only searching for that asshole ex of yours who made you this way. But yeah, I found out a lot more than I bargained for, Jessica," I say, lifting my brows knowingly. I'm not trying to be a dick, but I want her to know that she can stop hiding.

"Beautiful," she corrects on a heartfelt cry. "Slate, please. You can't look into me anymore. I'll have to leave if you do. Please don't make me disappear again." She pauses and her lips begin to quiver. I try to take another step forward, but once again, she retreats. "You're the only one who truly sees me," she whispers.

"What's going on? You have to give me something here, beautiful. Tell me something true!"

"You. Can't. Ask. Questions," she repeats very slowly, but it's not out of anger. She's desperate.

"Damn it, Riley! You have to trust me. What are you hiding?" I'm barely holding it together. I'm frustrated and angry and on the cusp of losing it all.

Her eyes are frantic and her entire body shakes as she pleads, "Stop. This is the whole problem. You're asking questions. They will take you away from me."

A cold chill of rage slides through my body at the very idea. "I won't let anyone take you away from me. Ever."

Her brown eyes light just before she drops her chin to her chest. "You won't even know it's happening until I'm gone," she whispers, and her shoulders shake with sobs.

I crack my neck, desperately trying to distract myself. She won't let me touch her as she breaks down in front of me. Screaming at her is only going to make her shut down, but I need some God damn answers before I lose my mind. I take a breath, praying for a magical calm to wash over me.

"Riley, you're mine. We've established that. No one, and I mean *no one*, will ever hurt you again. But you have to let me in on a little of the backstory here. I will fight the entire world for you, but I need you in my corner. I can't do this blind."

"It's the only way."

My frustration gets the best of me and I let out a long string of expletives. "You're right, beautiful. I can *see* you, but I can't *hear* you. There are too many lies and secrets echoing around us, distorting the real woman. I don't know who you truly are, Riley, but tiny flashes of that woman whisper around the room between us. I will find the real you among the echoes—and I will make her mine."

Her eyes fly to mine, and in a sad voice, she breaks me. "Oh, Slate.

That woman doesn't exist. All I am are the bits and pieces of static."

"Not to me, you're not," I say forcefully. "I'll stop with the questions, but make no mistake. I will find *you*. I need that woman. Not this façade you put on or the fears that overwhelm you. I'm talking about the woman you only show for the briefest of seconds when we are alone. I will search to the ends of the earth to find that woman—because I love her. I don't even know her real name, but I love her—fiercely."

"Slate," she breathes, shaking her head.

"Riley," I respond, taking another step toward her.

"Erica," I hear Dave interrupt from the doorway.

I turn around to find him standing behind me with defeat and grief painted all over his face.

"No!" she screams, rushing toward him.

"Her name is Erica," he clarifies, looking me directly in the eye.

"Shut up!" she screams, pushing him as hard as she can. My eyes go wide as I watch her detonate. "They will take him away from me! You asshole!" she cries, pounding on his chest. I loop a restraining arm around her waist, but she continues to wildly kick her legs and swings her arms. "I hate you. I fucking hate you."

"Good, because I fucking hate me too," Dave bites out. "But you know what? He needs to know you. And more than that, you need him to know, Erica."

"They'll make us disappear. You know that!" she cries, crumbling in my arms.

"I won't let that happen, I swear. Tell him all of it, babe. Free yourself as well." Dave nods to me and walks away, leaving me holding the pieces of the shattered woman I'm madly in love with.

CHAPTER CHAPTER CHAPTER CHAPTER Seventeen

Erica

I HAVE NO idea how long Slate and I have been lying in bed. He hasn't said a single word since he carried me in here, but then again, neither have I. I've been lying facedown, alternating between crying, sleeping, and wanting to puke at the idea of telling him everything. I don't think my past will send Slate running for the hills, but that doesn't mean I'm not worried that it will ultimately make him leave.

But no matter how long I wish I could put this off, I know it's time. I suddenly roll over to face him and find him propped up on an elbow, watching me.

"You ready?" he asks, and the familiar words make tears once again flood my eyes.

"I think so," I whisper as he lies down on my pillow, only inches from my face. He places a hand in the curve of my hip and gives me an encouraging squeeze. I suck in a breath and prepare to spill it all. "My name is Erica Hill. I used to be an emergency room physician—" My words are immediately cut off as Slate leans in for a deep and lingering kiss. He holds his mouth to mine while breathing me in and pouring his heart out with only a single kiss.

He pulls away, flashing me a crooked smile. "It's nice to meet you, Erica."

"Oh, God." I try to fight back the emotions, but the sound of my name coming from his mouth is just too much. It's a word I took for granted for almost thirty years, but now, it's something so incredible that it leaves me speechless.

In true Slate fashion, he holds me patiently, waiting for me to continue.

"Almost four years ago, I took a house call that changed my life. Everyone will tell you never to take house calls, but residents make shit for money. Combine that with over a hundred and fifty thousand dollars in student loans and just like everyone else without a rich mommy or daddy to lean on, I was broke. A guy I worked with did some after-hours stuff all the time. He told me the patient was some sort of hypochondriac that just wanted a doctor to tell him he didn't have a horrible illness. I would later learn that some people can be bought for mere dollars. My crooked-coworker asked me if I would be interested in some quick cash, and of course I said yes." I stop to laugh at myself. "Well, a few weeks later, they called me in the middle of the night, asking if I could come right away. When I arrived, I was escorted in by a large man who immediately cleared the room so I could do my evaluation.

"The patient who was described to me as a hypochondriac was anything but. He was obviously ill, probably cancer, but I'm not completely sure. I never even got a chance to ask any questions—I was just the distraction. As soon as everyone left the room, three men came in through the back, firing a single shot to the patient's head."

"Jesus Christ," Slate says, squeezing me tight.

"Please just let me finish."

He nods, but I know that, as much as he wants to know the rest, he doesn't want to *hear* it.

"My patient, Miguel Rodriguez, was a very prominent member of one of the largest drug rings in Miami. Which, by the way, is where I'm from," I throw in with a shrug, knowing that I point-blank lied to him about that months ago. "Well, Miguel's brother, Dom, decided to switch teams and work with Darren Wilkes, another prominent member of the drug world. Leo knows a lot more about this part than I do, but basically, Dom brought me in, playing the concerned-brother role as an excuse to see Miguel, then killed him in cold blood. I guess the cancer wasn't doing it fast enough. Dom ordered his right-hand man to kill me since I'd witnessed it."

Slate flinches at my words, but he doesn't say anything in response.

"I grew up with my aunt after my parents died when I was three. She was fifty-five when she took me in and passed away my first year of college. I have no family and I've always kind of kept to myself, so really, I was an easy mark for them." I pause, catching his eye. I know Slate, and this next part is going to hurt him more than it will for me to tell it. I toss his words right back at him. "You ready?"

He exhales and drags me in for a hug. He buries his head in my neck, and I can feel his heart racing against my chest. "Fuck, Riley. I am absolutely not ready."

"Erica," I correct him, needing to hear him say it again.

He lifts his head. "Is that what you want me to call you from now on?"

"It's kinda my name," I say with a broken smile.

"Okay then. Erica, tell me everything." He traces a hand up my back under my shirt.

I need to make sure he knows something first. The things I'm about to tell him will change everything, but before it does, I want him to know another truth.

"I love you. I didn't respond earlier, but I do."

"Fuck, Erica," he hisses. "Tell me you trust me?" he asks, and I can finally give him an honest answer.

"Completely."

Without another word spoken, he rolls me to my back, covering me with his huge body and kissing me with both reverence and lust. I'm not afraid as his weight settles over my body. Instead, I've never felt safer in my life. His warm tongue glides in my mouth and I roll my hips into his. He groans but all too quickly moves away.

"I just want you to know nothing you say is going to change anything, beautiful. So don't pull any punches. I don't want to have this conversation again."

I offer him a relieved smile. His words give me a little comfort, but he has no idea what he is getting into. It's easy to say that nothing will change *now*.

"Okay. Let's get this over with." He pulls me back toward him and we resume our position on our sides. This time, I tangle my legs with his, needing to feel him so I can't get lost in the past.

"How much do you want of this?"

"As much as you are willing to give."

I sigh. That was the right and completely wrong answer. "I was taken back to one of Dom's houses, where I was tied to a bed and raped by over eight men," I rush out as if it were like ripping off a Band-Aid.

I wait for him to react. Maybe back away and reconsider his desire to be with me, or even just to get angry. But it never comes. His strong jaw clenches as he grits his teeth, but otherwise, he remains emotionless.

"Just when I thought it was over, Darren Wilkes showed up. To call him a sick bastard would be the understatement of the century. He sat between my legs and took a knife, slicing up my thighs and over my vagina." I don't get the words out of my mouth before Slate explodes off the bed.

"What the fuck!" he shouts. His eyes are wild as he begins pacing around the bed, shoving a hand through his hair and cussing words I never knew existed. He finally stills but only long enough to throw a fist through the drywall.

I've been through enough therapy to know that none of this was my fault, but that doesn't change the fact that I'm embarrassed and ashamed all the same. I sit Indian style on the bed, knotting my hands in my lap while watching him unravel. Finally, after a few minutes, he snaps out of it and focuses his attention back on me.

"Shit, Erica. I'm sorry." He kneels on the bed and pulls me into his arms.

I go willingly, but for the first time since I met him, it feels awkward and forced. Slate wasn't supposed to ever know this stuff about me. Now, he knows too much.

I lean away, trying to collect my thoughts, but he stops me. "Don't do that. Don't pull away from me. I don't care, beautiful. This changes nothing."

I nod, but he's wrong. *It changes everything.*

"What happened to him—the man who did that to you?" he asks quietly.

"Leo killed him." His eyes go wide and he leans back to get a better look at my face. "Leo was an undercover agent for the DEA. He shot Darren while he sat between my legs. Then he killed his two guards and rescued me from that hell." Finally, the pent-up emotions escape my eyes.

"So you two are not related?" he asks while using his thumbs to dry the tears that steadily fall from my eyes.

"No. But I love him more than any bloodline could ever dictate."

"Okay, so how did you end up here? What are you running from now?"

"Leo was relieved from duty because of some of his actions on the day he rescued me—the same actions that saved my life. We both testified against Dom Rodriguez and were immediately moved into the Witness Protection Program. They tried to separate us, but Leo came with me, mainly because, back then, I was terrified of everyone in the entire world except for him.

"Over the years, Wilkes's brothers have found us three times. The first time, his younger brother walked right up to our door and knocked. Like it was nothing. Leo opened the door and Wilkes shot him in the chest while I sat on the couch completely helpless. He walked in, stepping over Leo, and grabbed me by the hair and dragged me out."

I pause as the memories overwhelm me. I break into a cold sweat and fight to keep myself from throwing up. After a few deep breaths,

I manage to continue.

"Of all the things that have happened to me, that might be the scariest moment of my life. I lived through being raped and assaulted once, but as he dragged me down the stairs, I knew I wouldn't survive it again. I tried to fight back and was mildly successful—until he punched me in the face, sending me into the welcomed darkness."

I peek up at Slate, who hasn't said anything, but not even a blind man could mistake the rage radiating off his body. His heart is racing and his chest is heaving, and there is an inferno blazing in his eyes.

"I don't remember anything else, but from what I hear, Leo stopped him. Killing yet another man to protect me."

"Jesus fucking Christ, Erica," he breathes.

"So yeah, unexpected knocks on doors scare me now," I try to say nonchalantly but fail miserably when the words catch in my throat. I'm physically and emotionally exhausted from the entire day, but I'm especially drained from trying to hold it together during this conversation. I just want it to be over—all of it. "I'm done. That's all my part. Can you get the other stuff from Leo tomorrow?" I say, closing the door on any further questions.

"I don't even know what to say right now," he answers. "This isn't an abusive ex-boyfriend. This is…"

"My life," I finish for him. "It sucks, but there is no escaping it. I live every day looking over my shoulder, waiting for them to find us again. But in the process of running, I found you. Slate, you made me feel safe, and I'm sorry I can't do the same for you. Just so you know, if you want to walk away from me and all of this now—I won't hold it against you. It would kill me to watch you leave, but it would destroy me if anything ever happened to you because of me."

"Shut up."

"I'm serious."

"So am I. Shut up." He kisses me, pushing me to my back, once again covering me completely with his body. Our mouths are both closed but it's by far the most passionate kiss I have ever received. "Tomorrow, we are moving to my apartment in Chicago. I'll talk with Leo in the morning about the logistics with the program, but I can't protect you here. From here on out, you don't lie to me. Okay?"

"Slate, you don't know what you are getting into. You can't protect me, period. I have an entire team of agents assigned to me and they still find us. They *always* find us."

"Erica, you are mine. I have absolutely zero plans of letting you go or allowing you to ever be hurt again. I'm not too naïve to admit that I'm treading in new waters with this, but you are highly under-estimating the extent to which I will go to keep you. This isn't some passing fling we have here. So stop acting like walking away from you will ever be an option again. That also goes for any ridiculous idea you get about trying to run to protect me." He gives me a pointed look that forces me to bite my lip. "From here on out, we do it all together. Got it?"

"I just—"

"Get your stuff. We are going to my place tonight." He stands up and heads to the door.

"Slate, maybe we need some space tonight. This is a big decision for you. Just being with me puts your entire life in danger."

"There is only one choice. Therefore, there is no decision to be made. Now, do *you* need some space?" he asks, crossing his thick arms over his chest.

"Maybe."

"Fine. You have an hour." He turns and walks out of my room, closing the door behind him.

"Jesus, he is bossy," I say to myself.

"Nothing new, beautiful!" he shouts from outside the door.

CHAPTER Eighteen

Slate

SPACE. SCREW THAT. Ril—Erica has lost her fucking mind. After that little get-to-know-you session, neither of us needs space, much less a night alone. Hell, I'll probably end up with nightmares tonight even with her tucked securely into my side. I don't actually know if I'll ever be able to sleep again.

"How bad is it?" I ask as I barge into Leo's room. He is sitting at the foot of his bed, tossing his phone in his hands. He's not relaxing or lounging—he was waiting for me.

He immediately stands. Leo is a big guy, but I still tower over him. "Really bad," he says as he walks to the small kitchen.

"Sorry, but I'm going to need more than that," I tell his back.

He pulls two beers from the fridge. "If she stays with you, we are officially being released from the program."

"What?" I slam my untouched beer down, causing it to foam all over the counter.

"I've been round and round with them tonight, and it's just not happening."

"Are they just going to leave her to die?" I grit out.

"No. They are going to try to scare her into leaving *you*." He lets out a loud huff then pulls a sip of his beer.

"I won't let her go. Tell them to fuck off."

"I would if I didn't think they would take me up on it. Slate, you are the epitome of everything we are supposed to avoid, yet she fell in love with you all the same. They aren't going to stand by and publicly fail while the media reports Slate Andrews's girlfriend was killed or worse—kidnapped."

"I won't let anyone touch her," I vow. "But I also won't let her go."

He takes in a deep breath and lifts his eyes to hold mine. "I'm going to advise they remove her from the situation."

A blast of adrenaline spirals through my body. I reach out and grab his throat, pushing him against the pantry door. I lean in close so Erica can't hear my eruption. "You even think about taking her from me and I'll feed you to the wolves myself. I will hunt until the day I die to find her. And trust me, I have the resources to make it happen, *Leo*." I spit his name like it's venom on my tongue.

"You're going to get her killed if you follow," he manages to bite out around my hand cupping his throat.

"Then don't take her. She stays with me."

"You don't know what you are talking about. She can't stay with you without protection. They will track her down."

"If we work together, we could do it. I have a place in Chicago. Maxed security system, private entrance, twenty-four-hour guard. Leo, we could make her safe." He stares into my eyes for a few moments as his face continually turns red from my grip on his throat.

It happens so fast that I can't even begin to tell you where I went wrong. Leo grabs my hand from his neck and spins me, pulling my arm hard behind my back and pinning my face against the same door I just held him against.

He leans in, speaking directly into my ear. "I want a team of my own men, unlimited funds, and for you to keep your fucking mouth shut and take care of *her*. I worry about her safety and you worry about her well-being."

It makes total sense but I'm no one's bitch. I slam my head back, cracking his nose and sending him to the ground. I drop to a knee beside him and once again regain my grip on his throat. "Deal."

He holds my eyes for a minute in an unspoken truce before I finally release him. I reach down, grabbing his hand and dragging him back to his feet. His nose is bleeding and my arm is throbbing from the restraint, but we both nod to each other in agreement.

"We leave in the morning. She's staying with me tonight."

"I'll let the big boys know," he says, pulling an ice pack from the freezer and pressing it to his nose.

"Hey, Leo." I stop him before he makes it to his room. "Will this ever end for her? I mean, is there a solution besides running all the time?"

"God, I hope so," he says with a resigned sigh. It's easy to forget that Erica isn't the only one whose life has been stolen.

"How much help has she had dealing with all of this? She is unquestionably not okay."

"She went through some pretty extensive therapy right after it happened. Then she called them all quack head doctors and refused to go back." He laughs. "Now she Skypes with a doctor once a month, but she needs more. See if you can talk her into seeing someone more regularly. Yeah?"

"Yeah, I'll see what I can do."

"University of Florida," she answers, dragging her nails over my chest.

"And what made you want to go into medicine?" I ask as we lie in bed.

For the last two hours, I've been getting to know Erica Hill. Jesus—she is *amazing*. When Erica talks about her life before that night, her eyes light and her entire demeanor changes. I only thought she was beautiful before.

"My parents died in a car accident. They were both killed instant-ly, but when I was young, I childishly thought, if they had had better doctors, they would have lived." She shrugs.

"Christ," I whisper.

"No, it's not as bad as it sounds. I was really young. I barely re-member them at all. I was just a little girl who dreamed of having a perfect mom and dad and the whole fairytale life. Anyway, it just kind of stuck with me. I remember when my first patient was rushed in from a car accident. It validated me. I felt like all my dreams had come true in just that moment. That's why I chose emergency medicine. It's not always fun or exciting, but at the end of the day, I felt like I accom-plished something. Some little girl's parents lived because I was there. I miss it." She swallows hard and looks up at me, barely hiding the tears sparkling in her blue eyes.

"We'll get you back there." It's not a lie, but it's definitely not a promise. I don't know that she will ever be able to practice medicine again. She seems to know that too because she give me patronizing nod and squeezes me tight.

"Can we stop talking? I just want to feel you." She slides her hand under the waistband of my boxers, gripping my swelling cock.

I'd love nothing more than to feel her too, but not tonight. I reach down, removing her hand. I've never rejected her before—and proba-bly won't ever again—but I can't do this now.

"Not tonight, beautiful," I say before kissing her forehead.

She blinks at me for a minute then begins nervously chewing on her lip. "Oh. Yeah. Um, it's been a crazy night. You've learned a lot of new things about me and I'm sure you need time to process." She suddenly rolls away from me.

Most nights, we sleep like this, so it takes a few seconds for me to realize that she isn't just settling in for the night. It's only when I feel the tiniest of shakes from her back that I realize that she is either crying or desperately fighting it.

"What's going on, Erica?" I roll her back over.

She doesn't try to fight me, but she covers her face with her hands. "It's already different."

"What is?"

"You and me." She sniffs, trying to collect herself. "I hate that you know now. It's already changing us."

"Yes, it is changing us, and thank Christ for that." Her eyes fly to mine. "For the first time since I met you, we have something real. No more lies or secrets. It's just *us* now. And tonight, I don't want to have sex because I don't want that *real* to even be in the same headspace of all that other bullshit you told me earlier." She looks away, and I realize that may not have been the best choice of words. "Look at me, beautiful. Tomorrow, we start over as Slate and Erica. And tomorrow, I'm stripping you naked and having my way with you for the very first time. So I suggest you get some sleep." I wink and her eyes flare.

"Slate, I'll understand if you need more time. I know this has to change the way you look at me at least a little."

"Oh it really does. Because tomorrow I'm going to be looking up at you from between your legs. Totally different view."

"Jesus, Slate."

"Nothing changes. So get that out of your head. I still want you just as much, if not more than I did before." I grab her ass and grind my hard-on against her just to prove it.

"Now that's just mean." She throws a leg over my hips and grinds right back against me. I let out a groan and rethink this whole waiting thing, but it's for the best.

"Go to sleep, Erica."

"Slate," she whispers just as I close my eyes.

"Sleep."

"Thank you."

I don't respond. I don't need to.

CHAPTER Nineteen

Erica

"ERICA," SLATE WHISPERS into my neck.

For the brief second before I open my eyes, I imagine that I'm back in my small apartment before that horrible night. Perhaps I'm tired from a long shift at the hospital instead of last night's emotional upheaval. But the one thing I take with me from reality into this fantasy world is Slate.

"Wake up, beautiful."

I feel the covers slide down my chest and his warm mouth latch onto my breast. Without opening my eyes, I play with his hair as his tongue circles my nipple.

"Mmm," I moan, arching my back off the bed.

Never pulling away from my breast, he shifts his body to lie between my legs. There is a sheet dividing us, but it does nothing to stop his hard cock from sliding against my clit. I lift my hips as he rolls his, making for the most amazing spark only Slate can bring me.

He drags his mouth up my chest and neck, pausing at my ear. "It's a new day, Erica."

It's a short sentiment. Nothing extreme. However one word rouses me into consciousness—*Erica.*

I open my eyes to see the golden eyes and crooked smile that I would recognize anywhere. His hair is disheveled and a thin layer of scruff covers his jaw. Yet, Slate has never looked sexier in his life. It's a new day, and even after all of the filth I divulged last night, he's still at my side.

"You ready?" he asks, enabling me to tell him yet another truth.

"Yes," I answer, and morning breath be damned, his mouth slams over mine.

He immediately uses one hand to push himself up to hover above me and the other to drag the sheet from between us. The morning sun is bright as he settles back on top of me, but this is Slate. For the first time ever, I don't care what he sees. I'm finally ready to bare it all.

He slides a hand down my body and ever-so-slowly drags it between my legs. Just before he rounds the final curve, he pauses to catch my gaze. I don't want to think about the scars or be nervous with Slate, but I feel it anyway. I clench my eyes closed and nod for him to continue. Only his hand never moves another inch.

"Erica, I love you. I never knew you before you had these scars, but that doesn't mean I won't spend my entire life trying to erase them from the inside out." My heart swells and my voice catches in my throat. "You see my nose, beautiful? Well, it's been broken three times. I swear, a few years ago, it was perfectly straight. I was a sexy bastard back then," he teases before becoming serious again. "Everyone has scars, Erica. Don't for a second think yours are any different based on how you got them. I love you—scars and all."

The hand that was only seconds ago trailing down my body shifts direction and slides back up and into my hair. As his mouth seals over mine, Slate Adam Andrews tells me a truth of his own without even uttering another word.

I allow him to kiss me for a minute longer, but only because it would be criminal to stop him. Slowly, I lift my left arm over my head, pulling on the hand he's using to support himself. He drops to his elbow as I guide his hand to restrain my wrist.

"I love you too. And I trust you." I take hold of his other hand and glide it down between my legs. The second he brushes over my wet core, we both moan.

He doesn't move as his eyes hold mine, but he immediately releases the arm I placed above my head. "Tell me to stop if you need to."

"I won't need to."

Slate

Erica's words fuel me forward. I suddenly sit up to kneel between her legs but never look down. I don't want this to be about the scars. She's nervous about my reaction almost as much as I am. I have a shit temper. I know that, when I see them, it's going to enrage me that someone hurt her in such a violent manner. I also know she will misconstrue that anger as some sort of personal judgment against her. If she is expecting me to sit between her knees and examine her old injuries, she couldn't be more wrong.

I just want to be with Erica.

My hands start at her knees, sliding up each of her thighs and spreading them wide as they go. My eyes remain locked on hers, being sure to give her no reaction whatsoever. Her breath catches as my hands meet the lines of puckered flesh running up the inside of her thighs. They are so slight that I've never felt them before in all the times we have been together, but then again, she has never let me touch her like this before either. Finally, I meet her heat and her eyes nervously flash around the room.

"Erica," I growl to catch her attention. My fingers slide over her wet folds, feeling the indentations where she was cut. My blood begins to boil, but I do my best to lock it down. "Fucking perfect," I whisper, pushing a single finger inside her. I drop my thumb to her clit, making slow circles. Her tense body relaxes as she closes her eyes.

"Slate," she moans, lifting her hips off the bed to meet my every stroke.

I finally drop my gaze to my hand moving in and out of her. The red lines are stark compared to her creamy, white skin, but what I can't tear my eyes away from is the way she freely undulates under my touch. Fuck, it's a beautiful sight to watch her apprehension melt away as she becomes lost in the moment. I can't take it for even a second longer.

I quickly push both hands under her ass and lift her entire lower half off the bed to meet my mouth. She lets out a startled squeak, but soon her legs relax over my shoulders. With a hand over her hips and one under her ass, I hold her to my mouth while I devour her pussy. I'm a desperate man. I thrust my tongue inside her, kissing and sucking every inch of her wetness. I flick her clit, starving with need to feel her come against my mouth. Not Riley or Beautiful, but to feel Erica come under my touch for the very first time.

Her body pulses around me as she rolls her hips against my mouth. With one last swipe of my tongue, she comes, calling my name as she hits her climax. It's not loud or wild. Instead, she says it with such reverence that it hits me in a place that's so deep I never even knew it existed before now. I slowly lower her back to the bed, continuing to taste her on the way down. She shoves a hand into my hair as I trail kisses up her stomach and over each breast. I slide up her body, covering her completely. I'm careful to read her reaction for any type of hesitance, but if she even gives it a second thought, I can't tell.

I reach toward the nightstand to retrieve a condom, but she shakes her head. "Don't. I started birth control as soon as you came back."

I lift a questioning eyebrow. "Then why have I been using condoms for the last four weeks?"

"Because I didn't want to hear you call me beautiful the first time we were truly together. I wanted you to be with *me*." Her eyes well with tears.

"You have to stop crying in bed or I'm going to develop a complex," I tease then kiss her gently. She quietly laughs as she swipes the tears from her face. "I've been dating a woman, and no, she wasn't always *you*. But in this bed, I've only ever been with Erica. This might be the only place you were ever truly honest with me."

She gives me the smallest smile and pushes her hips up off the bed, signaling to me that she's ready for more. I move a hand between us, and this time, she doesn't even flinch. Slowly, I guide my cock inside her tight pussy and she throws her head back against the pillow.

Rubbing my scruff against her cheek, I lean down and whisper, "Erica," into her ear just so there is absolutely no question in her mind about who I'm with right this second.

For well over an hour, I make love to Erica. It's not the normal hot and frantic sex we usually have, but that doesn't make it any less incredible. Every time she gets close, I ease up and keep her on the edge. It's slow and agonizing, but in the end, it gives us both exactly what we need—a connection without words, without lies, and without hurt. It gives us a new beginning.

CHAPTER Twenty

Erica

"HOLY SHIT!" I exclaim when I walk into Slate's Chicago apartment.

When I think apartment, even for a big, famous, rich guy, I think small and compact. But this place is the exact opposite. I knew Slate had money, but he seems like such a low-key guy that this place actually surprises me. It's huge. There's a private entrance and a scary security guard. I thought for a minute that Leo and I were going to be frisked before we were allowed to enter. Thankfully we weren't, because I know Leo never leaves home without a gun stashed somewhere.

Slate sent us first in case there were any paparazzi staking out his place. He says that it's rare for them to track him outside of LA but not completely unheard of. With his retirement announcement still fresh, he didn't want to take any chances.

"Well, it's definitely a step up from the last place," Leo says, dropping his bag beside me.

This morning, Leo officially withdrew us from the Witness Protection Program. I thought it would have been a long process with lots of paperwork to reclaim our identities, but not even three hours later, a manila envelope appeared on our doorstep with driver licenses, passports, and birth certificates enclosed inside. I am officially Erica Renee Hill again. I'm so freaking excited that I can't even bring myself to be scared.

"Did he tell you where we are supposed to be sleeping?" I ask Leo, who is currently typing numbers into the security panel, locking things back down.

"I'm gonna go out on a limb here and guess that you will be sleeping in his bed and I'll be in the guest room," he answers, being his usual smartass self.

"Do you think he really wants to share a room? That's like moving in together."

"You're kidding, right?" he asks with a slight laugh.

"No, I'm not kidding! I've never lived with a man before." He gives me the 'Oh, really?' look that makes me shout, "You don't count!"

"Babe, I'm pretty sure you got married last night. There may not have been a ring or preacher, but you definitely got hitched. I won't even begin to tell you how many zeros are in my security budget. Call me crazy, but I think he's serious about you."

"Shut up. I know he's serious, but living together is a totally different story. And wait. How many zeros are we talking?"

He laughs and ignores my question. "I'm gonna look around. Find that man's room, because I'm not brawling over why your bags are still in the foyer when he gets here."

I wander around his apartment in awe of how big this place actually is. From what I can tell, it consists of four bedrooms, five bathrooms, a rec room, a huge, open den/dining room combination, and a kitchen that would make any chef jealous. It's clean, uncluttered, and very minimalistic—just like the man who owns it.

I finally stumble upon a massive master suite that causes my jaw to drop. It's decorated with stark, white walls, but the curtains and bedding are blood red. The king-sized four-poster bed juts out from the corner. But how I really know this is his room is because it's the only one covered in pictures. I'm not just talking memorabilia from his fighting days either.

Slate is a different person in the public eye, but this room is filled with pictures of *my Slate* with various people. Some I recognize as his mom or his trainer, but what really steals my breath is the one of me smiling in a selfie. I remember him snapping it of us back when I thought he was just Adam Andrews. We were lying in bed, and my head is turned into his chest to hide from the camera, but my smile is unmistakable. If I didn't know it before, it's plainly obvious to any onlooker that I loved him even way back then.

"I love that picture," he says from the doorway.

"Shit!" I scream, spinning to face him.

"Damn, I'm sorry." He hurries into the room, wrapping me in his strong arms.

"Shit," I repeat into his chest, trying to catch my breath.

"It's just me, beautiful."

"Just so you know, the no-sneaking-up-on-me rule will always be intact."

"Noted." He kisses the top of my head.

"Any issues?" I ask, looking up into his amazing eyes and crooked grin.

"None. I stopped to drop off the rental and picked up food too. I hope you like Japanese."

"Oh please tell me you got sushi *and* hibachi. I haven't had Japanese since I moved from Florida."

"Well, I am absolutely on point tonight then. I'm pretty sure I got enough food to feed the entire building." He leans in, and I suck his bottom lip into my mouth, grazing it with my teeth as I release it. "Or maybe just enough to feed you." He smiles.

"Smart man." I laugh and head out of the room with Slate's arm pulled tight around my shoulders.

****

It's been an exhausting evening. Leo and Slate had a little security meeting while I hid in the bathtub with my Kindle, ignoring the out-

162

side world. I know I should be more involved with things like that. It is, after all, my life they are protecting, but I know myself. There are two speeds—dramatically obsessed and ignorantly blissful. For tonight, I chose the latter.

Leo's face was none too happy when he summoned Slate into the security room. Call me crazy, but I trust both of them. I am completely okay with them only giving me the pertinent information right now.

Slate and I are in bed after some absolutely amazing sex when I decide to finally ask him the one question I've been dying to know about.

"Will you tell me about your mom?" I whisper, kissing the underside of his jaw.

"Well that took you long enough." He smiles, sliding down so we are at eye level, facing each other. We have most of our serious chats in bed, and apparently, this is Slate's talking position. He places a hand on the curve of my waist and gives it a gentle squeeze.

"You don't have to…"

"It's okay, beautiful. I think it'd be good for you to know the real story. Google is filled with just as many lies as it is facts." He sucks in a deep breath, clears his throat, and begins to talk. "My mom was a housekeeper at a hotel. One night, she was called to change the linens on a bed, but when she got to the room, a man pulled her inside and raped her. He beat her then left her bloody and unconscious on the hotel floor."

I must have gone rigid because Slate immediately pulls me closer and tangles his legs with mine.

"She was thirty-seven and married with no kids at the time. The police and her husband were called to the scene. She was terrified and ashamed, so not only did she refuse medical care, but she also refused to cooperate with the police. Her husband was a piece of shit but seemed supportive at first. Well, until she popped up pregnant. The same day the doctor confirmed her pregnancy, he packed his bags and left. So two months after being raped and beaten, her husband walked out on her."

"Jesus." I sigh, and this time, I'm the one pulling him closer.

"Seven months later, I was born. She did the best she could. My mother never actually wanted to be a mom, but she loved me all the same. Because she never got any kind of help dealing with what happened to her, she lived a life of fear and solitude. Growing up, I didn't know any difference. It wasn't until I started school and I saw how vibrant the teachers were that I started to realize that something was wrong with her.

"When I was nine, her husband came back briefly. He wasn't abusive, but he was still an asshole. He got drunk one night and decided to tell me the whole story about my mom, but as you can guess, it was his side of the story. The fictional one where she was cheating on him and my 'father' justly raped and beat her."

"What the fuck!" I suddenly sit up.

"Shhh." He drags me back down and into his side. "Unfortunately, my grandmother was forced to fill me in on the real story at only nine years old after I started asking questions. Not long after that, he was gone again, but the damage had been done. As you can imagine, I had a lot of issues dealing with my newfound knowledge of how I had come to exist. I started acting out and getting into trouble. Then, one day, after getting into a fight at school, my mom sat me down and told me that I wasn't an accident, but that I was a gift sent to protect her." His voice catches and he clears his throat to cover the emotion. "Yeah. So anyway, you know the rest. I took the role of her protector very seriously for the rest of her life. When I got a little money, I spent it sending her to therapy and finally getting her the help she needed, even if it was twenty years too late. She never remarried or had more kids, but I think she was happy. She died two years ago after suffering a stroke in her sleep."

I don't say anything for a few minutes as I try to absorb everything he just said. Sure, it's a sad and tragic story, but it's also filled with love and triumph. And it forces me to ask him the real question.

"Do you think you're in love with me because of some ingrained need to protect women?" I ask quietly, unsure of whether I even want to know the answer.

He lets out a loud laugh. "Oh, Lord. Is that what you have playing in your head right now?"

"It's a valid question, Slate."

"Validity doesn't make it any less absurd." He laughs again but rolls me over so he is pinning me completely to the bed with his huge

164

body. "I will admit that, when I first met you, I wanted to help you. That woman who ran into my apartment all those months ago was terrified, and I won't lie. It immediately sparked some deep need to protect you. But that is absolutely not why I fell in love with you. I fell in love with you because you were smart and funny. You never once treated me like a commodity, even after you found out that I had money. But more than all of that, I fell in love with you because behind the fear was a strong, beautiful fighter too. Erica, I love you for your smart mouth, beautiful brain, and most importantly, because I've always wanted to role-play doctor/patient in bed."

I slap his back as he continues to laugh. "That was a good answer."

"It was, wasn't it?" He suddenly becomes serious again. "Are you worried that you only love me because I make you feel safe?"

"No, I know exactly why I love you." I lift my arms and wave them around the room. "Clearly, it's because you're loaded."

"Clearly." He begins tickling me only to silence my laughter with his mouth.

Four weeks later...

Slate

"I'M GOING TO the store. Do you need anything?"

"Erica, you don't have to go to the store. I'd feel better if you just let me call for grocery delivery."

"No freaking way. I need to get out of here. I'm wearing my dog collar and everything," she smarts off, lifting her wrist to show the bracelet Leo gave her the day after we got here. It has a built in tracking device and emergency alert button that calls the police and notifies all ten of Leo's men.

"It's not a dog collar. It's an emergency bracelet," Leo corrects from the kitchen while making a sandwich.

"Right. Yes, of course. How silly of me." She rolls her eyes but smiles up at me. "I'll take Johnson with me just in case."

"Damn it. I hate not being able to go with you." I pull her against my chest. "Almost as much as I hate those fucking brown contacts."

"Nope. You know the rules. If she goes out, she wears the contacts," Leo pipes in from behind me, but I ignore him. Yeah, I know the rules, but that doesn't mean I hate them any less. I've gotten used to seeing Erica's amazing blue eyes every day.

"I just need some fresh air, okay? I'll be back in less than an hour," she calls over her shoulder.

"I'll walk you down." I toss an arm around her shoulders and head downstairs. "Johnson," I call to the larger of the two guards standing at the private entrance to the building. "You let any anyone so much as bump into her, I'll kill you myself." He flashes me a shit-eating grin, revealing not one but two gold teeth. Where the hell Leo found these guys, I'll never know. But so far, they seem to know what they are doing. "Make it fast." I grab both sides of Erica's face and pull her in for a hard kiss.

"I love you," she says as she turns to walk away.

Johnson pushes the glass door open, but at the last second, I pull her in for another kiss.

I hate watching her leave, knowing that there is nothing I can do for her once she walks out those doors, but despite how much I would like to, I can't keep her locked up in my apartment for the rest of her life.

"Love you too, beautiful."

She smiles, dropping her sunglasses down on her face, and walks away.

As I exit the elevator, I run directly into Leo, who is waiting for me. He looks nervous and antsy, and it worries the shit out of me.

"What's wrong?"

His face is pale and he doesn't immediately respond. Quickly losing my patience with his lack of speech, I reach out to grab his shirt, but he grabs my wrist first.

"I just got a call. I think there is actually a way out of this mess." He runs a hand through his hair and laughs. "Oh my God, I think this might be almost over."

"What?" I breathe as the mere possibility makes my heart race.

"We need to talk, and quick—before she gets back." He moves over to the couch, where he sits down only to jump right back to his feet and start pacing.

"You're making me nervous. Start fucking talking." I stand with my hands on my hips.

"They don't want Erica. They want me."

"What?" I snap, taking a step forward.

"Just chill out and listen to me. The guy Erica and I testified against, Dom, was the reject of the Rodriguez family. He was a fucking idiot. Case in point: when he decided to pull a fast one on his entire family and merge with their enemy, Wilkes. Hell, the whole Rodriguez family would probably thank Erica for testifying against Dom after he killed his older brother. It's Wilkes's men who are really after us."

"Then why the hell are they coming after her? You're the one who killed Darren Wilkes."

"Because they have no fucking idea who the hell I am—but they think she does."

"What the hell?"

"My true identity was a tightly guarded secret as an undercover agent. But the Wilkes family assumes Erica knows since I took her with me when I left. The night everything went down, I killed Darren Wilkes and his top two, but there was a third man who survived his wounds. He ended up in prison on numerous other charges, but he was still able to get word out that I—or, really, Marcus—took her on my way out. And it appeared to him that she trusted me. They decided she was in on it with me from the very beginning. So Wilkes's brothers have been searching for us ever since. They know everything about Erica Hill and have been able to track her easier than they have me.

"I worked for Rodriguez when I was undercover, specifically Dom. And when he went down, they refused to cooperate and give Wilkes any of their security footage of me. Wilkes doesn't even have a picture of me. They only have the description given to them by some of the guys who met me—thirty-something, long, brown hair, tattoos, brown eyes, and of Mexican decent." He breaks into a thick accent while speaking smooth Spanish.

"You're white."

"Yeah, originally from Nebraska actually, but I tan up nice." He smiles. "The tattoos were fake too. But they don't know any of that. The one time the youngest Wilkes found me with Erica, he shot me in the chest and walked right over me, clueless to the fact that I was the man they were really looking for."

"Wait. Why haven't you just given them your name then? You could have gone off on your own and lead them away from her. You could have set her free years ago!" I roar.

"Maybe, but being alone made her even more vulnerable. They think she means something to me. Which she does—*now*. They would have tortured her just to draw me out. At least if we're together, I could always give up myself if we got into trouble."

"Jesus Christ. So how the hell is this going to be over? Get to that part. I don't want to hear the rest of this bullshit."

"So some serious shit has been going down, and it appears the last remaining Wilkes brother, Lucas, is fucking shit up for Rodriguez again. An official hit was just issued on his head. Lucas is the low man on the totem pole these days, but his ego is anything but. If Rodriguez manages to take him down, he will absorb all his men and we could finally be nobodies again. With Wilkes gone, we would be free of all of this once and for all."

"So, what? We just wait for Rodriguez to take out Wilkes?"

"Yep. And pray the cops don't get to Wilkes before Rodriguez has a chance to do it."

"How long are we talking here?"

"An hour…or ten years. I have no clue. But what's important is, for the first time ever, there's an end in sight. All we have to do is lay low and let the assholes extinguish each other."

"Do you really think this will work? I mean, won't Wilkes's men try to start something up on their own if he goes down?"

"Not unless they are fucking idiots. The Rodriguez family has only gotten bigger and more powerful over the years. Wilkes is the only one stupid enough to fuck with them. Once he is gone, all the small-time thugs and dealers will jump ship to where the money is."

"Rodriguez," I whisper.

"Yep," he confirms, finally stopping to face me. "We just have stay off Wilkes's radar until it's done."

"So are we telling Erica this?" I ask.

169

"Your call. But I don't want to get her hopes up."

"I'll tell her. She deserves to know."

"Shut up!" Erica squeals as I explain the situation to her.

Leo was right. Her hopes aren't just up—they are bursting through the roof.

"It's just a theory, beautiful. There are still a lot of factors that would have to happen to make it a reality."

"Slate, it could be over," she says as her eyes flood with tears. "OhmyGod, OhmyGod, Oh. My. God," she hurries out before jumping to her feet and running from the room. "Leo!" she shouts, rushing into his room.

"I see he told you." He laughs as she hurls herself into his arms.

"Seriously. This could really happen? Like really really happen?" she questions as he puts her down and takes a step away.

"It's a possibility, babe. Don't start applying for jobs yet, but it's a *definite* possibly."

"I want some wine. No, champagne!" She turns to me as I lean against the doorjamb.

I can't help but smile and enjoy her excitement. It's rare to see this giddy side of Erica, but that only makes it more beautiful when it happens.

"I could do a beer," Leo says from behind her.

"Let's do it." I pull her against my chest and head for the kitchen.

Three glasses of champagne later, Erica is still celebrating. She's talking a mile a minute and just all-around having fun. My heart tightens when I realize that I could possibly spend the rest of my life with this amazing woman. I'm not talking the frightened woman who is always looking over her shoulder, but rather this light and carefree version I see before me now.

"Let's go to bed," she says, straddling my lap.

I glance up at Leo, who is smiling, but he looks away when she starts kissing up my neck.

"Hey. Why don't you go out? Hit the city. I can hold down the fort tonight," I say to him as Erica's hands slide under my shirt. She begins to drunkenly giggle as I tease the edge of her shirt as well.

Leo shakes his head at her but finally nods to me. "Yeah. I think I'll do that. I'll take one of the boys with me. Cool?"

"Works for me." I stand, lifting Erica right along with me. She immediately locks her legs around my hips but turns to look at Leo.

"You'll be careful, right?"

"Of course, babe. Now go to bed. Your head is going to be killing you in the morning."

"Have a good night. Wear a condom. Do I need to give you the STD talk I used to give the kids who came into the hospital?" She laughs, making Leo groan and roll his eyes.

He pretends to be annoyed, but I know he's laughing on the inside. "I think I'm good, Doc." Without another glance, he heads out. "Be good, ladies and gentlemen."

Before the door even clicks behind him, Erica is attacking my mouth. Her hands are all over the place and she grinds against me.

"Fuck," I groan.

"That's what I'm hoping for," she says, dragging her tongue up my neck until she reaches my ear.

I bark out a laugh at her boldness but move as fast as I can to the bedroom. "Add champagne to the grocery list for tomorrow night. I'm suddenly quite fond of drunk Erica."

"Me too," she says, sliding from my hands the moment we reach our room.

She immediately drops to her knees in front of me, popping open my button on her descent. Just as quickly, she pulls my cock from my pants and sucks me deep into her mouth.

Strike that. I fucking *love* drunk Erica.

CHAPTER
Twenty-Two

Erica

I PRY MY eyes open, immediately wishing I could close them again. My head is pounding and I've never needed water more in my life. But I'm not too hung over to stop to appreciate Slate's naked ass as I crawl out of bed.

"Where you going?" he growls, clearing the sleep from his voice.

"Bathroom. Water. Ibuprofen," I croak out while holding my head.

I'm splashing water on my face when I hear shouting on the other side of the door. I fearlessly sling it open to find Leo yelling as Slate tries to pull the sheet around his waist.

"What the fuck were you thinking? God damn it!" he shouts, throwing a newspaper at Slate.

I pull on my bathrobe from off the back of the door and head over to figure out what the hell all the commotion is about. Then I pick up the paper off the bed.

"Oh my God," I breathe when I find a picture of Slate kissing me yesterday before I left for the grocery store. The headline reads: *Slate Andrews caught with mystery woman. Could she be the reason behind his sudden departure from professional boxing?*

"We have to go," Leo barks at me.

"We've been over this. I'm not leaving him," I respond, never tearing my eyes off the black-and-white image in front of me.

"Even dumbass Wilkes will be able to track down Slate Andrews. We have to leave," Leo growls while Slate remains surprisingly silent.

"Wait. Where are the rest of them?" I say, flipping through the paper. "There's got to be more than just this."

"That's the only one they published," Leo says, calming only momentarily.

"You can't see my face. His hands are covering it. No harm, no foul." I nonchalantly drop it back to the bed.

Slate slings his head to face me, and Leo gives me the most ridiculous look possible before snapping, "Are you still drunk?"

"No. But I'm not going to freak out over a picture of Slate's hands and a woman with dark hair."

"You can see enough," he responds, but it's Slate's reaction that really catches me off guard.

"He's right. You need to go."

"What?" Leo and I both question at the exact same time.

"We're so close to this being done. We can't afford something like this now. You need to go. I'll give you some money to set you two up for a while and continue with security, but you can't stay here with me."

"Stop," I squeak out as his rejection causes my heart to physically hurt. I know he's being rational, but what happened to the man who swore he would never leave me? The one who said he would fight until the ends of the earth for me? "What are you saying?"

"I love you. This is only temporary, beautiful. So get that hurt off your face. I'm sorry, but he's right. Wilkes would have absolutely zero issues finding me. There's an end in sight and I'm not going to fuck it up by being selfish enough to put you in danger."

"Bullshit! That's exactly what you did when we left the program. That's exactly what we *both* did. We chose to stay together and not let this mess dictate our relationship. I'm not leaving."

"Then I will," he says sadly. "You're right. That picture isn't too bad, and I don't think anyone could recognize you, but it's just the tip of the iceberg. Now the paparazzi are going to be on me twenty-four-seven. I've never had a public relationship before, and with the news of my retirement, people are dying to find a reason to explain why I suddenly called it quits. They aren't going to let up until they know absolutely everything about you. Wilkes may as well have just hired a hundred new men to track you. I'm sorry, but Leo's right. You have to go."

"Oh, so it's temporary, huh? What happens if Wilkes gets arrested before Rodriguez kills him? Or if it takes years before he can track him down? What then? Are you just going to stay away from me for years?"

"No. This will all die down eventually. People will forget about me as time passes."

"Oh my God. You can't be that stupid," I smart off, letting my true bitchiness fly.

In reality, I'm just pissed and terrified that, if he leaves now, he won't come back. I'm secure in my relationship with Slate. I believe that he loves me, but what if we separate and he realizes how easy his life could be with another woman. Someone who isn't broken, damaged, or ruined. Someone who wouldn't possibly get him killed.

"Excuse me?" he responds with almost as much attitude as I threw at him.

"They aren't going to forget you any more than they have Tyson, Foreman, or Ali."

"While I love your bitchy little compliment, I am hardly Ali."

"No, you're worse. You're mysterious and gorgeous, and you decided to walk away while you were at your absolute peak. Your fans aren't going to just forget about you any more than I could. But apparently I'm the only one who feels that way in this relationship."

"What the hell is that supposed to mean?" He raises his voice, but Leo jumps in the middle, ironically becoming the rational one of the group.

"All right, everyone. Just calm down. We can figure this out. You two stop bickering. No one is forgetting anyone. I may have overreacted. Let's just take a breath and talk this out. Erica's right. You can't see her face. I'm going to call in a buddy and see if he can flash a badge and see where they got that picture and, most importantly, if more exist. They may not be willing to tell me, but it can't hurt to ask. Now you two cuddle, fuck, *make love,* or whatever the hell you guys do in there. But just make up. Let me look into a couple of options and then we can figure it out—without name calling or being a bitch." He lifts a brow at me, but I only roll my eyes.

He walks out, leaving me with a very pissed-off version of my usually laid-back man.

"I need to go," he says flatly as I flop facedown on the bed.

"You're not going," I tell the bed.

"Stop being stubborn. You know this is the right thing to do this time."

"I don't give a shit if it's the rightest thing to ever exist. You're not going."

"Rightest thing to ever exist?" he says with a sigh while crawling up the bed to lie facedown next to me.

"There's a reason I didn't major in English."

He laughs and throws an arm over my back. "If anything ever happened to you, I..." He pauses before rolling me onto my side to face him. "I just need you safe somewhere. Do you think I can buy one of those underground bunkers from the 1970's?" I laugh and throw a leg over his hips. "I'm serious, Erica. I can't be the reason Wilkes finds you. Before, when we first left, all I could think about was spending time with you. But now that there's the possibility of an out, all I can think about is spending a lifetime with you. It's damn near crippling to think about losing that." He drops his head to my chest and sighs.

My heart squeezes as my attitude melts away. I scratch his back as we both lie in silence. My mind is racing, and if I know Slate at all, his is also.

"No one knows that picture is me, Slate. You know I am the first person to freak out if anything is even remotely threatening. But I'm more scared of losing you than I am anything else."

"You're not going to lose me. Just let me head back to LA for a little while and draw the attention away from you. We can put a cap on it if you want. How about three months? If Wilkes is still breathing in three months, we can rethink things. I'll come back or maybe we can head somewhere totally different. But we have to be smart about this. It's so fucking close to being over."

"I don't want to go three months," I pout. "What if you find another girlfriend in three months? She would probably be prettier than I am and love to be fawned all over by the paparazzi," I say teasingly, but the proverbial light bulb of genius goes off above my head. "Oh my God. Slate, you need to get a girlfriend," I squeal then fly up off the bed and dash out of the room. "Leo!" I shout, running down the hall.

"In here, babe," he calls from the security room.

Frozen on the screen is the video from yesterday that clearly shows a man taking a picture with a cell phone of Slate kissing me. He's standing just outside the door, but I don't remember seeing him at all.

"I'm pretty sure it was a fan. Watch." He presses play.

The man walks past, but as soon as the glass door opens, it catches his attention and he backs up with a broad smile. He instantly digs through his pocket for his phone and snaps a picture. But as I walk away, he never tears his eyes from Slate.

"Slate needs a girlfriend," I say as he rewinds the video, zooming in on the fan's face.

"Threesome? That's hot, babe. But I'm not sure Andrews could handle two of you." He turns to face me with a questioning look.

"No. Seriously. If he started publicly dating a short woman with brown hair, no one would question it. He was exposed by that picture, so let's out him completely."

"Have you lost your fucking mind?" Slate appears behind me, dressed in a pair of sweats riding low on his hips.

"Think about it," I plead, looking between the two men. "You could go to LA for a *week*, not three months, go out on a couple of very public dates, get your picture taken, and then come back home to *me*. No one has to leave and the paparazzi would stop trying to figure out who you are dating."

"That's probably the most ridiculous plan I have ever heard in my life," Slate replies, but my eyes never leave Leo, who is surprisingly silent.

"Tell him it would work," I beg.

"It would probably work." He shrugs. "And if it didn't, it couldn't hurt anything," he answers, turning his attention to Slate.

"No fucking way! Who exactly do you propose I date for a *week*?"

"I don't know. I'm sure we can find someone who would want to be seen with you." I smile, but he doesn't look even remotely entertained.

"I'm not doing it," he bites out while turning to walk away.

"It would buy us some time!" Leo shouts behind him, but Slate doesn't respond. He turns his attention back to me. "He's right you know—it's a ridiculous idea."

"But it will work."

"Maybe." He shrugs again. "Now, you just have to talk your boyfriend into cheating on you."

"It's not cheating," I say dismissively.

"It will be for him."

I wave him off and head back down the hall after Slate. When I walk back into our room, he's pacing around.

"Hey," I say as I shut the door behind me.

"I have spent my entire career avoiding the celebrity life."

"I know." I walk forward, wrapping my arms around his waist.

"I love you. I really do. But I'm not sure I can do this. I don't think just being seen with a woman on my arm will do it, beautiful."

"I know," I lie, suddenly realizing I didn't think this plan out very well. Managing my jealousy, while pushing him off on another woman, is not going to be easy.

He lets out a resigned breath. "The fight for my vacant title is next week. They would go nuts if I showed up with a woman," he says absently. It's as if he is forming the plan in his head even though he has absolutely zero intentions of following through with it. "I'm not sure I can do a week, but I can probably do a night."

I swallow around the lump in my throat and look up into his eyes. "Really?"

"One night, but if your harebrained plan doesn't work, we move on to mine. Deal?"

I smile in agreement but suddenly get very nervous. "What if she's amazing and you fall in love with her and never want to come back to me?" I try to lighten the mood, but it's a very real worry for me.

He laughs and pushes me back toward the bed. "Erica, I'm trying to figure out how to keep myself from cringing when she touches me and you are worrying that I'll fall in love with her?"

I fall against the bed, and he quickly covers me, sealing a kiss over my mouth while reaching toward the nightstand. He snatches his phone and dials while supporting himself on his elbows above me. I nibble on his neck as he begins talking.

"Mitch, it's Andrews. I need a date for the fight. Five four, brunette, dark eyes." He pauses to glance down at me, shaking his head. I can hear the man loudly chattering on the other end of the line, but Slate quickly cuts him off. "Yeah, yeah, yeah. Just make it happen." He hangs up and tosses it up the bed.

"Thank you," I whisper.

"Get naked. You can thank me that way." He smiles, pushing open my bathrobe with one hand.

CHAPTER Twenty-Three

One week later...

Slate

"SO, ARE YOU gay?" Bella asks as we sit in the VIP room, waiting for the fight to begin.

"No," I respond shortly while staring straight ahead at the TV showing the pre-fight interviews.

"Then why do you need a fake girlfriend?" She slides across the leather couch until she's sitting practically in my lap. Her perfume is suffocating, and it's all I can do not to openly gag.

I stand up and head to the bar positioned in the corner of the room. I've never been a big drinker, and I usually stick to beer when I do. However, tonight, I'm in serious need of something stronger. Hell, I'd drink rubbing alcohol at this point, but only after I poured it over my body to disinfect all the places she has touched me tonight.

I have no idea what the hell Mitch told her about this little setup, but she definitely got the wrong idea. I picked her up about three hours ago, and in that time, she has dragged her boobs across my arms no fewer that seventeen times. And that isn't even the half of it. I decided to be a gentleman and at least take her to dinner. I am, after all, using her to keep dangerous criminals away from my girlfriend. Dinner seemed like the least I could do. I also figured it couldn't hurt to get to know her a little better in case questions arose.

I'm a quiet guy, but I don't care how big of an introvert you are. You shouldn't be able to sit through a ninety-minute dinner and only utter six words. The first five being "So tell me about yourself?" The sixth was "Whoa" when she ran her foot under the ankle of my jeans and up my leg. I don't know when it became socially acceptable to rub your naked foot against someone's bare leg after knowing him for less than twenty minutes, but I've never been so glad to be off the dating scene in my life.

I might be overreacting just a bit. Bella isn't all terrible, but she has one major flaw that I can't get past—she just isn't Erica.

I pull out my phone and shoot her a text. I miss her. When Erica and I are together, she comes alive, but she isn't the only one. I had my own walls built up, but one glance at those blue eyes sent them all crumbling to the ground.

Me: I love you.
Erica: I love you too. How's it going?
Me: Vision Quest
Erica: Are you finally coming around to my way of thinking or are you having that much fun? I know you love that movie.
Me: I'm not weird like you. I watch GOOD movies to cheer myself up. So no, Vision Quest still rocks, but tonight is absolutely horrible.
Erica: Yeah. It's a Vision Quest night for me.
Me: I'm rethinking that three months thing. I hate being away from you.
Erica: Good. I hate it too.

"Hey, handsome," Bella says as she slides up behind me and—what do you know—rakes her boobs across my back.

"Hey." I pick up the shot I ordered and toss it back.

"I think they are ready for us." She rubs a hand up my chest. I quickly grab her wrist and gently peel it away.

"Save it for the cameras." I try to keep the annoyance out of my voice but fail.

"Just so you know, we need to make this believable. So if you wanted more than just that one kiss we discussed, I'd be okay with that. My agent's phone has been blowing up since we became an item." She dabs her lipstick.

"I'm glad this is working out for you. But one kiss, that is all. I swear, if you try for more, we will have a very public and embarrassing breakup when I walk out. I'm not trying to be a dick, because I really appreciate what you are doing here. But don't get any ideas of going off script, okay?"

"God, you are cranky."

"I can live with that." I move towards the door, but just before I tuck my phone into my pocket, I send out one last text.

Me: Heading inside to my seat. I love you. Don't forget that.
Erica: I love you too. Don't forget that.

Erica

"Hurry up, Erica! It's going to start soon!" Leo yells from the rec room.

The fight is about to start, and Slate just texted me that he was about to be seated—with his date. His agent Mitch found an up-and-coming actress to be Slate's girlfriend for the evening. Her name is Bella Sloan. She is gorgeous, and I hate her. She has really gotten into the role of being Slate's leading lady. She even spoke out earlier this week to a tabloid, telling them that she and Slate had been secretly dating for months.

I really fucking hate her.

For the last two hours, they have been doing snippets on Slate and his career. I watched them all at first, but then it just made me more anxious. So I went and hid in my bedroom for a while. I needed a few moments to remind myself that he is doing this for me—*for us*.

I curl up on the giant leather couch next to Leo. Grabbing a throw pillow, I nervously toy with one of the loose strings until I hear the announcer start talking about Slate. My eyes burn into the screen as the camera flashes to him sitting ringside, talking and laughing with his arm thrown around the back of the beautiful brunette's chair.

Leo must sense my anxiety because he reaches over, patting my leg. "What time is he getting home tonight?"

"Late," I answer quietly.

"You want to go out and grab some food when this is over?"

I turn and look at Leo, who never suggests we go anywhere in public.

"It's probably your last chance for a while. You're not going to be able to go anywhere when he gets back."

"I know."

"So? Chicago pizza and a beer?" he asks again, trying to keep my attention away from Slate on the screen. For that alone, I love him.

"Okay." I shrug and turn back to the TV.

For thirty minutes, we watch a fight, but I'm constantly staring into the background, hoping to catch a tiny glimpse of Slate and Bella. Finally, the camera finds them between rounds, and even though we discussed this moment in great detail, it still hits me hard. He casually kisses her. It's not one of the deep, passionate kisses I know Slate is capable of. It's brief but he sold it by pulling away and smiling down at her, allowing the moment to linger for a few seconds longer. I immediately turn my head and cover my eyes, physically unable to watch. The announcers and crowd go wild from watching Slate do something so public, but it kills me. Even though I was the one who asked him to do it in the first place.

"It's done," Leo says, flipping off the TV, not even bothering with the rest of the fight. "Let's go eat."

I may have tears in my eyes, but there is also a tinge of relief hidden in there somewhere. If only I could focus on that.

***

I sit on the couch and stare holes in the door. My leg shakes anxiously

182

as I wait for him to return. The last time I heard from him was just over an hour ago, letting me know that his flight had landed. It's four a.m., but I haven't been able to sleep without him—or probably more accurately, *because of him.*

Finally, he slings the door open, saying goodnight to the guard who followed him up and locking his eyes on mine. He's still wearing the same jeans and button-down he had on at the fight, and if possible, I hate that Bella chick even more. He's gorgeous and she got to enjoy it.

"Hey," I say with an unconvincing smile as my manners supersede my discomfort.

"Why are you still awake?" he asks, standing his ground—never moving forward even an inch.

I shrug, knotting my hands as I step toward him. "I missed you?"

He lets out a loud sigh before responding, "You have no idea. Come here, beautiful." He doesn't have to tell me twice. I hurry over, slamming into his chest.

"How was your flight?" I ask, but something feels off. He seems nervous and even a little bit angry.

"Long. I'm exhausted."

"Yeah. Me too. Do you want to go to bed?" I question nervously. *He's acting so freaking weird.*

"No, I want you to swear to me that, as soon as this is over, you'll marry me and we can move to a small city, where I only have to leave the house to go to the gym. I want a huge privacy fence where no one can take pictures. And a yard full of Rottweilers for those who are brave enough to try. Basically I want to live in a private little bubble with you and no one else—and especially not Bella Sloan." He rolls his eyes at the mere mention of her name.

I smile huge and immediately look down so he doesn't see how much I needed to hear him say that. Tears of relief sparkle in my eyes as I look up at him. "That sounds like a fantastic idea."

He barely brushes his lips over mine as he says, "It hurt to kiss her."

"I'm sorry you had to let her touch you."

"No, it wasn't that. It hurt when I looked up and didn't see your eyes. *That* was agonizing."

183

"Slate," I whisper only inches from his mouth.

"Kiss me."

I have no choice but to obey. His tongue rolls into my mouth, forcing a moan from my throat. I quickly climb up his body, needing to feel more of a connection.

I pull away only long enough to tell another truth. I say it just as much for myself as I do for him. "I love you. I know it didn't mean anything."

"Erica, you're wrong. It meant a fuck of a lot to me," he growls, leaning me against the cool wall. My back arches, thrusting my hips forward and causing us both to gasp.

"I'm sorry."

"It means that I get to keep you. That is *not* a sacrifice." His words hit me in that deep spot that only Slate knows exists.

"I love you," I repeat when any adequate words fail me.

"I will do absolutely anything to keep you, but I'm not doing that again. We'll find another way, but that was the one and only time I look up into eyes that aren't yours."

I quickly agree because I don't know if I can handle it again either. I know it was a stupid ploy, but it doesn't change that fact that it still hurt like hell.

"Take your contacts out. I can't stand them tonight."

Not willing to wait a single moment longer, I reach up and peel them both from my eyes, tossing them to the floor.

"There she is." He stares with such awe that it causes my chest to ache. He watches me for a few seconds until a mischievous smile plays on his lips.

"When you kissed her, I couldn't watch," I admit, burying my head into his neck.

"That's good, beautiful. If you could have watched, I really would have questioned this."

I immediately lift my head and find his lopsided grin. Yeah, the world is right again.

"You stink. Like perfume and cigarettes," I snip just to wipe the smile from his face, but it only makes it grow.

"God, her perfume was terrible. I stood outside in the smoking section just so I didn't have to smell her," he jokes before shoving a hand down the back of my pants to grab my ass. "Take a shower with me."

"Mmm…I can do that."

He walks toward the bedroom, never bothering to put me down. "So, do you think it worked?" he asks just as we get to the bathroom.

I unbutton his pants, and he pulls my shirt over my head, immediately leaning forward to suck a nipple into his mouth. I groan, swaying back, but his strong arm holds me tight against his mouth.

"You've been all over ESPN for the last four hours. I think you got more coverage than the actual fight," I say, slowly stroking his growing cock.

He flips on the shower before gliding his hand between my legs. Pulling me with him, he steps under the water.

"Now what?" I ask.

"Now we stay out of sight and wait, but we get to do that together." He continues tight circles against my clit, sending me close to the edge. Just before I come, he spins me around to face the wall and thrusts hard inside me. "Together," he repeats, quickly sliding out before slamming into me. It's by far the wildest Slate has ever been with me, but it doesn't scare me. It actually lights me on fire.

For two hours, Slate and I stay in the shower. He never stops touching me, even when we get to the bathing part. His hands roam over every curve of my body. They aren't always gentle, but they are never rough. By the time we head for bed, the sun is already blazing through the windows. I'm exhausted and probably could have fallen asleep hours ago, but as much as I needed to hear Slate's words of reassurance, I think he needed to *feel* my commitment to reassure himself.

CHAPTER
Twenty-Four

Two weeks later….

Slate

"CAN WE TALK for a minute?" Leo asks, walking into my bedroom. His eyes flash around the room, presumably looking for Erica.

"She's taking a bath," I say, answering his unspoken question. "What's up?"

He glances behind me at the bathroom door as he breathes a sigh of relief. He signals me to follow him into the hall. "I have to go somewhere for a few days. I'm not sure when I'll be back." He looks down and swallows hard.

"What's going on? Did something happen?" I take a step forward, but his eyes stay stuck to the ground.

"Look, I can't do this anymore. I just need to get away for a while.

She's safe with you. I've got a few things to do, and now seems like a good time," he replies, finally lifting his eyes to mine, and I immediately know that he's hiding something.

"You are so full of shit. Now tell me what the fuck is really going on?" I demand.

"Just tell her I went to run an errand, maybe close down the old apartment or something."

"I'm not lying to her. If that's the bullshit you want to tell, then do it your damn self," I bite out, closing the bedroom door just to be sure she can't hear the conversation.

"I can't live like this anymore," he says in a sad tone that is more alarming than the actual words.

"What the fuck is going on with you? You're not making any sense here. Are you going on vacation to clear your head or are you leaving for good?"

"I don't know yet," he snaps as his frustration wins over the turmoil. "Here. I wanted you to have this. It's the file I've been making since I was undercover. It documents everything from the first night I met Erica to the present. If anything happens while I'm gone, you turn that over to the police. I left the phone number of my contact at the program. If *anything* happens, you call them first, get her sorted, then you disappear. She won't leave you, but you have to swear to me that, if you can't get in touch with me, you will leave her in their custody."

"What the fuck are you talking about? God damn it. You are not leaving her like this. Not until you start making sense and tell me what the hell is going on," I bark, but he ignores me and continues to talk about Erica.

"It will break her heart to lose you, but you have to swear you will put her back in the program."

"No," I say simply, but that one single word makes him explode.

He suddenly pushes me back against the wall, holding a forearm against my throat. His eyes are feral and his chest heaves as he pins me. "God damn it. I'm not fucking around here. Swear to me!" he roars.

"What's wrong?" Erica questions as she rushes into the hallway. She's soaking wet and wrapped in her bathrobe.

As if a switch was flipped, Leo instantly transforms. He takes a step away, plastering on a fake smile as he turns to look at her.

"Hey, babe. Your boyfriend here was just pissing me off. Same shit, different day." He smiles and takes a step toward her. "I'm going to go run some errands. You want me to pick up dinner?" he says nonchalantly, blatantly lying.

Her eyes flash between us, but even as I stand stunned, Leo looks positively unaffected. It doesn't take but a few seconds before she lets go of her concern. Knowing Erica, she doesn't really want to know if something is wrong anyway.

"No, I'm going to cook tonight."

"All right. Well, I'm heading out." He gives her shoulder a squeeze, but his emotions manage to escape from behind the mask.

"Where are you going?" she asks, sensing his discomfort.

"I'm just going to hit the store, maybe pick up some movies. Any requests?" He gives me a nod and turns to walk away.

"You're lying," she calls as she follows him down the hall.

He walks towards the door, pausing only to pick up his duffel bag. "I'll be back," he says, never turning to face her.

"Since when do you need a bag to go to the store? Seriously, where are you going?" she asks, and I can see the panic escalating inside her. I try to pull her into my arms, but she bats my hands away. "Where. Are. You. Going?" she finally yells at him.

He turns around but he doesn't look at her. Instead, his eyes find mine. "You need to hold on to her. She can't follow me down and make a spectacle on the streets."

"Where are you going?" she yells again while stepping up into his face. But even though she's crowding him, he ignores her completely.

He holds my eyes from across the room and gives me one final plea, "Swear to me."

And with those words, I know without a doubt that this will be the last time I ever see Leo James. Where he is going and why are still a mystery, but as I look into his eyes, I know that he has absolutely no plans of returning.

"I swear," I respond even though I'm not sure I could ever let Erica go, but I have a feeling he needs to hear it.

He sucks in a deep breath and closes his eyes. A small smile of relief tilts the corner of his mouth as I can physically see the invisible weight lifted from his shoulders.

"Leo, please talk to me. Where are you going?" Erica begins to cry as she begs for the answers I can tell he has no intention of giving her.

He suddenly opens his eyes and pulls her into a hug, breathing in the scent of her damp hair. "I love you. You're safe now, Erica."

Just as quickly as he pulled her against him, he pushes her away and walks out the door. Tears are streaming down her face as she screams his name, but Leo never once looks back. She rushes into the hall after him, but I loop her around the waist to stop her from following him any farther. He's right—she can't go out there making a scene in the middle of the streets, and I sure as hell can't go down to stop her. She fights against my grip, but I hold her tight and carry her back into the apartment.

"You have to stop him," she says between sobs.

But what I only recognize now is that Leo was already gone before he ever even walked into the bedroom.

The day Leo left, Erica alternated between crying, pacing, calling his phone, and searching his room for clues about where he could be going. I had no idea what to do, and finally, I cornered her and gave her no other option but to lean on me. I didn't restrain her, but I made it clear that she's not in this alone. She finally relented and spent the night in my arms. She didn't sleep, but she curled in tight and allowed me to at least share her emotional burden. She loves Leo, and by all accounts, he loves her too. Which is why his sudden departure makes absolutely no sense.

Leo left all the credit cards I had given him when he took off. And while I wasn't really keeping up with the cash he spent, it doesn't appear as though he took any money either. Which, to me, means he went back into the program or knew he wouldn't live long enough to need money. Either way, it makes me really fucking nervous. However, right now, Erica has to be my main focus. He would have told me if there was any immediate danger. I refuse to believe that he would ever turn his back on Erica without being absolutely certain she was safe, but that doesn't mean I haven't beefed up security.

Johnson hired three new guards within twelve hours of when Leo left. I made him the new head of security, but I'm definitely keeping my finger on the pulse now more than I did when Leo was running the show. Erica has never really snapped out of her walking trance. She mostly just moves between our bedroom and the rec room. Her nose stays stuck to her Kindle or she just stares into space. Gone is *my Erica*, the funny one who laughs and jokes around. She isn't even the scared and timid Riley I originally met. She's just lost.

We haven't talked much in the three days since Leo's been gone, but every night, as she crawls into bed, she slides up beside me, holding me closer than ever before. I try to give her space to grieve, but it's killing me to watch. So the moments when she leans on me mean the world.

The minute Leo left, I locked the file he gave me away in the fireproof safe. I am the only person who has the combination, but it still needs to be housed somewhere else for safekeeping. Should anything happen to me—or, God forbid, Erica—I want there to be undeniable proof about where to point the finger. Today, I'm scanning it and emailing a copy to the only person I trust not to read it, Jimmy Douglas.

While Erica is lying on the couch in the rec room, mindlessly staring at some TV show that I know she has absolutely no interest in watching, I head to the office to send it out. I have no idea what's inside. I only know that Leo told me that he'd documented his time with Erica. Before now, I had no intention of actually taking the time to read it, but seeing her name on the very first page changes my mind completely.

For over an hour, I scour through Leo's notes from when he was working undercover with Rodriguez. Not having a strong firsthand knowledge of the underbellies of the drug world, I just assumed these guys were big-time dealers with even bigger connections. But to read Leo telling it, they are hardcore, whatever-it-takes murderers as well. They thrive on innocent lives to get them ahead and have no compunction in taking them out when their services are no longer required. Case in point—Erica.

I read through his notes, engrossed in the world he embraced as Marcus Torres. I told Erica I would never ask, and this is probably the roundabout way of breaking that promise, but I can't stop my hands from turning the pages. Then I read the one sentence I wish I could unsee. But no matter how hard I try, I can't erase the words written in Leo's handwriting scrawled across the page.

> I stood guard while at least
> eight men brutally raped her.

"What the fuck!" I shout, jumping away from the paper and shooting to my feet.

My mind whirls while I try to regain control. I knew he was there the night everything happened. He killed three men to rescue her, but what the fucking hell is this about him standing guard? Why in all my conversations with Erica and Leo has this topic never been broached? The only thing I can figure is that they are both hiding from the facts. My blood boils, but I know I have to finish. It's obvious I'm missing quite a few of the details from that night.

For the next three hours, I read every single letter of the notes he has taken over the almost four years they have been on the run together. I wasn't prepared for this. Erica's life hasn't just been stressful; it's been damn near unimaginable at points. And now that I know the truth, her undeniable attachment to Leo is disturbing to say the least. However, as I turn page after page, it's the very last paragraph that renders me completely speechless.

> August 4, 2014 - I was alerted by a man on the inside that Lucas Wilkes had not only found my true identity, but that he traced me to working as Slate Andrews's security advisor. I have but one option left to save Erica. No matter how drastic it may seem, she deserves to live free.

Oh God. What the hell is Leo up to? What drastic measure could he be taking to save her? I remember our conversation when he told me that Wilkes was searching for him and not Erica, and my stomach churns as I fear where he has gone. It never seemed right that Leo would just leave her unless he was planning to give himself up and set her free once and for all. *Shit.* What the fuck did he do?

I can't tell Erica about this. She's already having a tough time with him being gone, but this little hypothesis I have now would destroy her. I quickly decide to give it a week before bringing this up to her. Who knows? I could be completely off the mark here. Leo could come prancing back in with a tan from vacation tomorrow. But I have a sick feeling in my gut that I'm right about this one.

CHAPTER Twenty-Five

Slate

"ERICA," I CALL down the hall when I get out of the shower.

"In here," she says from the security room.

Before Leo left, I can't remember her ever going in there, but now, she spends almost every night staring at the monitors. I can't tell if she's afraid someone will break in without him or if she's just waiting for him to come home.

"Beautiful, you have to stop leaving this window open!" I tell her for the third time in three days.

"I need the air. I can't breathe stuck in this apartment all the time. I need to get out of here, Slate. I haven't been outside in weeks."

"It's not safe, Erica. Open the windows on the far side. These connect to the breezeway, and Johnson is going to have a stroke if he finds it open. You want to go out on the balcony?"

"What?" she says, shocked and immediately excited. "Leo was worried they would take pictures of me."

Shit. I didn't think about that.

"Yeah. He was probably right," I say, feeling like an ass as her face deflates. "Okay, how about this? What if I call the building and privately rent out the roof for the entire night. Johnson could clear it and block it off. I'll bring up some chairs and we can just lie out under the stars for as long as you want."

Her smile immediately returns, bigger than I've seen in days. "Oh God, Slate. That sounds amazing."

"I'll order some food too. Go get dressed. As soon as the sun goes down, we'll go up." I pull her in for a kiss, taking full advantage of her sudden good mood.

Three hours later, we lie on a blanket on the building's empty roof. We brought up chairs but quickly moved to the ground so we could be closer. Our legs are tangled together and she is squeezed tight against my side, using my chest as a pillow.

"Do you think he's okay?" she asks out of the blue.

I let out a sigh, not sure how to answer. Do I honestly think Leo's okay? No. But I can't tell her that. "I don't know, beautiful. I hope so."

"Me too," she says quietly.

Tonight is the perfect evening, and I'm seeing the first real flashes of Erica in days, but that only furthers my worries.

"Can I ask you something? Something you probably don't want to talk about?"

She sits up, leaning on one elbow to look me in the eye. "You can ask me anything, Slate. I don't have any secrets from you anymore."

I lean forward, kissing her on the forehead, feeling the pang of guilt for keeping my newest information about Leo from her. "I think you need more therapy."

She groans and lies back down next to me. "That's not a question."

"Okay, let me rephrase. Why don't you go to more therapy?"

"Because they told me I should leave Leo," she says honestly, shocking the hell out of me.

"Why'd they tell you to leave Leo?" I ask even though I know the answer.

"I saw the file in the safe, Slate."

"How'd you get into the safe?" I say, shocked.

"Leo gave me the combination in case of emergency."

"How the hell did Leo get the combination?" I shout while suddenly sitting up, forcing her to sit up with me.

She only responds with a shrug and the tiniest of smiles. "Anyway, I know you know everything that happened that night. So you know why they wanted me to leave Leo. I'm actually glad you read it. There were a lot of times I wanted you to know the truth but just couldn't bring myself to talk about it."

"I just read it tonight. Have *you* read it?" I ask nervously.

"I lived it. I don't need to read it." *Thank God for that!* She would freak if she read Leo's little 'drastic' line. "Did it explain why he sat by while I was being raped?"

"Erica, there isn't a rational reason why any decent human would ever do that. I know you think Leo has protected you all these years, but that's warped. He stood guard while men raped you just so he wouldn't blow his cover. That is fucked up, no matter how you look at it."

She let out a strangled laugh. "Is that what he wrote? That he didn't want to blow his cover? He is such a dick!" she yells into the night.

"Actually, he didn't give a reason at all. I just assumed."

"Well, you assumed wrong, Slate," she snaps. "Leo was compromised. Wilkes didn't trust him at all even though Dom did. Wilkes sent two men to watch Leo. They confiscated his weapon as soon as they walked into the house. There wasn't a single moment of that day that there wasn't a gun pointed at his back. He either had to play along or they would have killed him flat-out. I'll give you one guess what would have happened to me if they'd killed Leo."

"Jesus Christ."

"When it was Leo's turn, he managed to talk them into giving him his gun back just in case I got loose when he flipped me over."

"Flipped you over!" I roar, jumping to my feet.

"Leo never touched me, Slate," she says calmly from the ground.

I have no idea how she is telling this story without breaking down.

I wasn't even there and it's killing me to hear.

"Anyway, you know the rest. I don't have Stockholm syndrome or anything. Leo wasn't my captor who I suddenly fell in love with. He may have taken me there, but he did the very best he could to make sure we both survived. He won't forgive himself, so if you are on a mission to get someone into therapy, start with him."

"Erica, it's not right. You need to get mad and stop being so sympathetic towards him. Fine, he's not a horrible guy, but that doesn't mean it's healthy for you to be his best friend."

"And that is your opinion. It might be odd to others, but it works for us. Leo and I were forced together after that night. He hates himself for what happened, and as much as I needed him to feel safe, he needs to know I'm safe to be able to sleep at night."

"You both need help," I answer, settling back down on the blanket.

"Probably. But that's for us to decide."

"Just so you know, if I ever see him again, I'm going to fuck him up. It's my duty as your man to kill him for what he did. I'll let him live, just because I know you love him, but that's all I can promise," I say seriously, but she only laughs. I lie down and she immediately curls into my side. "Don't try to stop me, Erica. I'm serious." My words cause her to laugh even louder.

"Okay, Tarzan. You can do whatever you need to—as my *man*," she teases but rolls on top of me. "I love you."

"Christ, I love you too, beautiful." I lean forward to find her mouth.

It's a brief kiss, but only because she slides off me, settling once again on her side. She's right beside me, but her mind is a million miles away. I'm hoping she's thinking about our conversation and taking some of it seriously. Erica needs help. She's probably right about Leo too, but right now, I think he has bigger issues to deal with—like staying alive.

We lie in silence, staring up at the sky for a while before Erica says anything else.

"When all of this is over, where do you see us going?"

"Like physically moving or our relationship in general?"

"Both."

"I don't really know, because a lot of that depends on what you want to do. I can tell you that, no matter when or how it ends, I'm in this forever with you, Erica."

She squeezes me tight and sighs. "Sometimes, when I can't sleep, I imagine what it will be like to not live in fear anymore. I think of all these silly scenarios where you and I do the most normal things together. Things like going to a garden center to pick out flowers for the beds in front of our house."

"What kind of house is it?" I ask, rolling to my side to face her.

"Two-story, plantation style, with a big wraparound porch. I want a porch swing." She smiles, and I can tell she's envisioning it.

"What else do you want?"

"I'd like to go back to work. Although I'm not sure I'm cracked up for emergency medicine anymore. I'm too jumpy these days. But I was thinking... I know you fund several rehabilitation centers for abused women. I figured I'd be really great as part of the medical staff somewhere like that. Maybe my past could actually be beneficial to some of the patients who come in."

"I know a guy who could probably get you a job." I wink.

"That's what I was kind of banking on," she replies with a smirk. "What about you, Slate? What do you want to do now that you are officially unemployed?"

"Well, my plan was always to go back to Ohio and open a boxing gym for underprivileged kids. My mom almost went broke trying to keep me in the ring. Finally, my coach recognized that I had some talent and put me on a scholarship. I wouldn't have been able to afford to stick with the sport otherwise."

"So do you want to be like a trainer or just run the gym?"

"Nah. My place is in the ring. I'd hire someone to run the everyday operations. I really think I'd enjoy working with the kids."

"Do you want kids of your own?"

"Yeah, I definitely want kids...eventually. What about you?"

"I think I want just one, but I'm not ruling out more," she says nervously.

"I'm cool with only one." I tuck a stray hair behind her ear as she rushes out a breath.

"Oh thank God. I could totally see you wanting, like, five kids. I don't think I can do the big-family thing."

I begin laughing as she giggles beside me.

"You want to get married?" I ask, lifting an eyebrow at her.

"That better not be your proposal." She laughs again.

"No. I fully intend to get you a disgustingly gaudy ring and force you wear it everywhere when I finally propose."

"Oh, God. Please don't," she says, as horrified as if I'd just threatened to kill her puppy.

"Yep. Totally happening. I can't even tell you how excited I am to pick it out. It's going to be ridiculous."

"Slate, swear you won't do that!"

"I'm sorry. I can't do that, Erica. It's another one of my duties as your man," I joke.

"What? To buy me an ugly engagement ring?"

"Hey! Who said it was going to be ugly?" I grab my chest, feigning injury as she begins rolling in laughter beside me.

Yeah, even if it is temporary, my Erica is definitely back for the evening.

We talk for hours while lying on the hard ground. The blanket does nothing to soften it for us, but you won't hear me complaining. I love every second of it. We keep things light, as I suspect we have both had enough of the heavy to last a lifetime. Finally, Erica begins to yawn.

"You ready to go in?"

"No."

"You're about to fall asleep, beautiful."

"As soon as we go back inside, real life starts again. Can't we just say out here forever?"

"One of these days, I'm going to make the inside of those walls better than the outside. We'll have a *home* where the real life inside will be your sanctuary instead of your prison."

Her eyes glisten with tears as she nods. "I like the sound of that."

"Me too." I kiss the top of her head.

"Thank you," she whispers, but I don't respond. It would feel wrong to say anything, because I should be the one thanking her.

Slate

"MMM. WHERE YOU going?" I try to grab Erica as she slides out of the bed.

"Shh. Go back to sleep. I'm just getting some water," she whispers as she hurries out of the room.

Without another thought, I immediately fall back to sleep.

"Slate!" Erica screams, causing me to fly up off the bed.

Before my eyes even have a chance to adjust to the darkness, the hard metal butt of a gun slams down on the bridge of my nose. Pain explodes inside my head, but with Erica's screams still ringing in my ears, I don't let it control me. I still can't see my attackers, but that doesn't stop me from returning every blow they hit me with. My arms fly, wielding punch after punch, but what I can't figure out is how they remain standing.

Suddenly, I'm tackled from behind and forced to the ground. Even as I struggle against them, my arms are pulled behind my back and sealed in plastic zip ties. I continue to fight until light illuminates the room and an older man comes casually strolling in, dragging Erica by her hair. Rage and adrenaline overwhelm my body at the sight of him manhandling her like nothing more than a rag doll.

There are four men standing around me in various stages of injury, and even though my hands are bound, I still manage to escape their grasp and rush toward her. Tears are streaming from her bright-blue eyes, and without question, I know I will do absolutely anything to protect her. I never thought murdering someone would sound so appealing, but as I watch this man tip a gun up to Erica's head, it suddenly becomes my life mission to make sure he dies a painful death.

"Mr. Andrews, so nice to finally meet you. I'm a big fan," he says, pulling Erica's hair tighter, forcing her to cry out.

I recognize him as Lucas Wilkes from one of the photos Leo had in the folder. I instinctually take another step forward, but he shakes his head to stop me.

"No, no, Slate. I'm going to need you to stay right where you are." His smirk is disgusting.

"Give her to me," I growl but freeze as he slides the gun to her temple.

"I'm afraid I can't do that, and if you get any grand plans of trying to muscle your way out of this, I can assure you, I have no problem killing either one of you." He turns his attention to the men standing behind me. "Bring him to the living room," he bites out as he walks from the bedroom, his hand still firmly planted in Erica's hair.

My head spins as I try to figure out what to do. How the hell did they even get up here? But before I can really wrap my mind around the current situation, two men step up on each side of me, guiding me from the room. I don't fight them. I need to make sure Erica is safe before I can even consider fighting back again.

I'm led into the living room, where he is still holding her. His grunts deposit me in a chair and stand behind me. My eyes stay glued to Erica. She's crying, but the most alarming part is the odd level of calm she's wearing under the surface. It's almost as if she has given up and accepted this as the end.

"It's okay, beautiful," I say to try to snap her out of it—to bring her attention back to us. Even if I am bound to a chair, I need her to focus on something real before she gets lost in the fear.

"Beautiful! How sweet!" Wilkes laughs manically. "You know, Slate. I have been asking myself over and over how the hell a big time celebrity like yourself got involved with these two. I thought, on the way over here, that you were just a fool who hired the wrong man to run security. But now..." He pulls Erica to face him. "I heard you were a little whore. Are you sleeping with the boss? Tsk tsk, Erica. What would dear old Leo have to say about this? There has to be a reason all these men are falling all over themselves to keep you from me. Maybe I should take you for a quick spin to see if you live up to the hype." He leans forward, dragging his nose up her neck.

Bile rises to my throat as I bolt to my feet. Blinded by my uncontrollable anger, I sprint toward him only to be knocked to my ass by two of the men who were, seconds ago, standing behind me.

"Get your fucking hands off her!" I shout from the ground, but his smile widens.

"Now where's the fun in that? I'm quite enjoying the show." He moves behind her and very suggestively rolls his hips against her.

A blaze of rage erupts inside me again. I jump to my feet, head-butting the man on my left before charging forward. I'm not thinking straight, and it's only the sound of Erica's scream that slows me to a halt.

"Slate, stop!"

I look up and see that Wilkes has moved the gun from Erica and is currently aiming it directly at my chest. Part of me wouldn't even care if he shot me right now if it meant I could get my hands on him. But the idea of leaving Erica alone with him is the only thing that stills me.

"Please just stop!" Erica cries, completely breaking down for the first time since this whole ordeal started. Her body violently shakes and fear covers every inch of her beautiful face. "Please. Just do what he says for a minute." Her eyes are pleading. "Just one minute, Slate," she repeats.

I stare at her in confusion, but I can't catch my breath any more than I can process what the hell she is attempting to convey to me. But it's obvious that trying to bulldoze over these assholes isn't going to do us any good. I take the few steps backward, careful never to take my eyes off Wilkes, and sit back down in the chair. I suck in a few deep breaths to slow my racing mind. I need to formulate a plan, but the image of this man touching *my* Erica is holding me captive.

"Okay, Slate. Let's get to the point. As very entertaining as your little show was, I'm getting bored. Tell me where Leo James is at and I'll be out of here before you know it. Who knows? I might even leave your little girlfriend here when I leave."

"You are not taking her anywhere. Ever," I say menacingly, but it does nothing to sway his cheery demeanor.

"Last chance." He smiles, moving the gun back to Erica's head. "Where. Is. Leo?"

"I have no fucking idea where he is. He left us over a week ago," I bite out, but my eyes flash to Erica. Her chest is heaving, but she has the strangest look on her face.

"He's lying," she squeaks out. My eyes go wide as I look at her, confused. "If I tell you where he is, you have to promise to let Slate go. He's not involved in this."

"Oh, of course, my love. I would never harm your dear Slate. You tell me where Leo is and I'll leave Slate unharmed." He winks at me from behind her. *Lying son of a bitch.*

"Erica, what the fuck are you doing? Don't try to be brave here." I call out.

"I'm sorry. Don't be mad at me, okay?" She swallows before looking over her shoulder at Wilkes. "He's in the security room with two of his men. Just don't hurt Slate."

Wilkes's eyes go wide as his smile grows to epic proportions. "He's here?" He exclaims before leaning in and whispering, "This just got interesting." He nods his head toward the back hall and three of the four men head that way.

"I'm sorry," she whispers before squeezing her eyes tight and covering her ears.

"Erica?" I jump to my feet, immediately concerned about why she is apologizing.

Suddenly, I hear shots fired and shouting down the hall. Wilkes uses his gun to signal his last man to investigate before aiming it back at Erica's temple.

I stare down the hall, trying to figure out what the hell is going on. Leo's not in that room, but I have no idea who the hell is. Just as suddenly as it started, the whole room goes silent.

Wilkes yells, "Mark!" but no one answers. He nervously takes a step forward and shouts again, "Dan!"

With his attention focused somewhere else, I see it as my chance to make a move. I quietly rise to my feet, but Erica's head swings toward me. Her eyes are desperate but fearless as she mouths, "No. Sit down." The determination and bravery on her face has me momentarily willing to comply.

As soon as my ass hits the chair again, I hear a thick Spanish accent roll through the room. "Lucas Wilkes. It's so nice to finally see you again."

At the entrance of the hall, all four of Wilkes's men reappear. Only now they are unarmed, restrained, and being pushed forward with guns at their back. I've never seen the four new men who are escorting them. They are definitely not on my payroll, but they are clearly here to help.

Wilkes spins, pulling Erica completely in front of himself.

The group of men split as a young, well-dressed Hispanic man saunters into the room from between them.

"Mateo Rodriguez. What the fuck are you doing here?" His eyes are surprised but he never lets his smile falter. Wilkes swings his gun forward, pointing it at our newest guest.

"Looking for you, of course." He grins as three more men follow him—guns raised and aimed directly at Wilkes. "My new friend, Leo James, paid me a little visit this week. He informed me you were on the way here to find him. I have always wanted to visit the Windy City, so it was actually quite fortuitous." He pushes his hands into his pockets and shrugs casually.

"You are an idiot, Mateo! It was their testimony that landed Dom in jail. Now you are working with them? Have you forgotten about your family's honor? Because I sure as hell have not."

"Oh, I know all the facts, Lucas. I also know that Dom was a traitor and should count his lucky stars that he gets to serve a life sentence on the inside of a prison. Because, should he ever be released, he will unquestionably share your fate. So you see, I owe Mr. James quite a bit. He killed your stupid brothers *and* got rid of mine as well. Seriously, I don't know why he didn't come to me sooner. My apologies, Erica. It appears I'm a bit late to the party," he says, taking a step toward her.

"Back the fuck up!" Wilkes yells, but Rodriguez ignores him.

"I have to admit, Erica. I'm impressed. I have heard you are quite skittish. I had my doubts when Leo told me of your plan. But you managed to prove me wrong." He moves even closer.

"One more step and I swear I will kill her."

"I'm thinking that's not a good idea," Leo snarls, appearing a few feet behind Wilkes along with Johnson and two other men I definitely recognize.

"So nice of you to join us, Leo," Rodriguez purrs.

Wilkes immediately spins to face Leo, firing a shot before he even stills. Erica jumps, and for the briefest of seconds, Wilkes loses his grip on her neck. In a move so fluid I have no doubt it was choreographed, Erica drops to the ground. No sooner than her hands slam over her ears, Rodriguez's men fire their own bullets at Wilkes.

I watch helplessly as Erica lies on the floor while bullets buzz over her head. I try to call her name, but I can't even hear my own words among the chaos. After a few seconds, Wilkes collapses lifelessly to the ground.

"Son of a bitch!" Leo yells, covering his shoulder as it bleeds through his shirt.

I rush toward Erica, dropping to my knees beside her. "Fuck, are you okay?"

"I, uh… I think so," she says, fighting back the tears as she sits up and crawls as quickly as possible away from Wilkes's dead body. My hands are still zip-tied behind my back, but she throws her arms around my neck and buries her face in my chest.

"Someone cut him free," Leo barks. "Babe, can you come look at my shoulder?"

"Oh, God." She shakes off whatever emotions were just about to overtake her and runs to Leo's side.

My hands are freed by Johnson as the room moves in slow motion around me. Erica is frantically tending to Leo with a box of medical supplies someone magically produced. Rodriguez is ordering his men to take Wilkes's thugs back out the window in the security room, Wilkes is lying dead in the middle of my living room, and sirens from the street are screaming toward us.

"A word, Mr. Andrews," Rodriguez says, walking up behind me.

I can't focus on anything but Erica, but I somehow manage to drag my eyes to face him.

"We are gone, we were never here, and Wilkes broke in with the intentions of harming Erica. Your security officers were forced to kill Lucas Wilkes when he fired upon Leo." He drops three guns onto the couch beside me. "Ballistics will match one of those three guns to the bullet in Wilkes's head. By the way, they are all registered to you. You may be ticketed for not securing them properly." He winks. "Do you understand? Leo and Erica have gone to great lengths to prove to me you are trustworthy in this matter. Do not disappoint me now." He taps my shoulder and turns to walk away.

I have no idea what the fuck he just said, but all I know is that it ended with a bullet in Wilkes's head. Absolutely nothing else matters.

"Clear the room!" Leo shouts, standing back up.

"Erica! Leo! Should you ever find yourself in need again, you know where to find me!" Rodriguez shouts over his shoulder as he heads back toward the security room.

Erica runs forward, slamming into my chest. "Don't be mad," she says quietly.

"Oh, I'm fucking furious, but I can't for the life of me figure out why," I growl, looking at her with more anger than I ever thought possible.

"Well, the cops will be here any second, so aim your anger at the dead man on the floor. When they question you, remember everything happened except for the part where Rodriguez showed up."

"Jesus Christ, Erica, did you plan this?" I snap at her.

"Not now, Slate. We'll talk tonight." She blows me off.

I don't recognize this woman. There were just bullets flying around her, and now she is dismissing me as if I'd asked why we are out of milk.

Leo limps over even though it was his shoulder that was hit. He points down at the guns and says, "Pick those up and hand them to the guys. I need your prints on every single one of them."

I narrow my eyes at him but follow his orders. I'm not in any position to question him tonight.

Leo gives me the world's quickest brief, reminding me of what 'fictionally' went down tonight. Not even two minutes later, the room fills with at least a dozen police officers. They question us numerous times until Leo's contact at the US Marshal's office shows up, clearing us all. I'm not sure if they believe our story as much as they just don't give a damn that someone killed Lucas Wilkes.

They confiscated all of the weapons, but Leo assured me that they were in fact all legitimately (forged) registered to me. It seems Leo has been a busy guy over the last few weeks—even before he left.

However, it's Erica who surprises me the most. I'm pissed as hell that she blatantly played me for a fool, but I've never been so proud of someone in my life. To watch her transform from the terrified woman I first met all those months ago is utterly incredible.

She's far more of a fighter than I could ever imagine being.

CHAPTER
Twenty-Seven

Erica

"ARE YOU FUCKING kidding me?" Slate yells as I fill him in on how tonight came to be.

"Will you stop yelling?" I whisper-yell back at him.

We are, after all, in a suite in a downtown Chicago hotel. The last thing we need is the police being called on us yet again.

"You could have gotten us all killed!" he scolds, gritting his teeth.

I knew he would be pissed, and while I hate that he's mad, I'm so euphoric about how flawless tonight went down that I can't even hide my smile.

"Are you going to let me finish now?" I say, cocking my head to the side, but I'm sure I'm still smiling, which only pisses him off more. "So yeah, I may have drunkenly hatched this plan, but Leo and I were very sober when we put it into action."

"Fucking hell, get to the God damn plan. I can't listen to you tell me for one more minute how you and Leo devised this shit over beer and pizza."

"Right. Well, Leo has always said that, as far as he could tell, Rodriguez didn't hold any ill feelings toward either one of us for testifying against Dom, but we couldn't be absolutely certain. I know I told you the story about how Wilkes's little brother found us, but what you don't know is that it was a member of the Marshal's office who tipped him off about our whereabouts. He straight-up used us as bait to take down part of the Wilkes family. After that, I lost all faith in the program. If I'd had anywhere else to go, I would have gone. No questions asked. But we were both stuck.

"So while at dinner the night you were at the fight, and yes over a few beers, Leo and I decided we were sick of running and playing games with our own lives. I suggested using myself as bait to lure Wilkes out, but Leo being Leo, his first instinct was to protect me. However, within two hours, I talked him into it. Guilt is a hell of a tool," I say as Slate curls his lip in disgust. "Oh hush! It worked, didn't it?"

"Erica, this is not a game. You could have been killed!" he says, but once again, I smile, because I am no longer afraid.

I know how it turned out. This conversation before tonight would have had me rethinking everything, but they say that hindsight is twenty-twenty. And tonight, I see freedom.

"We both knew you would never go for it, so we decided to keep you in the dark. I love you, Slate, more than anything in the entire world. But I couldn't live like that anymore. Every single day, I lived in fear that not only something would happen to me, but worse that something would happen to you *because of me*. I knew you wouldn't allow me to risk my life, no matter how solid the plan."

"Damn right!" he snaps, but he finally sits down on the corner of the bed.

I settle behind him, wrapping my arms around his chest and burying my face between his shoulder blades. "Leo went to Rodriguez, who was all too willing to help as long as it ended with Wilkes's head."

"You knew where Leo was going when he left?" He sighs, grabbing my legs and pulling them around his waist from behind.

"I did. We staged the big exit. But if it helps at all, they were real tears as he walked out the door. I was worried Rodriguez wouldn't even humor Leo's plea for help and would kill him on the spot."

"The window in the security room?" he asks, and I can actually feel the pieces snapping into place for him.

"I was worried I would miss the call when Wilkes got there, so I left it open as much as possible."

"So just let me get this straight. Leo leaked his identity and the fact that he worked for me then left to *hopefully* get help from Rodriguez? What the hell would have happened if Rodriguez had actually killed Leo? He led Wilkes right to our door and then took off."

"We used the same twelve-hour rule we used in the program. If he was missing for more than twelve hours, I was to tell you everything, pack up, and leave. But luckily, Rodriguez immediately agreed."

"Jesus Christ, Erica. I don't even know what to say. It was stupid and irresponsible, but it worked. So as much I want to lose my fucking mind right now, I can't even be mad at you. I will say your ability to lie to me does not bode well for our future together."

"Yeah, well. At least we *have* a future together now," I respond dryly.

He sucks in a deep breath and pushes us both to the bed, turning to face me, assuming our talking position. "I always thought you were such a terrible liar." He humorlessly laughs to himself.

"Don't worry. I usually am. I just knew it was the only way out."

"God. I don't think I've ever been so scared in my life as when I saw him drag you into the room. All I could think about was how I had failed you, and because of that, I was going to lose you."

"You didn't fail me, Slate. You made me safe."

He laughs, shaking his head. "I didn't do anything. I was absolutely helpless tonight. It was the worst feeling in the entire fucking world."

"No. You did do something. You saved me. Maybe it wasn't tonight, but you gave me something to fight for, Slate. I used to be great in chaotic situations. I was always strong and levelheaded, but I lost that years ago. Do you think that frightened woman you first met hauling in groceries would have been able to stand there in Wilkes's arms without breaking down completely? I don't care if it was a carefully mapped-out plan. I would have lost control and been worthless when the memories overtook me. You gave me back the pieces that were stolen from me. You gave me back myself."

"You did that all on your own, beautiful," he says, leaning forward to kiss me.

"You're wrong, but I love you anyway."

Two weeks later...

"Indianapolis," Slate says, walking onto the balcony of our hotel only to freeze when he sees me.

Neither of us wanted to go back to his apartment, even after it was thoroughly cleaned. I may not have panicked the night Wilkes was killed, but that doesn't mean I wouldn't if I were living there again. I'm sitting out in the sun with my nose stuck in a book. It's not my normal romance read; instead, it's a medical journal. My license to practice medicine has long since lapsed over the last few years. Now I'm playing catch-up so I can hopefully start treating patients again as soon as possible.

"Um, you're blonde," he stutters out.

"I am." I smile up at him.

I went down to the hotel spa this morning and had my hair dyed back to its natural color for the first time in almost four years. The moment they turned me to face the mirror, I burst into tears. I spent a really long time pretending to be someone else, both physically and emotionally. But seeing myself with blonde hair and blue eyes while sitting in a public place hit me harder than I'd ever expected. I left with red-rimmed eyes and I was so embarrassed that I know I'll never be able to show my face in there again.

I run my hands through my hair, uncomfortably waiting for his reaction.

"Jesus, you are beautiful, Erica," he says softly, and I know he isn't lying just for the sake of a compliment. He stands motionlessly, staring down at me.

"You like it? I was worried you had a thing for brunettes."

He leans over, sucking in a shaky breath and kissing me hard while pushing a hand through my hair. He doesn't take it any deeper. He just holds me against his mouth, savoring the connection.

"I just have a thing for *you.* You should have warned me about this though. We have things to talk about and all I want to do now is take you inside and watch this sexy blonde riding my cock." *Yeah. He likes it.*

He finally takes a step back before adjusting his pants and clearing his throat.

"Later. I promise. Now what's this about Indianapolis?" I ask.

"Pack your bags, baby. We're moving."

I jump to my feet, spilling my coffee all over the ground. "Really?"

"Yep. I just signed on the space for the gym. It's not Ohio, but they have a great center that is dying to have you on staff. The director said you could start working with patients immediately as long as you are willing to have another doctor oversee you until you're caught up on all your licensing stuff."

"Shut up," I breathe.

"I also found some houses that I believe fit your criteria." He smirks, obviously proud of himself. "None of them have the porch swing, but I'm relatively sure I can have one of those added."

He steps over the puddle of coffee and sits down in the chair next to me. Pulling up pictures on his iPad, he goes through the specs on each house, always starting with security. I can hear him excitedly talking but I can't see anything as my eyes swim with tears. I lean forward, using my hair to curtain off my emotions.

I never in a million years expected to feel…well, normal again. I've been happy with Slate for a long time, but to be casually sitting outside, breathing easy, while the man I love searches through a dozen houses to make our *home*—it's overwhelming in the best possible way. I only thought he gave me back all the pieces of my life, but the truth is, Slate just keeps expanding the puzzle, giving me pieces I didn't even know were missing.

"Stop crying," he whispers, leaning over to kiss the top of my head.

I say the words I've probably said to him a million times since I met him. "Thank you."

He never responds, but he doesn't have to.

Five Years later....

"WELL, IS SHE running a fever?" I ask Slate while thumbing through the papers on my desk.

"Yeah. The thermometer said 99.8."

"That's not a fever, Slate." I roll my eyes and smile to myself.

"It may not be a high fever, but it's still a fever, Dr. Andrews. I don't think it's just her teeth. Her cheeks are all red too."

"Yet another symptom of teething, honey." I laugh but grab my coat and head out of my office anyway. "I'm on my way home."

"Good. No more working Saturdays."

"Yeah, good luck with that. Only four doctors—we all work a Saturday."

He groans just like he does every month when I have to work the weekend, but he quickly gets over it. "Be careful, beautiful. I love you."

"I love you too."

Slate and I got married the same day we moved to Indianapolis. It was a small, outside ceremony in a gorgeous garden with only Leo and Jimmy in attendance. Thankfully Slate didn't propose with a gaudy engagement ring, but I'm not sure I would have even cared if he had. Three weeks after Wilkes was killed, we were lying in our talking position in bed when Slate pulled out a very tasteful, oval-diamond ring.

His words will live with me forever. "The echoes are gone, beautiful. And the woman left behind is even more incredible than the one I fell in love with. Marry me, Erica." Of course, I said yes.

Life as Mrs. Andrews has been interesting. While I recovered my identity, I lost my life of anonymity. We have managed to stay out of the public eye for the most part. Some people may know who I am, but I definitely wouldn't say they recognize me at the grocery store. Slate still gets attention when we go out, but most people respect our privacy these days.

Eleven months after we got married, Adam Slate Andrews was born. He is perfect. I'm well aware of how cliché it sounds, but Slate is the most amazing father I have ever seen. His patience knows no bounds. Adam got my eyes, and because of that, Slate has never been able to tell him no. It's safe to assume that Adam is going to be hell on wheels when he gets older. He's a good kid though—at least for now. Adam loves his uncle Leo, even if he doesn't get to see him every day.

It was a huge transition for me to leave Leo. In a lot of ways, he was the only true friend I've ever had. Slate originally disagreed with our relationship, but after a bazillion hours of therapy together, he now accepts it for what it is. My relationship with Leo was grown from such a dark place that nothing should have been able to survive. However, sometimes even the darkness can't contain the most blinding lights. I love Leo like a brother. And it means the world to me that Slate, while he doesn't fully understand, accepts that.

The day before we moved to Indianapolis, Slate signed the papers to transfer ownership of the Chicago apartment into Leo's name. Leo tried to refuse at first, but after a private, hour-long talk between him and Slate, he finally accepted. My goodbye with Leo wasn't a short one. It killed me to leave him alone with all the guilt I knew he was still harboring. We may have been freed the day Lucas Wilkes was killed, but Leo never truly escaped. Slate insisted it would do him some good to be alone, and I can't say he was wrong.

Leo's life really took off after I left. Slate put him in touch with several of his Hollywood contacts, and he had no trouble securing his spot on the security scene. He's good at what he does, so it's not exact-ly a shock that he is successful.

While we aren't looking over our shoulders anymore, Slate isn't taking any more chances with me. Johnson was immediately assigned as my personal security officer. I would have preferred Leo, but he was busy starting up his new security company.

Our life was amazing, but despite claiming we only wanted one child, we both knew our family wasn't complete. Just under a year ago, Riley Renee Andrews finished off our family. She is the biggest daddy's girl in the world, and from day one, she's had Slate wrapped around her finger. She got his dark hair, but her hazel eyes are all her own.

Slate spends his days at the gym, and he actually has some pretty talented kids. He's done great things for the boxing community in Indianapolis. Above and beyond all of that though, I think he is finally happy. Slate loves boxing, and now he can actually enjoy it from behind the scenes and out of the limelight.

As I drive through the gates in front of our house, a sudden calm washes over me. Adam is running around like the madman he is. I watch as he giggles while stomping through the dirt. My eyes drift to the front porch, where Slate is swinging with Riley held tight against his chest.

"How is she?" I ask Slate as Adam careens into my legs. "Hey, buddy. Did you have a good day with Dad?"

He doesn't bother to answer me before taking off again.

"About the same." He stands to give me a kiss, but his face is worried.

"She'll be okay. I promise. It's just her teeth. Remember when Adam did the same thing?"

"I'm just glad you're home." He smiles warmly as he kisses my forehead.

"What do you want to eat for dinner tonight?"

"You," he says with a smirk.

"Jesus, Slate. You know, one of these days, they are going to understand you."

"It will be a sad day, beautiful. I know you love it when I talk dirty to you." He winks, and damn if he isn't right.

"I'm serious. You need to start watching your mouth," I lie. I'll actually rue the day when Slate stops talking dirty to me.

"Liar," he breathes into my ear, sending chills down my spine.

He hands me Riley, who is almost asleep, and jogs out to chase Adam in circles.

As I look around at our little bubble of the world, I can't help but remember how this all started. Our relationship was established on secrets and lies, but in the end, it flourished through truths. Slate told me years ago that we all have scars, and our relationship is no different. It could have very easily been ruined from the start, but he fought for me—even when I couldn't fight for myself.

Leo

"Hey, babe." I answer my phone to hear Erica sobbing on the other end. "What's wrong?" I immediately freeze in the middle of the busy Chicago sidewalk.

"It's a boy!" She laughs across the line. "We're going to name him Adam."

My whole body instantly relaxes and a smile spreads across my face. "Congratulations!" I say, laughing right along with her.

Suddenly, a tall blonde, fumbling through her purse and cussing, catches my eye. She's gorgeous, but her level of anxiety is what really makes me take notice.

"Are you coming up for the baby shower? Some of the nurses at work are putting together a little something for us in a few months."

"Isn't that for chicks?" I respond, never tearing my eyes off the blonde, who pulls out her cell phone, just to become more agitated.

"No. Slate will be there. You two can hang out while we gasp over baby clothes."

The woman I'm all but gawking at walks away, only to quickly turn back around and head in my direction.

"Erica, can I call you back?"

"Yeah. Yeah. Yeah. You can get off the phone, but you're coming to the shower."

"Okay. Send me the info. I'll be there," I reply just to appease her. "Bye, babe." I hang up and head toward the flustered woman. The closer I get, the sexier she becomes, and suddenly, I'm approaching her for a totally different reason.

"Excuse me, miss. Do you need some help?" I ask when I get close.

"God, yes! I'm late for an interview and I have no idea where the hell I am. The cab driver dropped me off here, but I think this is the wrong place. Oh, and my phone died, because *really*—that's the kind of day I'm having. You don't happen to know where State Street is, do you?" she rushes out then blows her hair out of her eyes with a huff.

"Yeah. That's, like, two streets back. You're not far. Come on. I'll walk you there."

"Oh, thank you so much." She sighs with relief.

I extend a hand toward her. "Hi. My name's Leo James."

"Nice to meet you. I'm Sarah Erickson."

The End

**Coming Fall 2014
Broken Course**

Leo James and Sarah Erickson
Can two broken souls mend each other, or will their pasts be
more than any love can overcome?

**Get to know Sarah Erickson in
Changing Course and Stolen Course
Available now!**

Acknowledgements

his book would be nothing without my betas. I can't stress to you enough how much these women keep me going. They listen to me whine when I can't figure out a character. They aren't afraid to tell me when something sucks. And most of all, they squeal with me on Facebook when I write something that works.

To Ashley, Bianca, Bianca, Tracey, Lakrysa, Adriana, Courtney, and Autumn, you ladies are the best betas in the world. I would be lost without you.

Then there are the bloggers. Seriously, you ladies are amazing!! I'm going to attempt to list a few, but let me be CLEAR, these are not the only bloggers I owe thanks too. So to every single one of you who has taken a chance on one of my books—THANK YOU!

Aestas Book Blog, Give Me Books, The Rock Stars of Romance, Red Cheeks Reads, K&T Book Reviews, Maryse's Book Blog, White Zin Bookends, Mixed Emotions Book Blog, Short and Sassy Book Blurbs, I Love My Ereader, The Book Hookup, Flutters and Flails, Biblio Belles Book Blog, Lovely Books, Nose Stuck In A Book, and Elizabeth Thiele (not a blogger, but lord that woman can pimp an author!)

To Autumn and Ashley: What can I say that hasn't already been said? I love you ladies. You listen to me ramble about my books and characters as if they were real. You deserve an award or a Caribbean vacation. I'll work on the latter.

To Danielle: Echo! Echo! Echo! I'm sorry. This book is not about a man standing in a cave. You will just have to get over it. I don't think I have the abilities to write a whole book about that.

To Jessica VW: Note to self. If you don't want me to spoil my books for you, you may want to refrain from drinking wine with me. Sorry about that. HAHA!

To The Vegetarians: You ladies are AMAZING! Thank you so much for reading and loving all of my books. I appreciate everything you do to spread the word. But most of all, thank you for the hot Nick Bateman pictures. That is how you know a good friend. The minute Nicky posts a new picture on Facebook, y'all are the first to share it. THANK YOU THANK YOU THANK YOU!

And lastly,

To my Husband: You are the inspiration for every one of my heroes—even the really tall ones. I love you! MmmMmm!

About The Author

Born and raised in Savannah, Georgia, Aly Martinez is a stay-at-home mom to four crazy kids under the age of five, including a set of twins. Currently living in Chicago, she passes what little free time she has reading anything and everything she can get her hands on, preferably with a glass of wine at her side.

After some encouragement from her friends, Aly decided to add "Author" to her ever-growing list of job titles. So grab a glass of Chardonnay, or a bottle if you're hanging out with Aly, and join her aboard the crazy train she calls life.

Facebook: https://www.facebook.com/AuthorAlyMartinez
Twitter: https://twitter.com/AlyMartinezAuth
Goodreads: https://www.goodreads.com/AlyMartinez

Made in the USA
Monee, IL
13 December 2024